"Make a place on your 'thriller' bookshelf—alongside Tom Clancy, Len Deighton and Ken Follett—for author Benjamin Spada's spectacular debut. 'FNG—A Black Spear Novel' introduces Sgt. Cole West as the Black Spear team confronts bio-chemical terrorism. Spada's crisp and credible prose takes you on a journey you won't regret!"

—Mike Murphey,
author of the award-winning
Physics, Lust and Greed sci-fi series

"FNG—A Black Spear Novel from debut author Benjamin Spada is a fast-paced roller coaster ride into the world of black ops. Edgy. Intelligent. Compelling. Film-worthy. And so real in terms of the catastrophic possibilities, it will make you tremble as you turn the pages. A 5-star read!"

—Laura Taylor,
6-Time Romantic Times
Award Winner

"Congratulations to novelist Benjamin Spada! He writes authentic, intense and visceral black ops fiction, while also providing just the right amount of back story to make his characters come alive on each page. I expect his debut novel—FNG: A Black Spear Novel—to develop a sizeable and loyal audience."

—Dennis Bowen,
author of *The Water Diamonds*,
Int'l Thriller Series, Book 1 of 8

FNG

A
BLACK SPEAR
NOVEL

BENJAMIN SPADA

FROM THE TINY ACORN . . .
GROWS THE MIGHTY OAK

www.acornpublishingllc.com
For information, address:
Acorn Publishing, LLC
3943 Irvine Blvd. Ste. 218
Irvine, CA 92602

FNG | A Black Spear Novel
Copyright © 2022 Benjamin Spada

Cover design by ebooklaunch.com
Interior design and formatting by Debra Cranfield Kennedy

Printed in the United States of America

ISBN-13: 979-8-88528-005-1 (hardcover)
ISBN-13: 979-8-88528-004-4 (paperback)
Library of Congress Control Number: 2021925114

For Jackie, always.
To the moon and back.

PROLOGUE

Loyalty only lasts so long. Matthew Lee-Ray was grateful for his agent and for how good she'd been to him over the years, but he was one phone call away from canning her. The headache he nursed already had his patience for bullshit running thin, and his agent's incessant calls were like barbed wire tightening around his skull. Felicia could be replaced, but Lee-Ray was the golden goose and it was *his* exposé documentaries that kept both their wallets lined.

He *finally* gave in and answered her on the fourth ring.

"Felicia, hey."

"Don't 'hey' me, Matt. I had you penciled in for a call fifteen minutes ago."

"Sorry. I've got a nasty headache, think I caught that bug going around." His bloodshot eyes and the scabs crusting his nostrils were clues enough to what he'd really been up to last night. He'd already popped a few aspirin and practically waterboarded himself with Visine, although neither helped. If anything, they'd made it all worse.

"Look, Matt, your contract with the studio has you on the hook for one more picture, but you haven't even pitched me your idea. You've got to give me something to work with here."

The barbed wire coiled tighter, and he squeezed his eyes shut to block out the pain. "I'm working on it, I just need a little more time," he said as he walked down his hallway to the bathroom.

The awards and memorabilia from his past films adorned the hallway walls and loomed over him as he passed. There was a poster from *False Democracy*, his debut which had shed light on voter disenfranchisement; another beside it was from *Uncle Sam's Club*, a controversial exposé on sexism and discrimination of women in the United States military. It had been his favorite project to date, though the backlash he'd received from the military and veteran communities had been intimidating to say the least. Thankfully, the same backlash and notoriety had fueled ticket sales. Who cared about the message or blowback as long as it filled theaters?

The memory of the media shitstorm brought a smile to his face. He opened the medicine cabinet in the bathroom, retrieving the bottles of aspirin and Visine. He popped two more pills in his mouth and swallowed them dry.

"I'm toying with the idea of a project on the inefficacy of over-the-counter medications. Big pharma is easier for people to hate than the Department of Defense, this time I'd like to make a movie that doesn't result in me getting death threats."

Admittedly, the first death threats had been staged by his assistant to build even more buzz about *Uncle Sam's Club*.

Lee-Ray took two more aspirin and then used the Visine. His eyes still ached like a son of a bitch. He ran a thumb and forefinger along them and rubbed. The mixture of drops and his own tears felt sticky.

"Ooh, I like it! I'll email the studio, this should buy us a little more time."

"Sounds good." He looked to his reflection; the studio's deadline was least of his concerns.

Blood. His eyes were leaking blood.

"Oh, fuck . . ."

He dropped his cell phone into the sink. He faintly heard Felicia asking what was wrong. Lee-Ray tried wiping it away but it just smeared across his cheeks. His heart hammered rapid-fire in his chest and a sick feeling brewed in his gut. Lee-Ray pulled his phone from the sink with blood-slicked fingers.

"Something's wrong," was all he managed to say before his whole body seized up on him. This time he fell down and cracked his head on the linoleum tile, his hands squeezed into fists, and his jaw clenched tight. His mouth snapped shut so abruptly, he bit off the end of his tongue. Blood filled his mouth and trickled down the back of his throat. The cell phone's screen fractured in his grip. Now blood dripped from his eyes, nose, and ears.

His fingernails dug through the skin of his palms. He longed to scream for help, but his jaw only locked tighter and tighter. He ground his teeth together until they finally shattered. Sharp fragments dug deep into exposed gums.

Tremors ran through his body. His back spasmed so hard, he felt a crack deep within him. The pain devastated him, and he passed out.

Machines beeping. It sounded like a hospital, but his clogged ears distorted everything. He thought his eyes were open but couldn't tell because everything was still black. At first he felt like he was having trouble breathing, but then realized some machine was doing it for him. An iron lung, maybe? Did those still exist? Bits of conversation drifted through the haze, but he couldn't make sense of any of it.

"What's happening to him? What happened to his eyes?"

"I . . . I don't know. I need to make a call."

"The blisters are getting worse, and he didn't have those lesions an hour ago."

Something clumpy dripped down his fingers. It felt like . . . *pieces* of his skin were falling off.

When he tried to move them, all he felt was a scraping sensation, as if his very bones were rubbing against each other. It felt like his entire body was dripping now. His thoughts grew cloudy again, and it became increasingly harder to feel anything, even terror.

Lee-Ray bobbed in and out of consciousness. The last thing he heard was an exchange between the doctor and a nurse.

"Doctor, I can't find a pulse."

Lee-Ray wanted to call out and let them know he was still here, but he felt so weak now, it took everything he had left just to string a simple thought together.

"Okay, call it. He's gone."

Lee-Ray wished to God they were right. But he was still alive, and he could feel everything as the sickness continued to course through him.

DAY 1
ROOKIE MOVES

*"No man is more unhappy than he who never faces
adversity, for he is not permitted to prove himself."*
—Seneca

CHAPTER 1

Black bars. This absurdity was the first thing I noticed about his uniform. Marine Corps officers wear shiny rank insignia on their collars in either silver or gold. When deployed or in the field, they replaced them with subdued versions of black or a dull brown. This was partly to avoid looking important; snipers knew to hunt for the bright metal rank insignias of officers. But I didn't expect to encounter any snipers in the cozy headquarters office here on home turf.

Yet here this guy was, two sets of captain's double black bars on his woodland camouflage uniform's collar. Stranger still, he didn't come off as naive. The way he walked through the doorway, his presence filling the room with a sense of icy command, made me second guess whether or not his uniform was wrong in the first place. His eyes were a pale blue, nearly gray. They scanned the office as if to challenge anyone who questioned him. Unfortunately, I was the only other person present.

I didn't like the way he was looking at me. Maybe he thought it was amusing to see a Marine like me stuck behind a desk. I'm admittedly one of those iron addicts you see at the gym, pushing the heavy weights like they were made of Styrofoam. While I might look like the kind of guy who could hold a machine gun in each hand, while simultaneously squatting with a tank on my back, here I was filing papers on the Commanding Officer's behalf. Some of the other guys have joked that seeing me working for the CO is akin to seeing Dwayne Johnson doing somebody's taxes for them. To be honest, I'm flattered by the comparison. I guess he and I do have the same haircut.

I've been in the Marine Corps long enough to be able to tell the difference between the two most common types of tough guys: there are the puffed-up talkers hoping nobody calls their bluff, and then the angry ones ready and willing for an actual fight. This man fit neither category. Whoever the captain was, he reminded me more of a lion you see in a zoo—out of place in its cage, looking quiet and disinterested, even lazy, while all along you know he would tear you to shreds if given the chance.

"Sergeant West." The captain said my name; it wasn't a question.

On reflex, I respectfully shot out of my chair. "Yes, sir?"

He put one hand in his pocket and somehow even that trivial movement came off as threatening. The guy was leaner than me by a good forty-five pounds, but still he made me tense.

"Do you know who I am?" he asked.

I glanced to his chest and noticed for the first time his uniform was void of any name markings. No name, not even a standard "U.S. MARINES" tape over his right breast pocket.

"Do you know who I am?" he repeated, his question void of condescension or cockiness. My confused silence seemed to be enough of an answer for him and the ghost of a smile crept across one corner of his mouth. "I may need your help with something." Without another word, he walked past my desk and through the door to my CO's office, shutting it behind him.

I'd only been on temporary duty to the battalion's office for a month, but even I could tell something wasn't kosher here. My CO, Lieutenant Colonel Tarly, was a hard man to like and an even harder

Marine to work under. So far, my duties came down to submitting paperwork, sending emails on his behalf, and making his coffee. Twice now I'd been reprimanded for not brewing it to his standard. Any prick that particular about his coffee was even more particular about who could just walk into his office uninvited. A voice in the back of my head told me I was going to catch some heat for this. Something about that icy stare of his, though . . .

Besides his strange uniform, there was nothing too remarkable about the visitor's physical appearance. Black hair clipped to a standard military fade, the hints of gray creeping in over his left temple, a aquiline nose, skin tanned from too much time out in the sun. He had the early thirties senior captain look of someone who's been in the service for some time, but there was something ancient behind those gray eyes of his.

I picked up the sound of a stifled yet clearly heated conversation sneaking out of Lieutenant Colonel Tarly's closed door. It wasn't uncommon. Tarly regularly chewed out enlisted and officers alike whenever he felt things weren't up to snuff. Except in this case his booming voice was drowned out by another. The captain, still muffled by the walls but demanding obedience, barked a single sentence. And then there was silence.

With a slow creak, Tarly's door opened and the man himself came out, followed by his visitor. There was something in Tarly's eyes that I'd seen in many of his visitors' eyes but never in his own: defeat.

"Sergeant Cole West," the CO said, as if reciting words from a practiced script, "your temporary assignment orders are canceled, effective immediately. Please go with Captain Vaun."

So now I had a name. But just who the hell was Captain Vaun, and what was he dragging me into?

CHAPTER 2

Cole West. 7:50 a.m.
Camp Pendleton
San Diego County, California

I hadn't even bothered to suggest following Captain Vaun in my own car. He'd simply unlocked his sedan and pointed to the passenger-side door. I figured this might be a routine interview or something, but it wasn't until we'd left the base gate headed for an unknown destination that my worry started to set in. I had no idea what was going on, but if Captain Vaun had enough pull to get Tarly to roll over for him so easily, I knew it was in my best interest not to ask any questions and just do exactly as I was told.

Stay cool, Cole, a voice in my head whispered. *He doesn't seem the type to play games.*

The voice in my head belonged to a friend I used to have named John Crow. I met John in Boot Camp, and he had become my best friend. Our careers in the military had taken us down separate paths, but John was always the golden example I looked to.

It was John who originally inspired me to take on martial arts; John who'd convinced me to reenlist and make the Corps a career. We'd never gotten lucky enough to be stationed together, but we still managed to keep in touch over the years. Even though we were pretty much the same age, it was always John who'd been the mentor when I needed him to be.

A few years ago John had taken his own life.

His suicide hit me hard, but not as hard as the thought of not having that friend to rely upon anymore. But even after all this time I could still hear him in my head. Sometimes it would be a whisper as simple as *Don't take that next drink, Cole—the drunk at the end of the bar looks like he wants a fight* or *Sit where you can face the door—this place doesn't look too friendly.*

Now I could hear his voice clear as day again. Telling me to notice the telltale bulge of a holstered pistol on Vaun's right hip. Urging me to take note of the knife I could see clipped into his pocket.

Normally I'd start to play out scenarios in my head about how I could disarm and disable someone. This was different. Nothing in Vaun's posture even conveyed hostility. He'd asked for my cell phone, which was a huge red flag, but I figured it was best to comply. In fact, he hadn't said a word to me after that or bothered to glance in my direction as he continued to drive.

Just play it safe, John would have said. *Let's see where he's taking us.*

Thirty minutes later I was in a nondescript office building, sitting across a table from Captain Vaun with my entire life laid out in front of me in several neatly organized manila folders.

"Cole Philip West," Captain Vaun said as he opened the first folder. He spoke before the folder was even open, which told me that he had probably memorized much of the information already. "Enlisted into the United States Marine Corps six years ago despite offers of ROTC scholarships and the chance to become an officer. You got top marks on all your tests. This could've given you your pick of any job in the Marine Corps. Infantry, Recon, Crypto-Linguistics, Cyber Warfare, Intelligence . . . yet you chose CBRN?"

Chemical, biological, radiological, and nuclear defense was my primary specialty. To be honest, it was a question I was pretty used to getting. People always want to know why you do anything regarding the military. If you choose a combat job, they'll ask if you're too stupid for technical work; if you choose the technical field, they'll ask if you're too cowardly for combat.

"I didn't want a high-risk job that would keep my mother worried every day," I said. It was a response I had become practiced in over the years.

Vaun blinked, obviously expecting more of an answer.

"Working in the chow hall is low risk," he said. It wasn't meant as an insult, rather he was stating a fact. "Plenty of other jobs available for that. Why CBRN?"

I paused to think. "Biological agents and chemical weapons frightened me. Growing up it was all that was in the news. Anthrax this, Sarin gas that, Ebola outbreak this, Coronavirus that. I wanted to know more about them; I wanted to fight them."

This time my answer appeared to be sufficient. Vaun flipped through a few pages, then looked down at the packet again. "You know the old joke, right? What the rest of the military thinks of CBRN? What it *actually* stands for?"

I bit the inside of my cheek and took a breath. "CBRN. Can't be really necessary."

"Does it bother you when you hear that?"

"No, sir," I lied. "CBRN Defense is an insurance policy. It only becomes necessary when the shit hits the fan. If the rest of the military doesn't feel like we're a necessary asset, then I can at least take comfort in knowing the world isn't in that bad of shape."

Vaun nodded. "You said you chose CBRN partly because you didn't want to worry your mother. Did that feeling change after she died?"

It took a second for my brain to process what he'd said. A spark of anger lit in my chest, all the blood in my veins running hot. With one sentence his line of questioning had gone from cookie-cutter information readily available in my military record to the realm of uncomfortable private matters.

"She died in a car crash shortly after you enlisted. Did you consider transferring to another field after that?"

"No. Sir."

Vaun closed the folder and opened another. "What about when your father, a police officer in San Francisco, was shot in the line of duty? Why did you not consider following in his footsteps once your contract was up? You're on your second enlistment already, but you probably could have made detective by now, or a federal agent of some kind." Those nearly gray eyes of his broke away from me for just a moment to read another line from the paper in front of him. "Interesting. Says here you weren't even present at his funeral."

Sorry, John, but I couldn't take it any longer. "Excuse me, sir, but what does that have to do with whatever *this* is? And while we're on the subject: Just what the hell is this, anyway?"

Vaun leaned back in his chair with a tired sigh. "I'm trying to understand you, Sergeant West."

"Why?"

"I'll explain soon enough."

"How about right damned now? I'd say I've been pretty patient and more than fair so far." I stood up so fast, the chair I'd been sitting in nearly hit the wall behind me. "Even in the military I've got rights. Either start explaining what this is, or I walk out of this room."

"Believe me when I tell you that it is in your best interest to stay calm," Vaun said.

He seemed utterly cool, but I could see that threatening presence of his just below the surface.

"Sit down, Sergeant."

I heard John tsk tsking now that I'd let my temper show.

Vaun let the room be silent while I took a seat, and when the tension refused to break he folded his arms across his chest and continued. "You have no combat deployments or experience," he said, not even bothering to pretend he needed to read from any of my records. "And yet you've been regularly recommended for promotion by all your superiors."

As a Marine, that was a bit of a low blow. In the end, nobody really gets to choose whether they do or do not get to go overseas. Any Marine worth a damn actually wants to deploy and go do what they signed up to do. Unfortunately, some are just never afforded the opportunity. In my case, it was just bad luck of enlisting right as U.S. involvement in the Middle East was beginning to draw down.

"Why would you choose to reenlist if there wasn't a fight for you to be in?"

My brow furrowed as I answered, "Because one day there might be. I'd rather still be in a uniform and ready for it, instead of going back to the civilian world and pretending that there isn't a threat still out there."

Vaun uncrossed his arms and reorganized all the manila folders back into their neat little stacks. "Insurance policy," he began. "That's what you called it, right? If the world gets bad enough to the point where anthrax and nerve gas is readily being used, well then you would be the just-in-case response. So, tell me," he said and pulled another folder out from a bag next to him. This one, however, was jet black. "What would you do if I told you things are much worse than you thought, and that the shit has already hit the fan? What would you do if I said that we're long past that day?"

He let his last statement sink in. He gave me time to gauge the depth of what he was saying, to measure whether I was even ready to believe it.

"Who are you, really? CIA?" I asked. "NSA? Counter-Intel? Secret Squirrel Squad?"

Vaun tilted his head back like a poker player taking one last look at his hand, and then gave me that smug half smile. His face went blank. "I'm with the Black Spear initiative. You might have heard of us?"

Ah, shit.

CHAPTER 3

There are days in your life when you're hit with that proverbial fork in the road. Most of the time you aren't aware of it until after it's far behind you. Both of my parents dying had been like that. So had deciding to enlist, but today wouldn't be like that at all. I could see this fork in the road clear as day, and it came about with those two simple words. Black Spear.

It explained what Vaun had said to Tarly in his office. A name-drop that silenced every smart-ass remark I would have made in any other circumstance.

Black Spear—a name spoken in hushed whispers in every branch of the military, while often joked about by the junior ranks in the same way they joked about the Men in Black. It was the great bogeyman of the military community. Assassinations. Espionage. International subterfuge. Destabilizing and deposing dictatorships. The type of shit that would've gotten Tom Clancy and Robert Ludlum hard.

Throw a stone at a group of Marines and you're bound to hit a guy who knows a guy in Special Forces or CounterIntel. But nobody knew anyone in Black Spear. The reason why is quite simple: Black Spear wasn't supposed to exist. People said it was bad luck to even say the name. When I was new, I was warned that just Googling "Black Spear" was a surefire way to end up as a missing person's case. Talk of them emerged like rumors passed around on a smoke break, a dark shadow people tried to lighten up by painting as a joke.

But it was here. And it was real. And I sat in a room with a man who had me fully convinced that it was no laughing matter.

"I don't have time to do the song and dance of trying to convince you," Vaun said. He seemed weary, as if this was an exchange he'd had many times before and had grown tired of. "I shouldn't need to tell you we don't exactly carry badges for this sort of thing. If you want me to call—"

"No," I interrupted.

The captain gave a slightly surprised tilt of his head before I continued.

"I'm in an unmarked warehouse. I count one pistol on your hip and saw a possible second in the small of your back. The only Marines authorized to be armed when stateside are Military Police. Not even they can carry two pieces, and never concealed. You're definitely not a cop. Whatever you are, you're on another level. My CO outranks you two times over, yet you won a dick measuring contest with him so easily, I was ordered to go with you. No questions asked. No explanations given. I'm convinced."

Vaun sighed and chewed his jaw for a moment, "Good. That saves us some time." Without a word he stood and walked towards the door. When he opened it, he glanced back at me. "Let's go, West."

I moved into pace beside him as he tucked the manila folders under his arm and entered the hallway outside. The black folder remained at the top of the stack.

"We're older than most people think," Vaun said, his voice echoing off the empty hallway walls.

I thought it gave everything a grandiose feel.

"Don't ask me how old, because that answer is a little tricky. Over the years the Black Spear initiative has fallen under several different organizations. The OSS back in the forties, the U.S. Marshals before that, and the CIA most recently. History might look a little different to you if not for most of our files being redacted."

"Does Black Spear still fall under the Agency?"

"Not anymore. After 9/11 we went through some restructuring. I don't need to tell you that officially we *don't* fall under anyone. Department of Defense, State, Homeland Security, et cetera. Not existing helps expedite and simplify things. We've dismantled entire terrorist networks before the State Department could hold a meeting to approve any action. While we don't exist on the record, if we did have a mission statement, it would say something along the lines of being a special counter-terrorism task force dedicated to stopping threats of certain extreme natures under the discretion and direct authority of the President."

"Extreme?"

Vaun mulled it over, and then decided not to explain at all.

"Who knows about Black Spear?"

My question actually got a laugh from Vaun. "You tell me? How many of your friends have heard of us?"

I nodded. "Nothing for sure. But everyone's heard the name."

Vaun stopped in the hallway as we reached an observation window that showed a large warehouse area below.

"Exactly. Look out in that warehouse and you'll see two former SEALs, a couple ex-Delta guys, and a few Feds we pulled from Homeland. We have a program that flags anyone with certain qualifications or recommendations. We can pull from all agencies, all departments. Even state and local. Once upon a time I was in the Corps just like you, hearing the same legends. Bottom line, we're the Bigfoot of black ops. Nobody thinks we exist, but everyone's heard of us."

I looked into the open warehouse area and spotted the handful of personnel Vaun had identified. They all wore identical simple black combat dress. The warehouse had half a dozen tactical vehicles and various cases of weapons and ammunition opened up. I was about to ask what they were gearing up for when Vaun continued down the hallway and cocked his head for me to follow.

"That's Achilles Squad," explained Vaun. "Oh, and here's your cell phone back."

He handed it over, and I slid it into my pocket.

"It shouldn't come as a surprise that we can't have you contacting anyone. We're blocking all incoming and outgoing signals anyway. It definitely wouldn't end well if it started ringing in Mister Rourke's office."

Vaun made sure I picked up on the name-drop. I went for the bait, asking the question anyway. "Who's Rourke?"

"*Mister* Rourke," he corrected. "He's the Director, our direct liaison to POTUS. And just to give you a warning: don't play with this man. He doesn't have the patience I have."

In the brief amount of time I'd known him, Vaun hadn't once struck me as patient. That same grin I'd seen at the corner of his mouth appeared again, and I realized we were standing outside an office door. With a simple knock Vaun opened the door and looked at me with what could almost be considered amusement. Or was it pity?

"Good luck in there."

CHAPTER 4

Jax. 2 days ago
Terminal Grounds

The desert was hot today, but heat was something he'd been tempered in long ago. Lately he found that the rolling dunes before him were exactly what he needed in order to be drawn into his thoughts. He imagined most people experienced a similar sensation when staring out at the ocean's endless waves. He'd never cared much for beaches, though. It was something about how their very idea evoked feelings of relaxation. Soft sand, a cool breeze, and a gentle warm sun. But his soul was not one born for leisure.

In contrast, this desert, as were the others overseas he'd grown to intimately know, was hard. Its sun was unforgiving, and there was an eternal sort of strength to the sands here that he readily drew from. He knew that sometimes the men walking the grounds below would catch him on the catwalk, staring. Even then he wouldn't break his gaze upon the sands. His thoughts were too important to become distracted. The mission and the cause were too pressing.

His shoulder-length dark brown hair was slicked back and his full beard, though long, was clean and well-maintained. Abraham Jackson, known simply as Abe to his friends and Jax to his troops, was a born leader. Jax honestly believed that in a thousand possible lifetimes, he still would've found his way into the military. Service was often referred to as a calling; it was one he'd eagerly answered when he'd come of age. From the second he'd enlisted, he'd felt that he'd truly found his niche in life. While other men oftentimes grew discouraged with military life and frequent deployments, he'd thrived on it.

Jax had cut his teeth in Iraq, he'd done his time in Afghanistan, and despite how skilled a warrior he was, he'd been passed over for promotion until the end of his contract. Four fucking years of back-to-back combat tours, spilling blood in a sandbox nobody gave a shit about, and all without ever strapping on a second chevron. Since he'd never picked up rank beyond Lance Corporal, he was denied reenlistment.

He was a "Terminal Lance"; one of thousands of Marines every year who simply hadn't managed to get promoted before their time was up. "It is what it is," is what he'd been told by countless superiors who appeared sorry to see him go, yet not concerned enough to raise a finger about his dismissal from the Corps. His entire chain of command watched as he'd been forced out. "Thank you for your service, now you're on your own."

Jax understood the importance of putting a group before the individual, but he also had enough perspective to know that deeming him unworthy was a mistake. That thought had put a brand on his soul that even now hadn't healed. Pain can drive a man to great things.

When he'd been forced out, Jax had felt lost for a time. He was a warrior through and through. Yet he'd been considered worthless by the very organization that had become his family. After a time Jax grew sick of his own self-loathing and used it to fuel a new goal.

Upon a suggestion from one of his friends, a fellow Terminal Lance he'd served with named Rob Batson, Jax had formed a support group for veterans like himself. He'd called it Terminal; it was a cheeky joke that drew in a particular demographic. Originally, Terminal had been geared towards deterring suicide and unemployment through outreach. Build the community in order to build the network of support. However, what started as a tight-knit few quickly grew into a sizable organization. Spurred on by Jax and Batson's influence, Terminal had blossomed into their very own military outfit.

By associating with military humor pages and other similar social media groups, Terminal was able to expand its recruitment efforts to an even larger pool. The convenience of digital networking had played a pivotal role in finding the veterans they needed.

Disillusioned. Disappointed. Frustrated. Most importantly: trained. In the military there was a position for every job you could think of. There were trigger pullers, wrench turners, armorers, logisticians, communications technicians, medical personnel, and even meteorological specialists. Each year thousands of military personnel were processed out of every MOS (military occupational specialty). Some were discharged voluntarily; others less so. Terminal didn't discriminate against the circumstances.

In the beginning Jax personally handled recruitment. Each and every man had been approached one at a time. Now, he had an entire team going off a nearly foolproof script. One of their members with a Master's in psychology had even helped Jax perfect it. He had his men sitting behind computers pushing out private messages over Facebook, trolling the lobbies of VA centers, rubbing elbows and buying drinks at the local VFWs, and even doing house calls. They'd gotten recruitment down to a science. It always started casually. Looking for work? That disability payment late again? Wife left and took the kids? Not everyone responded eagerly, but that didn't matter. Eventually those who were interested got the final message: "You should meet Jax."

All it took from there was one all-expenses paid bus ticket to meet the man himself, and Terminal's numbers grew—one by one.

Jax allowed himself a smile as he looked across the open ground of his compound to see all the men training. Some practiced hand-to-hand combat, others field-stripping and -cleaning weapons, and still more unloading the latest shipment of cargo from trucks. All these warriors were his. The military hadn't had any use for them. Like himself, they'd been cast to the wind. Warriors without a war. But Jax was cooking one up just for them.

Turning from the view, he opened a door and entered his personal office. Batson waited inside as expected. The big man gave Jax a firm handshake then sat in the chair before Jax's desk.

"Went off without a hitch," he said.

Jax nodded. "Good. And we made sure to pull the Visine bottle from his office?"

"Yeah, boss. Got rid of it with bleach, just like you said." There was a shade of disappointment on his friend's face. Jax didn't have to ask what it was for. Batson was a fighter. He wanted to get his hands dirty. He wanted to pull triggers and twist knives, not do this covert stuff.

But even he understood necessity. There would be a time for all that before long. "Soon, Bats, soon," Jax reassured him. His friend gave an unconvinced nod. "But until then we need to be careful. They're going to be looking into Lee-Ray. We need to ensure that the only breadcrumbs we've left behind are the ones we want them to follow."

Batson stood and left Jax with his thoughts. A long time he'd been laying the foundation for this game. If all went to plan, he was already two steps ahead of the player on the other side of the game board. Jax was excited to face the opposition.

CHAPTER 5

Cole West. 9:00 a.m.
Black Spear Site
San Diego, California

Just two people were in the room: one large man in a suit and a woman with a tight-lipped frown. "Good morning, sir," Captain Vaun said. He rendered a salute to Rourke, then nodded at the woman. "Ms. Mason."

"Captain," the woman replied. She wore a black blazer atop a pencil skirt. When she stepped closer to Vaun to take the folders, I saw a hook-shaped scar that cut all the way from her right eyebrow down to her cheekbone. She took the stack of folders. Rourke dismissed Vaun with a curt nod.

Meanwhile, I stood there, wondering exactly what I was supposed to be doing.

"Kara, give us the room, please," Rourke muttered.

Kara Mason passed the documents to her boss before leaving. The contemptuous look she gave me on her way out told me there would be no workplace romance between us any time soon. I reminded myself that I was in the company of killers. And I should assume everyone—even Rourke's assistant—to be dangerous.

Rourke was a massive man. There really wasn't any other way to put it. His tailored three-piece charcoal gray suit hid his muscled frame, but he still looked strong enough to strangle an elephant.

His office was little more than functional. Spacious, yet empty. Desk, computer, and two leather chairs. Adorning the wall behind him was what I could only assume to be Black Spear's emblem; a large omega symbol with a long spearhead in the middle, all in black. The spearhead cutting through the symbol made it resemble a sinister eye. Oftentimes, units would get artists to paint their emblem at the front of the company office. This looked haphazardly blasted onto the wall with spray paint and a stencil. No motto underneath. No "Department of International Assassination" or anything like that. It was a simple enough statement that they were both the very tip of America's spear and its last option. Ominous in its simplicity. This organization wasn't inclined towards aesthetics. And neither was he.

Rourke held the folders in a hand that looked more at home taking an axe to a tree than handling office papers. He had a wide jaw and hard-squinted eyes that reminded me of pictures of old bare-knuckle boxers. His thinning hair was buzzed close to his scalp and his face held scars nearly faded away from years ago. Though he was only maybe an inch or two taller, he seemed to tower over me.

"Take a seat," he ordered in a thick Brooklyn accent. One of his hands slapped the folders onto his desk and then swatted them away as if they were junk mail. "So, you're the new guy." His eyes narrowed to a squint as they met mine for the first time. The irises around his pupils were a dark brown, nearly black.

From the way he glowered at me, I couldn't help but feel like I'd done him some wrong. I stupidly opened my mouth to say something, but he caught me off guard.

"A CBRN Marine Sergeant," Rourke continued, his accent making it sound like Sah-jent. "You know what CBRN stands for right?"

"Can't be really necessary," I said.

Rourke frowned, probably annoyed that I'd managed to steal the punchline from him. Good. Fuck him, the joke was getting old today.

"Look," he said, "Captain Vaun's Cerberus Squad is down a man. We need somebody of your *expertise*." The way he said 'expertise' made it sound more like he was describing which type of herpes I had. "We've come across something. Something bad."

Rourke reached for one of the documents. He set the manila folders aside and instead grabbed the black one.

"Take a look," he said.

When I flipped it open I wished I hadn't. "What the hell . . ."

The first few pictures were of a man in a hospital bed. The plastic sheets surrounding him indicated an isolation of some sort. Blood leaked from his eyelids and the corners of his mouth. A second photo showed a close-up of more blood dripping from his ears.

"Ebola?" I asked. The hemorrhaging from eyes and ears could be a sign of something from the *Filovirus* family. Having a CBRN background meant I was more than familiar with Mother Nature's nastier inventions. Rather than answer my question, Rourke instead waited for me to flip to the next images. "Oh. Definitely not Ebola, then."

The second set showed the man's skin had grown red and inflamed, with lumps spewing white pus across the man's body. Fluid seeping from corrupted flesh had stained the hospital bed a rotten yellow. I fought the gag rising in my throat lest I embarrassed myself in front of Black Spear's head honcho.

"Meet Matthew Lee-Ray," said Rourke, "Film director, warrior of social justice, and as of yesterday our case zero."

I looked more closely at the photos, realizing the victim was indeed the famous director. His face had contorted into such a grisly mess of infection, I hadn't recognized him. I'd caught a few of Lee-Ray's films. Although they weren't my cup of tea, I never would've wished this on him.

"Tell me what you think, Sergeant West."

My mind tried to come up with something that made sense, but the symptoms themselves contradicted each other. "It's weird, sir," I said. "These symptoms . . . The first picture makes me think it's a viral hemorrhagic fever like Ebola or Marburg, but then the infection ravaging the skin is more like smallpox or advanced bacterial staph infection. Those are wildly different pathogens. The layman tends to group bacteria and viruses under a single umbrella, but the reality is they're not even similar in size or structure. Hospitals are easy to catch cross-contamination in, though. If you go in for treatment of one bug, you're likely to pick up another while you're there. It's not impossible for him to have picked up two simultaneous infections."

"In this case that is highly unlikely."

"Why's that?"

"Sergeant West, those two sets of photos were taken mere hours apart."

My eyebrows narrowed, and I flipped back and forth between the photographs. No way that was possible. Even in cases with severely compromised immune systems, infections didn't spread that quickly or severely. As unbelievable as it was, the time stamp in the corner confirmed it. Vaun's words from just minutes ago came back to me.

What would you do if I told you things are much worse than you thought, and that the shit has already hit the fan?

Then I saw the third set of photos.

"Those were taken just sixteen hours after he was admitted to the hospital. When it was clear this wasn't something . . . *normal*, he was transferred to a contained facility at Reagan Memorial in Los Angeles where he promptly expired," Rourke said. "He started hemorrhaging internally, all his organs and blood vessels began to fail. At the same time necrosis set in and effectively rotted him away at the surface. His heart rate was so weak by then, we can't even exactly pinpoint a time of death."

What had in the earlier pictures looked like a very sick man now resembled a rotting corpse. The skin appeared to be completely flayed away, the exposed tissue beneath had gone a yellowish brown as the infection burned through the musculature. Hands had decayed to nothing but bloodied bones, and all across his arms, legs, and face there were patches eaten away just as deep. Knowing that this man was still alive when these pictures were taken made it even worse.

"Twenty-four hours after he arrived at the hospital, all that was left of him in that bed was bones and soup," Rourke muttered. "Not long after that, the bones themselves began to deteriorate. We had to act quickly to preserve the evidence we could. We've already started running a cover story of him expiring abruptly from severe pneumonia. Thankfully, he wanted to be cremated so we already passed along someone else's ashes for his next of kin to pick up."

I wondered whose ashes Black Spear had handed over, but I figured it was better not to know.

I reorganized the photos in the black folder and then gently closed it. Part of my unease left now that they were out of sight, but at the same time I knew my dreams would be haunted tonight.

I pushed the black folder back towards Rourke. "You want my professional opinion? This is some next-level shit. Mother Nature is pretty cruel, but she doesn't work this quickly. Everything about this has the signs of a chimera virus."

A chimera virus was a term used to describe a spliced-together microorganism. There were promises of medical benefits to them, but the greater concern was their application to biological weapons. Like the beast of Greek mythology, a chimera was hybridized with the most frightening aspects of various separate organisms. "Something like this had to be cooked up in a bio-lab, so we're looking at characteristics of multiple distinct pathogens. I've heard rumors of experiments in China and Russia to splice viruses and bacteria with fungal spores. I think this is proof that chimeras aren't just rumors. This had to be engineered." A question popped into my head, going off like a bomb and stopping my thoughts in their tracks. "Is this contained?"

Rourke gave me a stare, his face revealing nothing. "Yes and no. For obvious reasons, we're keeping most details from the public. An American citizen, and a celebrity no less, was just made the victim of a covert bioterror assassination. And, so far, we have zero leads. Lee-Ray's isolation held at the hospital, but we immediately sent samples to one of our labs for analysis. So yes, we have it contained. But since we have no idea who this came from, how it was developed, and whether there are any viable treatments, I'm hesitant to put much weight on that 'yes.'"

The door behind me creaked. Captain Vaun and Ms. Mason had returned. Vaun had since changed out of his cammies and switched to simple black tactical pants and a collared shirt.

"Okay, New Guy," the Brooklyn Gorilla said as he leaned back in his chair. "Now that you know a little bit about what we're up against, you need to make a decision. If you're in, then you're right in the thick of it with us. If not, then you go back to Camp Pendleton and go on pretending you don't know what the real monsters in the world are. You can return to your boring career counting the days till the end of your contract. Just know this: if you choose to walk, and you so much as utter a word to your priest or your barber about today? I will suicide you, and I will bury them."

His facial expression left no room for doubt.

"I don't suppose this is something I can mull over a beer tonight and get back to you?"

"Sergeant, you make a decision right here and goddamn now. Time isn't exactly on our side. If you aren't interested, I already have a long list of other more qualified candidates eager to fill this role."

I heard what Rourke was saying and had to process it. All my life I'd been preparing for something, though I knew not what. Now it was here. I was terrified, and every logical part of me screamed to get out and go back home. Back to where it was safe.

But the darker part of me, the deeper warrior side, knew that wasn't an option. Burying my head in the sand wouldn't erase the danger. I needed to see this through, just as I needed to see just how far down the rabbit hole I could go.

"I'm in."

★ ★ ★

Darren Rourke watched Captain Vaun and Sergeant West leave his office and gave a ten-count before letting out a deep sigh.

"Well, he's certainly unqualified."

"There are other factors beyond qualifications," Kara said.

"Name one thing he has that the other candidates don't."

"A recommendation from someone we trust."

He looked away from her, and she smiled slightly at the little victory she'd gained.

"It's Vaun's call," he said. "In the meantime, feel free to keep your greatly appreciated opinion to yourself."

"You don't keep me here for my impeccable looks," she said while absentmindedly tracing a fingertip along the scar on her face.

Rourke glanced back and forth between photos of Lee-Ray and excerpts from West's personal file. "I would share your optimism, but it's my job to address these threats as promptly and covertly as possible, not cater to hope and belief in someone's potential."

"Ha, nothing of the sort. But it's *my* job to provide you with an alternative perspective whether you want it or not. Let Vaun have his fun. Either you'll be surprised by the results, or you'll be satisfied knowing you were right from the beginning. Sounds like a win-win to me. Will there be anything else, sir?"

Rourke shook his head, and Kara departed to handle other matters. Things were not going his way. This virus had shown up unannounced and left as much of a trail to follow as a ghost. On top of all that he had a fresh recruit in his ranks to worry about who, in Rourke's very experienced professional opinion, was far too unproven to be part of Black Spear.

No deployments, nothing even remotely remarkable. If anything, the most memorable thing Rourke could ascertain was that Cole West was very *unmemorable*. And yet, he had to admit there was still something about him that struck a chord.

Rourke didn't know a single word that could entirely capture what he was after. He was looking for a warrior born, someone who was a fighter in his blood whether or not he'd been proven yet. Good soldiers were a dime a dozen. But Black Spear didn't need robots who blindly followed orders; he needed men with a primal instinct that generations of evolution and civilization had yet to strip away.

Black Spear's operators needed to think outside the box by default, because the very nature of the threats they faced did not fit within the box of standard thinking. They weren't even in the same realm of normal. He needed men who could look at those photos of Matthew Lee-Ray and not break, people who could be faced with the absolutely impossible and carry on as if it was business as usual. Rourke hadn't truly been listening to West give his analysis on Lee-Ray's virus; in point of fact, he'd been studying his eyes. Looking for that animal side.

Surprisingly, West didn't crack. Rourke would have been willing to bet that the Sergeant would freeze when faced with Lee-Ray's photos. Any normal person would and should freeze in terror if they'd gazed upon them. But West hadn't. He'd kept looking at them and examining the symptoms as clues. Then at the end he did something even more peculiar. He'd made a joke. "Next-level shit" he'd called it.

He opened the top personal folder for West and examined his profile photo. Rourke had been in this game longer than anyone, he had a knack for being able to see to the core of people. But he wasn't sure yet if West had what it took. If Vaun was wrong, at least there were other candidates. Thinking back to the long roster of other potentials reminded him of a quote by the Greek philosopher, Heraclitus.

He recited the ancient saying to himself perfectly from memory: "Out of every one hundred men, ten shouldn't even be there. Eighty are just targets. Nine are the real fighters, and we are lucky to have them, for they make the battle. But the one . . . one is a warrior, and he will bring the others back."

That's what Rourke was after. The one.

"Time will tell, New Guy," Rourke sighed. He hoped Vaun knew what he was doing. This shadow world they fought against wasn't very generous when it came to second chances.

CHAPTER 6

Cole West. 9:18 a.m.
Black Spear Site
San Diego, California

Vaun escorted me out of Rourke's office and back towards the large warehouse. I kept glancing over at him to gauge his mood, but came up empty each time. I'm pretty sure a blank canvas has more expression than him.

"Be honest with me. Were you ever actually in the Corps or does the uniform just help you get around on base?"

Vaun paused at the bottom of the stairs. The look in his eyes and the way his head tilted was nothing short of predatory. I imagine for him it would be like if a mouse got curious and started annoying a lion with questions. Funny, since I outweighed the lean Captain by an easy forty-five pounds and a couple inches. Instead of saying anything at all, he simply reached up to his shirt collar and pulled it down. There on his left breast was a faded black tattoo of an eagle, globe, and anchor. The hallowed symbol of the United States Marine Corps.

"Semper fi," he said, deadpan. Vaun fixed his shirt, stuck his hands back in his pockets, then cocked his head back towards the warehouse.

A high stack of wooden crates and weapon boxes was in front of me, and as I turned the corner I came into an open area with three men standing around several metal-topped tables. They weren't the same ones I'd seen earlier that Vaun said belonged to Achilles Squad. These must be his own team. The Cerberus Squad.

They all wore the same nondescript uniform consisting of black tactical pants with a plain black T-shirt. All of them had been in the process of gearing up for something. Thumbing rounds into spare magazines, adjusting holsters on rigs, and function-checking rifles.

The one facing me from the table was built like a strongman powerlifter, taller than me by a head and a half with easily fifty-plus pounds of muscle on top. His hair was buzzed to a military fade but kept longer on the top, his light brown eyes squinted at me as I approached. Somewhat olive skin, I figured him to be of Italian descent. His face, already set with a frown, pulled into deeper scowl when he noticed me. Evidently he was an unfortunate carrier of that disease they call Resting Asshole Face.

The guy who had his back to me noticed the change in Asshole's posture and turned about. "As I live and breathe," he half-chuckled in a Texan accent, and spit some brown dip-spit into a water bottle he held. "We got a fucking new guy."

The Texan was shorter, he had a round face with a pig-like upturned nose, and a fancy douchebag haircut complete with a comb-over and razored-in shave at the part. Maybe I was just jealous, because he actually kind of pulled it off while I'd been shaving my hair to the scalp for years. Whatever, something about him was just rubbing me the wrong way. He sneered at me before wiping a bit of brown spittle onto his sleeve.

The third at the table had dirty-blond hair that, despite being cut short, still showed curls. Of all the people in the area, myself included, he was the leanest in build. Also, he was strangely the only one in the room smiling. Mr. Happy had a big old grin on his face as if Vaun was bringing a new puppy home.

"Everyone was new once," someone beside me said. There had

been a fourth hidden in the shadows. A Japanese man stepped into the light and leaned upon the wall of crates as he stared me down. This one had his jet-black hair pulled into a top-knot and a pair of thin Ray-Ban prescription lenses on the bridge of his nose. I'd take him for a hip school professor if it weren't for the large knives sheathed on either side of his hips. Top-Knot broke off his stare with me to look at Vaun.

"Who is he, Captain?" asked Texan. He circled me like a shark. "Uniform says Marine. So, what? Special Forces? Scout Sniper? There isn't enough room for two EOD guys on the squad. I don't like sharing my detonators."

I became entirely uncomfortable as the only person in the room wearing an official military uniform. My mouth went dry as all eyes fell on me.

"CBRN," answered Vaun.

A resounding groan came from the group.

"Bullshit," said Texan, "We've got no Talon and now we get *him*? That ain't gonna fit the bill, Captain. We can handle the mission on our own. We don't need him slowing us down, and you know it."

Before I could say anything in my defense, Asshole pointed an angry finger at Texan. "There's no bill to fit," he said. His voice was pure Southside Chicago Italian.

"You know what I meant," said Texan. "Okay, New Guy, tell me: where've you been deployed?"

I was about to answer but instead clenched my jaw shut. My patience was running thin, and I wasn't exactly in a mood to justify myself to anyone anymore. They asked me to be here after all. The ghost of John's voice was in my head shouting at me to remain calm. But it was getting quieter by the second.

My silence was enough of an answer. The Texan shook his head in disgust as he took a single pace towards me.

"Nothing worse than a Jarhead who thinks he's the shit but hasn't *done* shit." He jammed a stubby finger at my face. "All 'oorah' this and that and cocksure of yourself. But you've never been in *our* world." He gave my shoulder a shove. My heart rate quickened and my hands balled into fists at my side.

"You're CBRN, huh?" he said. Another two-handed push, harder this time. I heard John's voice reminding me that they were trying to test me, to see what I was made of. The Texan stood close enough that I could smell the sickly-sweet wintergreen of his breath. He took the wad out of his lip and he dropped it right on my boot, making sure to look me right in my eyes. "I mean, you *do* know what CBRN stands for, right?"

His smile disappeared as my fist smashed into his jaw.

"Can't be really necessary."

Sure, it was a sucker punch. Sure, it was dirty fighting in the purest of forms. But damn it felt good to knock that look clean off his face. A half-second later all hell broke loose. My mind logged everyone's reactions. I saw the Texan crash into the table. Asshole began to lumber towards me, and Happy grinned from ear to ear.

I was ready. Weight on the balls of my feet, both hands up to guard, shoulders loaded and ready to fire off. Bring it.

There's that age-old piece of advice you hear about going to prison. If you want to survive you just need to find the biggest meanest guy and knock him out on day one. I guess you could say my logic behind cold-cocking a black-ops soldier was the same.

Now you've gone and done it, John's ghost said. But there were other things he would've said as well. He would have urged me to look at my surroundings and see what could be used as a weapon. Form a plan so that I wouldn't just be reacting to theirs. The corner of a table or the leg of a chair could be made just as dangerous as a pointed elbow or curled fist. All that mattered was being able to see what was available.

Asshole was the first to make a move as I finished deciding my plan of attack. A huge fist tore through the air towards my face, but I parried with my forearm and it glanced off. Before he had time to follow up, I dropped in low, countering with two quick hooks to his side and an open-palmed liver shot into his ribcage.

Their mistake had been in thinking me inexperienced. Thanks to John's encouragement, I'd been studying martial arts for years so that I could still handle my own if the need ever arose. And right now, the need was strong indeed.

It looked like the hits I'd landed on Asshole only made him madder. A solid liver shot is enough to drop most people, but he was so big I felt like I was fighting a mountain. He lashed out with a knee that contained so much power, it took both of my arms slapping down just to block half of it. Despite being built like a damn wrecking ball, he was explosively fast. The blow pushed me backwards into the Texan, who'd managed to shake the stars out of his eyes. To be honest I was glad he was back on his feet. I would've been a little disappointed if Black Spear's operatives went down that easy.

Also I really wanted to hit that guy some more.

"Your girlfriend won't recognize you after we're done," Texan said as he wrapped his forearm around my neck. One: I may have bitten off more than I could chew. Two: I didn't actually have a girlfriend, or even so much as a romantic interest for that matter. That little bit of knowledge actually hurt more than his choke did at the moment.

Before he could get it locked in fully, I hooked my hands in and dropped my weight down to one knee. Texan was sent flipping over my back and into Asshole, who caught him as if he weighed nothing. He gave a simple grunt then tossed him aside.

Something slammed into the back of my ribs. Oh yeah, there were still two other opponents in the room with me. I spun around while simultaneously throwing an elbow. Happy blocked it, grinning ear to ear the whole time. There had been nearly no force behind Happy's kick, he could've easily coldcocked me if he'd wanted. He was enjoying this little dance. I side-stepped to adjust my angle so that Happy and Asshole were to my left and right instead of in front and behind me.

I remembered the fourth man and risked a look over my shoulder, but Top-Knot was still leaning against the stack of crates. He was just cleaning a fingernail and remained unconcerned with the brawl around him. Vaun was similarly uninvolved, choosing to observe from several paces away.

I put my back to the table just in case Vaun or Top-Knot decided to enter the fight and take me from behind. I was outnumbered and in over my head, so it would take something drastic for me to remain on top of things. I grinned when an idea came to mind.

Happy lunged forward, and at the same time I reached behind me to grab the Texan's dip-spit bottle and threw it. The brown filth sloshed all over his chest and up into his face.

"Ah fuck, dude, that's not cool," he said. In that moment of disgust and confusion, I delivered a push-kick square into his chest that sent him sprawling into a wall of crates.

I grabbed one of the fully loaded rifle magazines from the table and held it in a one-handed grip like a knife. I've trained with fighting sticks, knives, and open handed, which meant as long as I had something to hold I knew just where to hit people to make it hurt. Admittedly a majority of that experience was gained from receiving hits in those very places myself.

Asshole was unimpressed and threw a mean wide left. I struck out with the magazine and hit inside of his hook, slamming the hard metal down then up into his forearm. In the same instant, I pulled my hand back and delivered a strike to his temple.

He responded with a right haymaker that hit me above the brow. The blow knocked me back and stardust exploded in my vison. I stumbled over my feet and tried to regain balance, but the world itself was spinning on its axis all wrong.

I grabbed the edge of the metal-top table to steady myself while my other hand clamped onto my eye. It was already swelling up. "Oof, that looks like it hurt," the Texan said. "You can lay there and cry if you want, go ahead and run to tell mommy and daddy the other kids were being mean to you."

As if I even had any family left alive who could listen. Fuck it, if I was going down at least I'd give them a few more marks to remember me by.

Happy was to my left by the toppled crates, and he glanced over in our direction. He shook his head as he tried to wipe the globs of dip spit off his T-shirt. "He's all yours, bud. This shit is vile."

I wasn't sure if he was talking to me or Asshole. Good, now it was just down to me, Asshole, and the Texan. If Vaun or Top-Knot chose to get involved, my odds would look even less fun.

"Big bad Black Spear guys getting the business from a guy like me?" I said. I outstretched my hands to either side, leaving myself wide open. Texan roared and threw a flurry of punches, snarling like a rabid dog the whole time. Just like I wanted him to.

I ducked the last blow, spun behind him, and kneed him twice in the back right at his kidney. Immediately he crumpled down into a ball and sputtered out a few gasps of air.

Before I could finish him, two arms strong as oak wrapped around me and pinned my arms to my side. All the air was forced from my lungs, and it felt like my head was going to pop right off my body.

Somehow the Texan had managed to pull himself to his feet. Maybe it was the sound of me struggling that pulled him out of his pain, or maybe I just wasn't giving these guys enough credit for how tough they were. All the same he got up with a glint in his eye that worried me.

These guys were no-shit killers. They're the ones who do the things Uncle Sam can't even admit happen. And here I was picking a fight with them. I'd thrown caution to the wind in the most epic of ways. Would they really kill me for what I'd done?

As if to confirm my fears, the Texan walked towards me and slammed his fist into my gut so hard, I thought I was going to puke my intestines up. Without giving me a second to recover he followed it up with another punch that finished turning my stomach to jelly. This time I did throw up, but at least it was all over his boots. Little victories.

"I wonder when the last time you lost this bad was," he said.

Every ounce of me wanted to hurt him more. Fuck him and his stylish haircut. I wanted to put my boot in his face and smash that button nose of his into paste.

Instead, all I could do was wheeze while Asshole squeezed the life from me. My vision swam with black. Blood from my whole body was being pushed up into my skull. The pressure rose to a point where I thought my ribs were bound to snap and pierce a lung. Then, just as I was wanting to tap out and beg for forgiveness, Asshole's hold on me softened.

"He's had enough."

I found my feet and sucked in a precious lungful of air. I wanted to take the out he offered me. It would be so easy . . . Part of me wished to crawl back to Camp Pendleton and lick my wounds, but a bigger part of me knew that I was the FNG, and this was the only chance I'd ever get to prove that I was worth a damn.

Mustering up the last bits of energy I had, I spun around and jumped into Asshole. I came in with my knee raised, driving it into his chest. Simultaneously, I wrapped one arm around the back of his head while driving an elbow into his jaw with the other. The blow I delivered with my knee knocked the wind out of him, and the elbow made his eyes bulge as the sudden strike overloaded that little reset center of his brain. The big man toppled backwards and fell.

Sweat beaded on my head and I forced my tired hands to raise up into a guard once more while I turned to face the last man.

"Seriously, though," the Texan said, "what the fuck are you *doing* here?"

Instead of coming up with a witty one-liner to piss him off again, I actually thought about what he was asking. I thought about the girlfriend or wife I didn't have. I thought about the family that was all gone who wouldn't mourn if something happened to me. I thought about how close I'd come to losing this fight just now, and how it was the first time in a long time I'd taken a stand for something. I thought about how little meaning there was in my life that I didn't just coast through on autopilot. It was a lot to consider in a moment like that, yet it gave me an answer to his question.

"I've got nowhere else to be."

This time he came at me without anger; he'd already seen what that got him. We traded punches with each other. He threw a left and right that I quickly parried, then countered with an uppercut. He snapped me in the cheek with a cross. I boxed his shoulders. We were both running on "E", our punches sluggish. Desperate to take me out, he threw a heavy roundhouse kick.

It was his last mistake. I saw the kick coming and stepped into the attack to cut off its power. I blocked the blow and wrapped my arm around his knee, forcing him to balance on one foot. Then I grabbed him about the throat, and choke-slammed him to the hard ground. He didn't get back up.

All three were down. Asshole was trying to reboot his systems, Mr. Happy was sprawled along some broken boxes, and now the Texan was decked in front of me. I tried to catch my breath and breathe the hate out of my lungs.

I spat blood out of my mouth and rubbed my jaw. I took a few steps away from the Texan and then knelt on the ground to pick something up. It was the glob of dip he'd tossed onto my boot earlier. I walked back and dropped it right onto his chest.

I would've laughed to myself if I wasn't so beaten down and tired.

On shaky legs I walked back towards where Vaun stood. The stone-faced bastard still refused to show any hint of being impressed. He just stood there with his arms across his chest. Then, ever so slowly, he cast his gaze towards Top-Knot.

Well, fuck.

Top-Knot took his glasses off and slid them into his pants pocket. Sighing, he pushed off the box and turned to face me. "You're pretty good," he said and lashed out with a chop so impossibly fast that everything went white before I felt it connect. I was already blacked out before his next three hits landed.

Vaun allowed himself the smallest of smiles once West fell to the ground. *Damn*, he thought, *that was some shit.*

When he'd told the squad to antagonize West, this wasn't exactly the result he was expecting. He wanted to see if there was fight in this candidate after all. In hindsight, maybe it had been a little unfair of him to not let the rest of Cerberus Squad know that West was proficient in martial arts. Vaun's team had also just gotten back from another mission this morning, so he chalked West's overall win to them being off-guard and exhausted. Any way you cut the cake, though, this guy definitely had some skill.

"If you just wanted to see him unconscious I could've saved you some time," Kara harrumphed behind him. "Your boys are sloppy today, Captain. You should've just let me had a go at him while we were upstairs."

Vaun wasn't sure how long Kara or Mr. Rourke had been watching, but he hoped they'd seen some of the show.

"I wanted to test him, Ms. Mason," Vaun said. "Not kill him."

"Why him?" Rourke asked. "I've got an All-Star list of candidates that have years more experience from every military branch and federal three-letter department imaginable. Green Berets, Navy SEALs, and

Marine Raiders all with multiple combat tours. CIA field operatives with over a decade of wet work. I even have international augments from our allies being offered as support. And yet you chose him to fill out your squad's roster."

After a pause, Vaun turned to Rourke and looked deep into his eyes. "You know why, sir."

Rourke's stare flickered with uncertainty. "You better know what you're doing, Vaun."

Vaun looked to where Sergeant West lay unconscious. "He came highly recommended."

"Captain, I just had his belongings on Pendleton boxed up and brought down here. I'd appreciate it if you didn't kill him before he unpacks. I hate wasted efforts." Rourke turned his nose up at West's crumpled body once more before walking away. "However pointless those efforts may be."

The man left Vaun alone with his mostly unconscious squad. "I'll try and keep him in one piece, sir."

CHAPTER 7

Jax cracked his knuckles then clasped his wrists behind his back as he walked. He'd donned what he considered to be his uniform as leader of Terminal. Woodland camouflage trousers that were faded from years of hard use, but instead of the matching top Jax wore the green coat jacket of his Service Alpha uniform. None of his many ribbons adorned his chest. The only personal decoration he'd kept were the matching set of Lance Corporal chevrons sewn onto each shoulder.

His people needed to see, to know who he was. Not which deployments he'd gone on or how much combat he'd faced while there, but the low rank he'd held. A single chevron stripe with crossed rifles underneath. The junior enlisted: the true driving force of the United States military. Someone who still got his hands dirty. A worker. Not one of the higher-ranking officers, who forgot what it meant to be on the frontlines.

The heels of his spit-shined black boots clanged on the metal floor beneath him with every purposeful step. "I know what they want. And it's almost time."

Batson, his closest friend and for all intents and purposes his second-in-command of Terminal, nodded slowly. Unlike Jax, Batson wore nothing from his Marine days. A leather bomber jacket with the sleeves cut off, dark brown tactical cargo pants, and steel-toes were Batson's choice of clothing. That and his big Fu Manchu mustache made him look more like a Hulk Hogan biker thug than a decorated veteran.

"They're ready, Jax. You built this army, and now they're waiting for the word."

Jax knew they were. All of the men were champing at the bit to take action. Even though nobody wanted to make a move until Jax said so, at its core, Terminal was a community and everyone had a say. That was one thing he found everyone appreciated about being part of Terminal: there was no rank. While Jax was accepted as their leader, nobody was really in charge of or the boss of anyone else. Authority was given freely out of respect, and respect was only earned through deserved action.

"I said they're ready, Jax," Batson repeated.

Jax paused in his tracks. He ran a single hand through his slicked-back hair and then waved it at Rob dismissively.

"Our opening salvo has been fired," Jax said. "That self-righteous prick Lee-Ray was the perfect little guinea pig."

A smile escaped Batson. Personally, Jax hated when Batson smiled. It crinkled up the big man's mustache in an unsettling manner. He also displayed both top and bottom rows of teeth when he grinned, which resembled a snarl rather than a smile. Selecting Matthew Lee-Ray as their first field-test subject had been Batson's idea. So in this rare instance the strange smile was excusable; everyone in Terminal hated that Hollywood director, after all.

"No updates in the news yet, though."

Now it was Jax's turn to smile. "Of course not, they don't want to start a panic. I'm sure they're already looking at whatever samples from his corpse they managed to sponge together."

"Should we be worried about that?"

He clapped Batson on the shoulder. "No. Whatever they find out should only frighten them more. Even *if* they were able to learn anything from what they mopped up, it'll be too late." Jax's voice dropped, going cold and dripping with certainty. With conviction. "They can't stop what's coming. Moses is going to make their world bleed."

Batson flinched at the mention. Just barely, but enough for Jax to notice.

"Are you ready for this?" Jax asked.

"Till the end, brother."

"Good. Task your team. It's time."

As Batson's heavy boots sounded his departure, Jax closed his eyes and felt the weight of this moment wash over him. The gravity of it was not lost on him. He allowed himself to really savor it all before the wheels picked up speed.

Soon Terminal would unleash its wrath across a country that had turned its back on people like them. Jax was fully aware that in the coming days he would be painted a villain by the media, but he wasn't going to lose sleep over it. In time, history would see the truth of coming events. Jax considered his actions, though cruel and brutal, necessary. The cause was just.

Blood would flow. People would die. And Jax would revel in it all.

The absence of details in the media coverage for Lee-Ray's death nagged at Jax, though. Yes, they'd covered the story, but no cause of death had been released. Speculation ran rampant on everything from drug overdose to heart failure. Nearly every celebrity had made some statement of remembrance, but no images of a necrotized corpse yet.

Terminal's mission was grounded in attention. If their actions were being hidden from the public, then their goal was at a standstill. The finest men in this country had been betrayed by their own fucking government on a daily basis, and the general public refused to even bat an eye in their direction. So far, their opponents had managed to keep everything under wraps. It didn't matter. Jax knew that very soon they would no longer be ignored. Nobody had listened before. Jax intended to make it impossible for them to remain unheard.

CHAPTER 8

Cole West. 9:32 a.m.
Black Spear Site
San Diego, California

Sometimes you just have to hit someone in the face. Any guy with stress management skills as poor as mine knows that when the crap of life begins to pile up into a heaping brown mountain of shit, the only way to let off some steam is to punch someone. Real fucking hard. Usually, it works and you walk away feeling better. Then, there were times like this where instead of walking away you find yourself flat on your back.

Waking up from getting knocked out is kind of like coming to after a night of heavy drinking. Your head hurts something fierce and everything is hazy for a moment, but as you stare at the ceiling you eventually piece it all back together.

"FNG's stirring," the Southside accent said.

My whole face throbbed. I pawed at it gently with my hand, the Asshole's punch from earlier had left my eye swollen nearly shut. I knew I had managed to get a few licks in, so I smiled while pulling myself to one knee.

"Okay," I said. "We'll mark that up as a tie."

It took a few seconds for the ground to decide it wanted to be made of concrete and not Jell-O. Everyone else had found a way to pull themselves together quicker than I had, and they all watched me like hawks. Or maybe vultures, waiting to tear my corpse to shreds.

"This day is off to an interesting start," said Captain Vaun.

"I'm not sure what the routine is for black-ops induction," I said, laying on the sarcasm as thick as possible. "Does this count as hazing? I know the DoD usually frowns on that stuff."

"You had your chance to walk away, Sergeant."

All humor vanished from my tone. "I'm *not* walking away." There was nothing back on Camp Pendleton for me to walk back to anyway.

Vaun considered that over for a second. Then he nodded, as if agreeing with himself on something, and walked past me to the four men in the combat garb I'd just duked it out with. "If you're sticking around, then I guess you should meet the rest of the Cerberus Squad."

The first person Captain Vaun pointed to was the big Asshole who'd nearly crushed the life out of me. He stood over six and a half feet tall and packed with mass, the same scowl and furrowed brow from earlier. His build was more akin to Ser Gregor Clegane than what I'd expect of an elite soldier. "Corporal Brandon Taggart, Marine Corps," Vaun said. "Six years with Force Recon. Don't let his size fool you, he's got a lot of brain in that head of his."

"It's just Tag," the big man said. "Nice to meet you." The grimace never faltered for a second.

Next Vaun pointed in the direction of Happy. He went ahead and introduced himself on his own with another smile. "Daniel Kelly. Not bad. You actually got some moves, New Guy."

"Kelly is acting second-in-command," said Vaun.

Kelly's grin grew impossibly wider. It was so infectious, I caught Tag's frown break for a second.

Following Kelly was my personal favorite: the Texan dip-spitter. "Staff Sergeant Derek Hodges. Eight years with Army EOD. Since Black Spear got him to join up, he's switched from defusing and disarming explosives to more . . . *offensive* applications."

"Demo expert," cut in Hodges. "So basically if you don't like loud noises, you might want to stay away from me, New Guy."

"Pretty sure I got a close enough look when you were snoozing on the ground a minute ago." Despite the swelling on my face, despite the beatdown I'd received earlier, and despite how completely in over my head I was with everything, it felt good to smile at him.

"Watch yourself," Captain Vaun said. Those gray eyes of his stared holes straight through me. Immediately my smile disappeared. Vaun gave a slow two-count pause before he spoke again. "Realize that the men in this room have faced things you couldn't imagine. Realize that, despite getting in a few lucky hits, you're still a rookie. And a liability."

There's a fine line between confident and arrogant, and I realized I'd missed a step and crossed that blurry line with my remarks.

"If you really want, I could have you go another round with Billy?"

At that, the Japanese man with the glasses stepped forward and extended his finger and pinky, making the Hawaiian Shaka sign and shaking it. Vaun slapped him on the shoulder as he walked over to the table. "Billy Ho has been on loan to us for a while, but he's fitting in very nicely with Cerberus."

"Just happy to be here, coach," Billy said with a mock salute.

I did my very best to etch everyone's names into my memory. I was good with names and faces, always have been, and I recited them back to myself in my head. Captain Vaun is in charge. Kelly is acting LT. Billy can kick my ass, Tag could bench press a house, and Hodges genuinely disliked me more than all the others. Off to a good start so far.

It dawned on me that I was the only one in an official military uniform; they were all in simple black fatigues. "Am I supposed to change?" I asked.

That seemed to amuse everyone. Vaun signaled Kelly, who walked towards me.

"All right, New Guy, follow me." Kelly took us away from the gear prepping area. "Where did you train hand to hand? Couldn't quite place one style."

"Little of this, little of that," I said. "A friend of mine convinced me to try Jiu-Jitsu, then when he got bored of that, we started learning Filipino Kali and Muay Thai. I've taken a few boxing classes and done a couple seminars of just about everything. All just tools for the toolbox, you know?"

Kelly nodded. "Impressive. Maybe Billy will give you another shot at the title one day. Try not to be too bummed, I think the Captain and Ms. Mason are the only ones I've ever seen take him in a sparring match."

"Ms. Mason?" I asked. "Rourke's secretary?"

"*Mister* Rourke," Kelly corrected. "And she's not just his assistant, she's his bodyguard, too. Definitely not a good idea to call her a secretary to her face. Or even say it when she's in the same hemisphere as you. You *do* know she was the first female to pass SEAL training?"

"I thought there weren't any female SEALs?"

Kelly gave me a knowing smile. "You can try and tell her that, but I wouldn't recommend it."

We reached a locker room, and Kelly knocked on one of the lockers. "This one's yours, bud."

Each locker was labeled with what I assumed to be a combat callsign: Blackbars, Forty-Seven, Crash, Kage, and Boomerang. I figured Blackbars to be Vaun's, but didn't have a clue who the others belonged to. Mine didn't have anything; not even FNG. I guess they didn't figure on me staying long enough to earn one.

I opened my locker and found a full set of tactical cargo trousers, a black UnderArmour shirt, and a pair of combat boots. They were the perfect blend of indiscernible law enforcement agency without any distinguishing labels. We would look like authority figures without any official markings. After a quick check I was pleased to find they were just my size. I really shouldn't have been surprised. If they were able to glean every bit of information about my life—from my parents' deaths to my damn ASVAB scores—then finding out my boot size must've been a cinch.

It's troubling when you realize how little of your personality *can't* be found in a digital world. A search of my banking records would tell them the last movie I saw or how often I indulge in a cheeseburger. Pinging the GPS history in my car could create a complete map of my comings and goings. Hell, peeking at my Amazon purchase history alone would give them a decent chunk of who I am. Books on philosophy, frequent orders of Valhalla Java coffee, and the occasional comic book. Even I could see the inference someone else would make: I'm desperate to find meaning, drink too much caffeine to overcome my own jadedness, and I'm still naive enough to believe in the ideals of superheroes. Being objective enough to do a fair self-assessment was just one of the more annoying skills I'd picked up over the years.

My paranoia spiked at the thought that Black Spear had acquired every survey and questionnaire I'd ever filled out. In the modern internet age, everything was recorded. What was that old saying? The internet is forever. Yeah, and Black Spear had an all-access pass to it.

Before I could start changing, Kelly snapped his fingers to get my attention.

"Wait, hold up!" he said, "Almost jinxed the whole damn thing." Before I could ask what he meant he slipped a digital camera from his pocket. "It's tradition. Always gotta snap a picture of that deer-in-the-headlights look of the new guy on his first day. Especially with that shiner Tag gave you."

I had no other option but to laugh at myself a little bit. Right now my face looked like purpled crap, so I guess, yeah, it would be a pretty good representation of how I felt right at the moment. I smiled at Kelly and flipped him the middle-finger as he said "Cheese!" The camera flashed and my one solid eye had to squint shut.

Kelly laughed. "Oh, yeah, that's a good one. Definitely gonna laugh at that a few years from now. I'll send it to you so you can remember this, too."

"Remember what . . . ?" I questioned more to myself as he was walking out of the locker room. I grabbed the fresh clothes from the locker when I realized Kelly had stopped in the doorway.

"To remember the day you left the Marine Corps, bud," he said. He gave me a peculiar shrug.

There it was, though. The elephant in the room with us. The quintessential point of no return. All I had to do was take that step over the edge.

I took a second to look at the squared away Marine in the mirror one last time. Satisfied, I meticulously stripped off the old clothing and donned the black. My new reflection stared me down, attempting to look confident.

"Welcome to Black Spear," I said. I told myself I was ready for what I'd just gotten into. It was a lie, one that not even the man in the mirror found convincing.

CHAPTER 9

Jax stepped to where Batson briefed the group, moving as quiet-footed as a cat. They huddled around a table littered with maps and surveillance photos, but there were no briefing sheets or unnecessarily long written orders for the men to read. This was Terminal. There was no need for red tape and bureaucracy, all there was *was* the mission. As long as the mission and their roles in it were understood, there was no need to add steps between A and B. It made Jax think of something he'd seen on a bumper sticker about the United States Marine Corps: *USMC: Uncomplicated Shit Made Complicated since 1775.* Terminal didn't have that problem.

"The remains have been brought to this building here," Batson said and jabbed a finger at one of the photographs. "The outside makes it look like just some cheap office space, but Garza here cased it and there's more to it than that."

"I don't know about you, but last time I had a physical, the doctor wasn't touting one of those," said Garza. He pointed to one of the photographs he'd taken, it showed one of the suited men transporting the remains into the building. The man had a submachine gun in hand. "I was working the security gig at Reagan Memorial, and watched the cameras just like Jax said to. I snuck a peek at what was left of him before some suits came in to wipe the security tapes clean. The remains weren't pretty. Whatever they sponged together into those jars is in that building, though."

Batson nodded and continued his mission briefing. Jax didn't need to listen. After all, it was his briefing he'd passed down to Batson. He walked behind the ring of men surrounding the table. Most didn't notice him; they were too focused on hearing their assignments.

"Garza, I want you back at the hospital for your shift," said Batson. "The rest of you . . . I need six shooters with me. We're hitting that building. We let them have a peek at some of the cards we hold, but we don't need them looking too far beyond that glimpse."

Garza bit his lip for a second then shook his head, "Bats, I want a part in this. I'm not going to go drink shitty coffee and twiddle my thumbs while everyone else gets some."

Everyone looked to Batson.

"I said I wanted you on your next shift." He stared at the table, then slowly shifted his gaze to Garza. "Is that a challenge?"

Jax smiled and watched the others tense up. Since Terminal had no formal rank structure, everyone was equal. There were no orders. If someone needed something done, they could request it by saying, "I want you to do this," but it was never a command.

However, anyone could challenge anyone else if they disagreed. If no one backed down from their position, then the challenge would begin. The stakes of the challenge depended on the size of the disagreement, so it could vary anywhere from a simple rock-paper-scissors best out of three, to full-contact hand-to-hand. Jax had once seen a newer recruit knock three teeth from another man's mouth, because he wanted his spot on a mission. These little trials were not uncommon, but so far only one person had ever challenged Batson. No one challenged Jax. Ever.

"Not a challenge," Garza said. "I just wanted a piece."

Batson thought it over, his unfaltering gaze set to combust Garza on the spot, then he looked past him to where Jax stood. He shrugged. It was Batson's call to make. Thinking to himself for just another moment, Batson nodded. "Okay, fair enough. You did your part and brought us this much. You're in. We're pushing out in two hours. Security personnel at that facility is light, according to Garza's recon, so small-arms only. I don't want to risk anyone getting pulled over by a cop for a speeding ticket and getting caught with a goddamn RPG that'll lead back to the Grounds."

They all gave resounding grunts and nods of approval. "Go grab some caffeine and get ready."

Batson pounded his hand onto the table like a gavel to dismiss them. When everyone had left the briefing room but Jax, the big man let out a long-winded sigh.

"You were the one who told me they were ready, brother."

Batson's shoulders dropped. "They *are* ready. I just can't help but wonder if this is how all those assholes felt, you know?"

"Which assholes?"

"Every asshole that was ever in command of us. Everyone who ever gave us orders that could've gotten one of us killed."

"Nobody gives orders to anybody in Terminal."

"You know what I meant," Batson said, smirking.

"I know what you meant," said Jax. "But that's the price of the cause. The difference between us and those assholes is our guys know what we're in this for. This isn't for foreign interests, or political greed, and they know that."

Jax stepped away from the table and opened up his jacket. Around his waist was a leather gun-belt: he kept a six-inch KA-BAR bowie knife sheathed on his right hip; holstered on the left was a .45 Colt 1911 pistol.

"Do you see this gun?" Jax asked. He drew it from the holster and held it in the palm of his hand. Its gunmetal finish was cleaned and buffed to a near mirror shine and its redwood grip, though pockmarked with wear and tear, had not lost an ounce of its charm.

Batson nodded.

"Remember our last pump together? The Lieutenant who wasn't worth a damn?"

"Second Lieutenant Kim. He made some pretty crappy calls."

"Exactly. Like when he led us straight into that ambush. I'd already dragged three of our guys back to the convoy when I found him with this," Jax held the 1911 out for Batson to get a better look. "Everybody knows it's illegal to take personal guns on deployment, but regulations always apply differently to higher-ups. Nobody cared if he broke the rules. There he was with this pretty .45, shooting and shooting . . . and hitting nothing. I mean not a damn thing. So I threw him down, took it, and used it better than he did."

"If I remember correctly, that little assault with Kim is what ended up killing your chances of reenlistment."

"Sure, but I still managed to swipe his pistol. I held onto it all this time. Told myself it was right to take it, because only an officer worth a damn—a *true* leader—should own it. And here I finally found one." Jax extended his arm towards Batson, holding the gun by the barrel. "It's a good thing you're questioning yourself. It means you give a fuck about those men."

Batson examined the 1911 closely, working the slide and admiring how smooth the action was. "I don't know what to say. Thanks, brother." Batson was never the silver tongue, but his simple words held volumes behind them.

"With Lee-Ray we gave them a taste of what we can do, now we show them how far we're willing to go."

Rob Batson's eyes darkened with a cruel eagerness for the fight to come. "Hell, yeah, Jax."

CHAPTER 10

Vaun was just beginning his mission brief as I left the locker room. "Simple pickup and delivery," he said. "We'll be transporting the Lee-Ray remains to Angel Site in Los Angeles. The new guy is just tagging along to assist in transit. If containment is compromised at any time, he's up to bat."

Up to bat. It made what I would have to do sound incredibly easy. The closest I'd come to dealing with a leaking weapon of mass destruction was when I'd had to assist in patching a bulk chlorine container headed to the pool on base. If I'd messed that up the worst that would've happened was some bleached uniforms and a little chemical burn. I tried to take comfort in the idea that if anybody had fail-proof containment equipment, it was Black Spear.

"HazMat suits already loaded?" Vaun asked, to which Tag nodded. "Good. We'll suit up when we reach the pick-up site. I don't want some passerby on the freeway to see us kitted up while en route and raise questions."

"Angel Site is understaffed," said Hodges. "Sounds like we're not going to have much back-up on this."

"Back-up is as needed. Any other questions?"

The squad stayed silent. I did my best to remain unseen.

Slowly, Hodges raised his hand in the air. "Yeah. Whose pocket does the new guy have to hold onto today, sir?"

That got a few chuckles from everyone. I pretended to find something interesting to look at on the floor while fantasizing about choke-slamming Hodges again. Picturing my boot heel grinding down on his throat eased me down a bit.

"You want to can the clown act here?" asked the Captain.

The laughter stopped at once.

As it turned out, Kelly drew the short straw for who got to babysit me. Thankfully, he didn't literally make me hold onto his pocket, he just pointed towards the open bay doors of the warehouse when Vaun told us to mount up. The squad rode in two separate blacked-out SUVs. When Vaun led us out to them, I hadn't thought they were anything special. But upon a closer look, I could see that the shiny black paint job only slightly hid the armor plating, and the dark tinting disguised the reinforced Plexiglas that made up each window. Billy assured me there were plenty more prizes in the back in case the party got real fun. His words, not mine.

As we sped north on Interstate 5, I reexamined the two other members of Cerberus Squad that rode with me. We all wore the same dark clothing. No insignias or unit patches, no markers of who we were. Black pants, matching T-shirts, identical Walther 9mm Concealed Carry Pistols holstered on our hips, and two extra magazines each. The Walther CCP held eight rounds, had an ergonomic grip, and a two-tone black and silver finish. No extra bells and whistles required. I didn't doubt that Black Spear had access to some very fun bang-bang toys, but for now our loadout was decidedly low-key and our appearance purposefully indistinguishable from any federal agency. Camouflage through vagueness.

The ride had been silent so far. Kelly had a radio earbud but there was no communication with Vaun in the lead car.

"Hey, West," Kelly said with a glance over his shoulder. "You can clearly handle yourself in a fight, but do you know how to use that thing?"

I looked down to the 9mm holstered on my hip. "Yeah. Highest range score in the unit."

Kelly whistled to himself and nodded to Tag.

"Think he can shoot as well as he fights?" Kelly asked.

Tag responded with a simple grunt and his grip tightened on the steering wheel.

I'd quickly picked up on the fact that Tag communicated entirely in an eloquent selection of grunts. The low drawn out ones meant disapproval; short ones seemingly meant "okay."

"By the way," Kelly said and looked up at the rear-view mirror to meet my eyes, "that shit with Hodges's spit bottle? I'm sending you my dry-cleaning bill."

"It was three on one, had to improvise."

Tag grunted, exhaling through his nose sharply at the same time. I think that was his way of laughing.

Kelly made a disgusted face. "Yeah, well, just between you and me, you should know that the Captain had to do some serious vouching for you to keep Hodges from going megaton on you."

"He really doesn't like me, huh?"

"It's not every day a new recruit wrecks the squad, bud," Kelly said. "But I'm sure Hodges is a little annoyed you didn't have to go through the indoc like all the other recruits."

"Indoc?"

Kelly rolled his window down and held his hand out, waving it up and down like a sailboat catching the wind. "Yeah. Indoctrination. Sounds a little like brainwashing, I know, but it's more of a rundown of how things go. The dos and don'ts."

"This may be my first black-ops outfit, but I get the gist of things." Saying that made me remember when Vaun took my cell phone. When I looked down to it now, I saw that it still wasn't showing any bars of service. Somehow even the camera had been disabled. I made a mental note to request he undo whatever digital voodoo he'd done next chance I got.

"Okay, so I've been trying not to ask too many questions," I said. "But I just gotta know, where exactly are we headed?"

For a split-second Kelly and Tag looked at each other. A silent conversation played out across their eyes, then Tag shrugged and Kelly nodded. They kept quiet to me, though. John's voice whispered, suggesting that they were just driving to some remote area to whack me. I was thinking about all the different ways a man could die horribly when Kelly broke the silence. "Mister Rourke showed you the pictures . . ."

I nodded. "Yeah, definitely going to lose some sleep over those tonight." Now the thought of getting driven to the middle of nowhere to get a bullet put in my head sounded charming by comparison.

"We're going to one of Black Spear's off-site labs. Matthew Lee-Ray's remains were brought there. That's why we need you, new guy, because we just might need your . . . *professional* opinion on some things." The way Kelly leaned on the word showed that he thought my opinion was anything but. Guess I couldn't blame them.

"My professional opinion?"

"Sure, if you have one, that is."

"Whatever killed him had aspects of Ebola, flesh-eating viruses, and smallpox. My professional opinion would be to turn this car around and head as far away as possible."

Kelly kept silent.

Tag grunted, it was a short one.

CHAPTER 11

Batson tried to figure out the feeling that he had right now, but he just couldn't quite grasp it. "Good" wasn't specific enough. "Motivated" wasn't exactly it, either. The word "vindicated" came to mind, but he wasn't fully sure what it meant. Batson wasn't stupid, but there was a reason that Jax was the brains behind Terminal and not him. He wished Jax was here to explain exactly what it was he was feeling. Justified, maybe?

Batson knew that he was doing exactly what he was put on this planet to do. He felt like a square peg finally getting put back into a square hole. That was it. Maybe he didn't know what the right word was, but he definitely knew how to describe it.

Many people enlisted into the Armed Forces due to a lack of options, but not Batson. Of all the luck, he'd been born into an incredibly wealthy family. The Batsons owned a very large import/export company that had shipped cargo all over the world for over seventy years. But the boring life of an heir didn't interest young Robert, so despite all of his father's objections he left home to find his own way.

Batson had always been one to work off the sweat of his own brow and the gnarled callous of his hands. It's why he'd had such success in the military and why he'd promised his father he'd never come back to work for him. In fact, when Batson was on his second deployment overseas and received a message that his father had passed away, he wasn't even fazed.

Inheriting his father's company and position was never something he wanted. Sitting behind a desk, wearing an expensive suit, writing checks for everyone else? No thanks. Within a week he'd sold off all the company assets and pocketed enough money to make most corporate accountants blush.

But once his time in the military had come to an end, he'd become truly lost. Attempts at joining private military contractors had gone bust, a few security gigs were disappointing, and prior service recruiters for Uncle Sam all ignored him. If it weren't for Jax, Batson would still be in that freefall that so many vets wound up in. He wasn't too proud to admit he owed everything he was to Jax.

Nodding triumphantly, Batson shook his thoughts away and came back to reality. Once again in the present, he heard intermittent gunfire down the hall, a few screams, and the clatter of spent rounds raining onto the linoleum floor. Shit, how he'd missed these sounds.

Batson's grip tightened on the 1911 Colt. Security in the building, as Garza had reported, was extremely light. Batson had been on point. The armed sentry at the door was confused when Batson entered the front door. In that half-second of confusion, Batson brought his .45 pistol to bear, thumbed back the hammer, and unloaded a double-tap into the man's face. All in one half of a second. The grouping was perfect, right above the man's brow.

If Jax was the brains of Terminal, then it would be fair to say that Batson was its fist. He towered over nearly every member of Terminal, and he knew that most were intimidated by him. And rightly so. It was the reason Batson was first through the door. It was the reason the first kill was his by right.

Before the guard's brains had time to trickle down the wall,

Batson's team was moving in. This lab was small and only had two entrances. His men entered through both and started to fan out. What little opposition that existed was quickly snuffed out.

It was a thing of beauty. For years Jax had been forming Terminal, Batson had been training them, and now he finally got to see the men in action. None of them were green. While Terminal had its fair share of men with noncombat backgrounds, all of the ones Batson had brought on this particular mission were seasoned veterans. Two were infantry, one was Force Recon, another was former Green Beret, and Garza had been Army Airborne. All men of action. All men of considerable skill.

In a strange sort of way Batson wished this mission had been more challenging. The scientists and doctors could barely run away before they were cut down. One lab assistant with a bit of spunk actually tried to fight back with a long IV pole. The Green Beret had knocked the pole away with one hand and ran a large hunting knife through his gut with the other. Batson watched as that blade stabbed again and again.

The men were eager, that was for sure. Batson was certain they were just letting off the steam of being away from fighting for too long. Too much pent-up aggression. In the service there were rules of engagement and a set code of conduct. Terminal had none. So if the big Green Beret wanted to do the man with a knife instead of a bullet? Batson didn't care, just as long as the mission got done.

He walked slowly down the blood-painted hallway. A lab technician in a ruined white lab coat crawled towards him. The entry wound in the man's lower back and the dark red trail behind him told Batson he'd taken a bullet to the spine.

At the end of the hallway, Garza walked towards the injured man. In his hands he held a small 9mm submachine gun. "That's right," Garza said and fired off a shot. It snapped into the tile next to the man's leg, "Keep going, you're almost there!" He let off a short burst and the bullets cracked into the linoleum by the man's head.

Batson took one step forward, aimed his weapon with one hand, and squeezed a single round off into the back of the technician's head.

Garza looked up at him with equal parts shock and confusion.

"We're professionals," Batson muttered. "Professionals don't waste time."

With that, Batson reached into his pocket and pulled out a small rectangular device. No larger than a cell phone, with a stubby antenna, and a small lever clicker. Batson ran his thumb along the explosive detonator and felt his lip twitch as he fought back a smile. A one-pound block of C-4 was enough to completely destroy the average size house into a ball of nothing but fire and rubble. For this small office building? Batson's team had brought in a dozen blocks. Two were planted at every corner and another four in the central lab. Any chance of pulling anything useful from Lee-Ray's tissue samples was about to quite literally go up in smoke.

The Green Beret, a simple man named Franklin but who was called Moose by everyone, walked up to Batson. "Explosives planted, no witnesses," he said. Moose was massive. He towered over even Batson, but much leaner. Less of an Incredible Hulk, more of a Lurch from *The Addams Family*. Batson wasn't scared, but he was still glad the big lug was on his side.

Once more he found himself running his thumb along the detonator. In war, he'd personally seen just about every kind of explosion there was. Breaching charges to take off doors, IEDs that took out friendly vehicles, and anti-personnel mortar fire that literally shredded enemy combatants. But this, right here? This would actually be the first-time Batson got to set the fireworks off himself.

A big smile, the type he knew Jax hated, slipped across his face. Hell, he just couldn't help it.

CHAPTER 12

Jax's breath frosted before him. All that kept him warm was his green coat. Normally the select few allowed in this section of the compound wore self-contained HazMat suits. Uncomfortable, bulky, but they managed to keep you warm. They also managed to keep the wearer safe from the Moses-1 samples in the room.

Jax held one of the sealed Moses-1 vials and felt the power in his hand. He always had an appreciation for the tools of war: the meticulous precision of a properly zeroed sniper scope, the rewarding comfort of a sharpened blade, and even the awesome, unequaled might of nuclear weapons. But what he held in his hand right now could only be described in one simple word: beautiful.

He peered at the substance within the glass. Unlike the tropes of Hollywood movies, it didn't glow a sickly green nor was it adorned with a skull label. Moses-1 resembled little more than a rust-colored solution. And yet its simple appearance betrayed its virulence.

Moses-1 was a genetically engineered virus, hybridized together from a smorgasbord of the CDC's worst biological agents. Initial symptoms less than ten minutes after exposure were somewhat mild. A little blood from the tear ducts was the first sign of the virus spreading. At the second stage of infection, slight hemorrhaging effects inherited from the Ebola virus caused bleeding from all orifices. From there the effects progressed rapidly into the third stage. The body's central nervous system is triggered into a series of violent seizures by the infection, some of these powerful enough to cause spinal fractures.

Moses-1 attacked the eyes with particular ferocity. That, combined with the onset of blistering, often led to the eyes actually bursting. Even his right-hand man Batson had been horrified when shown pictures of test subjects with hollowed-out sockets. As the virus continued to ravage the host body, the blister-like smallpox symptoms were eaten away by a characteristic taken from an accelerated form of *necrotizing fasciitis*. That was the fourth and final stage of infection: a complete and total viral crash. Essentially, Mose-1 devoured the flesh of its host body while the organs and blood vessels hemorrhaged internally.

Jax had heard once that if you had just enough VX nerve gas to fill the eye of Lincoln on a penny it was still toxic enough to kill a man within ten minutes. Jax liked that as a gauge for how deadly Moses-1 was. VX only spread minimally beyond its initial release area. But Moses-1? Hell, that was the beauty of a virus. All you need is one person dosed and their own body turns into a little virus factory, pumping it out on an assembly line until they finally crashed and bled out hours later.

Not everyone in Terminal had even been made privy to Moses-1's existence. Despite Batson's disapproval, Jax deemed it best not to show the men their full hand yet.

Jax's thoughts were interrupted by his vibrating phone. He placed the virus back into the refrigerated storage container before answering. Batson. The clean-up of the medical facility was complete.

Lee-Ray had been dosed with less than one microliter of the virus and it was still fatal. By Jax's estimation, an entire container possessed the potential to cause casualties in the hundreds of thousands. Lowballing, of course. And that didn't even count secondary and tertiary infections. Those numbers would elevate into the millions. And that would still leave Terminal with five other vials. Who said math wasn't interesting?

He took one last look at Terminal's crown jewel, wondering how many millions would have to die for America to do the right thing.

"Ashes to ashes," Jax said to himself. "Dust to dust."

CHAPTER 13

The building was just coming into view when it exploded about a block away from us. One second the medical facility was there, and in the next it disappeared in an expanding ball of fire. Just... gone. Erased. A one-story building, staffed by over twenty research and security personnel, reduced to rubble in an instant. The orange blast punched into the sky, flinging a dense wall of black smoke outwards in every direction. Heat, pressure, and noise converged into a total sensory overload that I struggled to comprehend.

The shockwave rocked our vehicles, and I saw Tag's massive arms fight against the steering wheel. Tires shrieked, the vehicle swerved towards the sidewalk, and then Tag wrestled the SUV back onto the road as a pedestrian gaped at our windshield.

The radio in Kelly's hand squawked to life. "This is Blackbars. We just went hot. Callsigns only."

Kelly's nice-guy smile disappeared and was replaced with the mask of a stone-faced killer.

Tag's knuckles went white on the steering wheel.

"Copy," Kelly said.

Blackbars was Captain Vaun's callsign. During our drive I'd

picked up information on Cerberus Squad. Kelly had explained to me that, prior to being recruited into Black Spear, Captain Vaun had practically spent more time deployed or in the field than he'd spent stateside. The man abhorred an office. He'd grown so accustomed to wearing the black rank insignias, it became all he wore in uniform. It was a curious practice he brought with him when he joined Black Spear.

"Get your party favors ready, Forty-Seven," Vaun said. "I don't know what we're getting into, but I don't want to be surprised."

Kelly was Forty-Seven, a name borrowed from an infamous assassin from a popular video game. So far Kelly had struck me as too friendly to warrant such a name. Kelly looked over his shoulder at me, wordlessly pointing to one of the black Pelican cases behind my seat. I popped it open and looked inside.

"Nice," I said. An FN SCAR Mk17 assault rifle sat snugly inside. The SCAR was a beautiful weapon. Unlike the standard issue M4s and M16s, the SCAR used the heavier 7.62mm round. Real hole-punchers. It was fitted with a scope that looked like it cost even more than the rifle itself. I reluctantly passed the weapon to Kelly in the passenger seat.

"The shotgun is Boomerang's," Kelly said as he did a weapon-check on his rifle.

Corporal Brandon Taggart was nicknamed Boomerang because, in his six years with Force Recon, he'd been demoted on four separate occasions. The man had a penchant for insubordination. It was his unsurpassed skill with digital systems and unparalleled ferocity in a fight that kept him from being administratively separated. The chevrons on his collar had been like boomerangs, tossed away but they kept coming back. Kelly had said that the stories behind Tag's demotions were all worth telling, but Tag simply grunted when I asked for one. I guess I didn't even rate to hear them yet.

"Hands off my shotgun, New Guy."

Oh yeah, I also didn't deserve the creative energy required to think of a good callsign yet. I clicked the Pelican case's latches back into place and swallowed my pride. It's just the way it was; these guys were all top-rate and I was admittedly way out of my element. I also wasn't viewed as fit to carry anything beyond the 9mm sidearm yet. I tried not to be too upset about it. In all honesty if Cerberus Squad was as good as they were supposed to be, any bad guys who got in our way would be dead before I'd get a chance to get in the way. I probably wouldn't even have to so much as draw the pistol from its holster.

"Forty-Seven, Crash has eyes on an oncoming vehicle," Vaun said.

Crash was Hodges. Apparently, he didn't have the best driving record. There was a white van approaching with a blacked-out windshield. When something disastrous happens, it's a natural human reaction to stare. You see it in rubberneckers on the highway when there's a wreck. You see it when pedestrians simply stare at a man on a ledge who takes that long fall to the pavement. So when a building explodes in broad daylight and a vehicle drives away without even pausing, I'd classify that as suspicious.

"If this shit gets hot you're staying in the car. You listening, bud?" Kelly said. His seriousness was completely different from the grinning man I'd fought earlier.

"Yes, sir."

"Cut the 'sir' crap. I'm just filling in for the Captain's Lieutenant. That doesn't make me one."

I looked through the windshield at the van barreling toward us. It was just half a block away from Vaun's vehicle. As the distance closed I saw our lead SUV pull over and all three Black Spear operatives hopped out. Hodges had a shotgun laid across the hood aimed at the oncoming van. Next to him was Billy, his pistol drawn and outstretched in a two-handed grip. Steady as a rock. I hadn't yet heard Billy's callsign, but after the beatdown he delivered me earlier I wasn't quite ready to approach him about it.

There was still a chance this was a misunderstanding, so Captain Vaun took a step away from the SUV and fired a single round into the air. Warning shot.

The occupants of the van did not respond as passively. As soon as Vaun pulled the trigger, the van side door slid open and a man leaned out the side with a submachine gun in hand. Vaun ducked back behind the safety of the SUV as bullets peppered the asphalt around him. The few pedestrians that were still nearby scattered to avoid the wild and aimless gunshots.

Hodges pumped out three shells from his shotgun in rapid succession. The first hit the left headlight, the second hit the side paneling, but the third clipped the thug's arm. Before Hodges could manage a fourth, the van opened up the throttle and sped past their SUV. Right in our direction.

Kelly scowled. "And here I thought the day was going to be boring."

The buckshot-pelted van sped at us head-on. Ever so casually, Kelly rolled down his window. He leaned out of the window and brought his scope to his eye when his radio squawked.

"Forty-Seven, this is Blackbars, I need one alive enough to talk."

With his right-hand holding the pistol grip of the rifle, Kelly used his left to thumb the radio. "Copy that."

The rifle cracked and the tinted glass on the driver's side of the white van's windshield puffed a crater. From this distance, I could see the driver's head snap back before the inside of the windshield was painted a chunky red. Kelly leaned back into his seat, face not showing any reaction. "There's still the guy with the submachine gun in the back."

It had been an impossible shot. Most marksmen can't pull off accurate shots against a target moving that fast, let alone when inside a vehicle moving at the same speed. Kelly hadn't broken a sweat.

The van swerved around and drifted into the oncoming lane, but then regained control and roared past us. Tag hit the brakes and cranked the steering wheel to the left. The tires squealed against Tag's efforts to break the laws of physics through sheer strength. My head thrashed to the side and struck the window, reminding me of the bruised condition of my face. My blackened eye screamed at me and my aching teeth clattered together. Then, as if by miracle, the back end of our SUV whipped around and Tag floored it.

"He's headed to the freeway, Kelly," Tag said. "You want to slow him down?"

Kelly frowned and narrowed his eyes. The on-ramp for the interstate was just after this block, and I knew we couldn't risk civilian vehicles complicating things. The van's side door slid open in front of us again and this time two men leaned out to fire at us. One was the submachine gunner from before, holding his weapon in a blood-soaked arm. The other was a brutish man who fired a nickel-plated 1911 Colt. The bullets smacked across our windshield, but the tempered glass barely showed a blemish. Kelly and Tag's eyes met, and for a split-second Kelly's smile returned.

The van was nearly to the on-ramp when Kelly leaned out the window once more. I saw him take a breath, slowly release it, and then pull off two quick shots into the rear window of the van. I assumed they were just suppressing fire, but a moment later the goon with the submachine gun slumped out of the side door.

Kelly quickly sat back into his seat. "Oh shit, try not to—!"

The man crashed into the front of our windshield with a wet crunch. His body flattened against the tempered glass as if he were made of red putty. Before he slid under the bumper, I noticed the entry wound Kelly's shot had left on the side of his breast. Heart shot.

Tag grimaced at the sight, then casually flicked on the windshield wipers to clear the blood off.

The man with the .45 wasted another round testing the armored windshield. It definitely paid to be on the side of things that had the military black budget and high-tech gear. Kelly took his position again, this time aiming for the tires. After a single shot, the back-right tire exploded, but somehow the van's driver managed to steer to the on-ramp.

Kelly tossed his radio to Tag, who promptly hit the push-to-talk button. "Blackbars, this is Boomerang. We're about to get eyes on from the public."

"Roger that, Boomerang. I'll see if we can—"

"Cerberus, this is Father," a deep Brooklyn voice cut in. Rourke. "Nearby State Troopers are already en route to halt traffic. We'll be wearing FBI badges for this one. Handle it. Father, out."

The van hurtled onto the freeway like an injured mare fleeing on hobbled but spry legs. Its tire shredded and the rim showered sparks on the pavement behind it. The high-speed air rushed through Kelly's open window and turned the inside of our SUV into a whirlwind. There were only a few other cars on the freeway, which was a miracle in and of itself in the Los Angeles area. All the same, Kelly couldn't sight up a shot as the van swerved around the other vehicles.

"Get up there, damn it," Kelly said.

Tag grunted and weaved around the light traffic, trying to get alongside their van. We came up behind it on their left, and the man with the .45 aimed to shoot at us again.

But this time I was the one who fired out the window. The Walther kicked in my hand as I squeezed off a couple shots. I wasn't expecting to have Kelly's accuracy, but as our distance closed it had made it easier. The bullets ricocheted off the paneling of the vehicle, enough to convince the .45 guy to duck back inside.

Kelly looked back at me, surprised. "You ever shoot anyone before, New Guy?"

"First time for everything," I said.

Kelly smiled. "Well, it's just like the movies. Put the bad guy down, nothing to it."

I nodded, hoping it was going to be as easy as it sounded. Hoping more that it wouldn't come to that. The van slowed, the shredded tire keeping it from escaping, and we continued to gain on it.

"Fuck 'em if they can't take a hint," grumbled Tag. He whipped the steering wheel to the right to execute a PIT maneuver. Our SUV slammed into their left rear tire and the whole back end of the van fishtailed. It slid sideways and the open sliding door turned to face us. I saw in that short half second the bewildered look on the .45 man's face as the van went into a roll.

Tag hit the brakes to put some distance between us and the heap of metal that toppled away from us. After what felt like an eternity, the van came to a rest on its side, the sliding door now open to the sky. A few passing vehicles sped by it; one clipped the front end then came to a stop, and two more slowed behind the wreck. Concerned citizens just in the wrong place at the wrong time.

"Shotgun. Now," Tag growled.

I opened the latches and tossed it up, both Tag and Kelly already exiting the vehicle with weapons at the ready. Kelly risked a glance back to me as I opened my door and stepped outside.

"Yeah, yeah, I know. Stay back," I said.

Kelly and Tag cautiously approached the crashed vehicle when a hand holding a compact SMG pointed out of the side door at them and lit up with a long burst of fire. Both men ducked behind the cover of one of the stopped passenger vehicles, but the car's occupants were sprayed with rounds. The man in the driver's seat slumped over, his head coming to a rest on the horn. Its blare went on and on.

While Kelly and Tag took cover, four men climbed out of the overturned van. Three from the side door and one through the destroyed windshield. I saw them fan out in opposite directions in a flanking maneuver. They were practiced and they moved fluidly. In seconds they'd have my teammates boxed in. Despite my concerns— and ignoring Kelly's silent order—I moved up from the SUV.

The two Black Spear operatives were outnumbered. I couldn't just sit back and watch. Kelly screamed at the people who had stopped their vehicle to get the hell out of there. An old man and his granddaughter hurried away as the goons from the van fired wild shots in their direction. Somehow, they got away unscathed.

I could see the huge man with the .45 leaning out from behind the wrecked van. He wore a leather bomber jacket that had the sleeves cut off and a moustache on his face that was pulled into a snarl as he fired again and again.

Two men were circling around towards us from the left. I spotted one, a younger Hispanic-looking man with a MAC-10, shooting blindly over the hood of a car. His partner steadily closed in on us. The MAC-10 kept us ducked behind cover, while the other continued to flank us. And then he was there, right in front of us, his handgun pointing right at Tag's head.

A triumphant look crossed his face but then Tag took the slightest step backward—and Hodges's SUV smashed into him at full speed. Whatever Hodges's driving record looked like, it was getting another note in it for sure today.

Before either of us had time to react, the one with the MAC-10 cleared the distance. I spun as fast as I could when I heard the machine pistol firing, but I couldn't move fast enough. Someone behind me grabbed my shoulder. Kelly pulled me out of the way, screaming, "Get down!" He took one of the rounds to the shoulder and fell back while I squeezed off a shot. It hit the shooter in the chest. He fell back, gasping as he slammed into the pavement.

I gripped my pistol in both hands. The shooter wore a ballistic vest, but my shot still knocked the wind out of him. His weapon clattered away, just barely out of reach.

"Don't fucking move," I warned as I trained my weapon on his face.

His fingers grazed the grip of his lost MAC-10.

I stepped closer, never taking my eyes off the sights. "I don't want to kill you, man."

He reached out with impossible slowness. His fingers wrapped around the grip of his gun. My pistol bucked in my hand. I hadn't even meant to pull the trigger.

The shot wasn't clean. It didn't hit him between the eyes and instantly turn off the lights, or make his brains explode out the back of his head. Instead, my shot landed just below his left nostril. A small red dot. Blood pooled out of it in thin little rivers that ran down his upper lip and down both sides of his face. I stared into his eyes as they went wide. Faintly I sensed shouting and tires peeling away from us. But the only thing I was focusing on was him. He made snorting choking sounds. I realized he was trying to breathe through the fresh hole drilled through his nasal passages and into his skull. Every time he made that snorting sound more blood coughed out of that little red dot in his face.

I watched as his whole body shook. He twitched once, twice, and then his eyes rolled into his skull and he was still. So still. The blood continued to drain from the dead man's head.

Kelly had lied to me. It had been nothing like in a movie.

CHAPTER 14

Mr. Rourke. 11:45 a.m.
Black Spear Site
San Diego, California

Darren Rourke watched the satellite imaging from his computer and rubbed at the ache flaring across his jaw. Everything considered? The situation could be worse. Civilian casualties were minimal, and Rourke himself had disabled all traffic cameras in the area. His right-hand, Mason, was handling the coordination of local police and state troopers under the guise of false FBI credentials. The agency's Director was on Rourke's speed-dial and knew the drill.

Rourke was a man of decided calculation. And by his calculations Cerberus Squad had performed acceptably.

The medical facility, on the other hand, was a complete and utter loss. It wasn't the deaths of twenty-seven men and women that troubled him, but the tissue samples that had been destroyed. There hadn't been much left of Lee-Ray to begin with. Now, any chance of devising a countermeasure had been consumed by the flames.

Mason walked back into his office and crossed her arms in her typical impatient manner. Given that she was one of maybe three people on the planet who had his utmost trust, he allowed her these little moments of contempt.

"Local assets are on scene. We'll run a gangland story for the

Interstate, scheduled demolition with backdated permits for the medical facility."

Rourke nodded. "Someone's playing with us, Mason, and I am less than amused. They used Matthew Lee-Ray like a signal flare to show what they were capable of, and then just as quickly snuffed out any clues."

"We're quite skilled at uncovering more, sir."

"I feel like I'm playing poker. We caught a peek at the other player's hand and then all the cards disappeared."

Mason pursed her lips. "I've found that the best solution when someone cheats me at cards, and hides an ace or two up their sleeve, is to cut off their arms. Hard to hide things up your sleeves if you don't have any. Card analogies aside, these shooters were sloppy. We'll catch them, sir."

"I know we will, but that's not what concerns me," Rourke said. "If we'd managed to retain just one sample, we could have our best scientists working around the clock to break the virus down and develop an antidote of sorts. Our own efforts to minimize awareness of the virus to the public put us in a bind."

Kara Mason had worked for Rourke long enough to pick up on every silent cue he had. Knowing that he needed some space to think, Mason exited his office without explanation or a needless request to leave. Courtesies and overt formality were hardly the biggest reasons Rourke kept her by his side.

On the positive side of the scales was Captain Vaun's new recruit. Sergeant West had no place in the gun game he had found himself in, yet he'd managed to hold his own. Any other person in this situation would have hidden in the car when the shootout had gone to the freeway. West had done the exact opposite. In the end, he'd even managed to take down one of the shooters. A headshot, no less.

Though Rourke was still hesitant to say that West could hack it with Black Spear, he could safely admit that his opinions on him were beginning to shift.

Black Spear dealt with threats akin to nightmares on a regular basis, but something about this new case made Rourke's jaw hurt. Lots of things tended to cause that old wound to spike up. Lousy bureaucracy and the unavoidable politics that intruded into this line of work tended to cause just a small noticeable throb.

The big aches, the real pains like he felt now, always happened to come around when Black Spear had a real problem on its hands. It was Rourke's own personal superstition, and he had learned over many years of experience to trust the old wound. He pulled a small pill case from his jacket pocket, tapped two pills into his palm, and gulped them down dry to quiet the pain.

Something big was coming Black Spear's way, and like it or not, the team stuck at the center of it had a rookie still on his first day. Rourke forced himself to stop rubbing his jaw and sat in his office in silence, mulling over what was to come.

Rourke was a man of deliberate calculation. At the moment, West was just one of many undetermined variables fogging up the equation.

CHAPTER 15

Cole West. 11:57 a.m.
Interstate 5
Los Angeles, California

I don't know how long I kept aiming at the dead man on the ground. I was aware that time was passing but I couldn't make myself holster the gun. Flashing red and blue lights were in the distance from the state troopers securing a perimeter, per our FBI cover story.

I didn't care about any of that. All I could focus on was the body before me.

Dead, by my bullet. This made it real. If there was a point of no return, I knew I'd just punched my ticket with the pull of a trigger.

"Your hand is gonna start shaking soon. Better holster that," a voice said behind me.

I slammed the pistol into my holster as if not holding the gun would take me out of this moment. When I turned, I was surprised to find that it was Tag who had spoken. His voice had been so soft, so damn gentle and reassuring, you'd think he was a friendly youth pastor rather than a three-hundred pound walking mountain.

"It's not like a movie," he said, his eyes on the body. "Kelly just says that because . . . well, I guess because it helps that first time."

I nodded, but then my eyes went wide. "Kelly? Is he—"

"Yeah," Tag cut me off. He planted a hand on my chest to keep me from sprinting away. "He's good. Are you, though?"

I gave an unconvincing nod. Tag saw straight through me. I forced everything I was feeling down deep where it couldn't hurt, because this wasn't the time nor place to process anything, then clenched my jaw and tried again. It must've worked because he cocked his head over his shoulder and started leading me towards an ambulance.

"He took one round to the shoulder; through-and-through. Our docs are looking at him now."

Kelly was already being loaded up into the back of an ambulance on a stretcher. Two paramedics were treating his gunshot wound while yelling information to each other so quickly that I couldn't hear any of it. A question came to mind of just how many medical personnel Rourke had on tap to respond to a scene so quickly. A lump got caught in my throat as I stared at his red-soaked bandages. Before I managed to say anything to Kelly, a hand latched onto my shoulder and wrenched me around.

"You motherfucker!" Hodges screamed. He was close enough that his wintergreen spit flecked my cheeks. "I saw what happened! Kelly took that round for you!"

Blood rushed to my bruised face and pain seared anew. I tried to speak, but Hodges shoved me hard in the chest and I staggered, my back hitting the side of the ambulance.

"You couldn't watch your own ass and now one of the guys on *my* team is out of the fight. Because of you."

As angry as I was, I had nothing to say. The bullet Kelly had taken was meant for me after all. Tag stepped forward, and I readied myself for another round of verbal abuse. Instead, he pulled Hodges close and spoke mere inches from his face. "The new guy is on *our* team." Their staring match lasted a full five seconds before Tag spoke again. "Take a walk, bro."

Hodges backhanded the side of the ambulance then stomped off.

The paramedics closed the backdoors of the ambulance and sped away. As the flashing lights tore down the freeway, I looked at Tag, "Thanks."

"Didn't do it for you," he said. "Just as I told him: like it or not you're on my team. I look out for people on my team." With that he walked away. I followed alongside him.

We came up to Vaun's SUV, the front end dented and painted with blood from where Hodges had run head-on into one of the shooters. Said body was a ruined mess under the front bumper, and Billy was at the moment having a hard time wrenching it from the undercarriage. Meantime, Vaun leaned against the open driver's-side door, a finger pressing on his small radio earbud. Billy managed to unstick the crushed corpse. He knelt beside it.

A military helicopter circling above buffeted us as it descended. "That's our ride," Vaun said, "Cleanup crews will take care of the vehicles. Rourke wants us debriefed, then we're hitting the two that got away. We've got a drone tracking them now."

"We still get dibs?" Billy asked, not sparing an instant to pause his cursory examination of the dead shooter.

"Officially we are still an active team for this. We're down a man, so Achilles Squad will back us up."

Tag scowled. "As long as we get dibs. I'm looking forward to asking these guys a few questions."

"Oorah," Vaun said with a dark look in his eye. "Our ride is here. Let's roll, gentlemen."

As I started to turn, Billy held up a hand.

"Yo, hold up. You might want to see this, Captain."

We all moved over as Billy undid the buttons of the dead shooter's shirt. Images of an English bulldog, a skeletal grim reaper holding an M16, and a set of chevrons were still visible on the bloody mashed flesh. We all knew what they were. The tattoos weren't signature marks of any Mexican cartel or radical Islamist terrorist group. This guy wasn't some Russian agent wreaking havoc on our home soil. Every single one of the tattoos were familiar military moto pieces. The shooter was one of our own.

Forty minutes later we were at Angel Site. There were several Black Spear stations across the country, and Angel Site was the resident stronghold within Los Angeles County. It was minimally staffed, which is why a San Diego team had been assigned to retrieve the samples in the first place. I didn't know the name of the site in San Diego; everyone on my team just called it Home.

We were led not to a briefing room, but down to one of the basement levels. There we found the morgue and Doctor Tanya Phelps. I quickly learned that she preferred to be called just Tanya or maybe Doc, but never Doctor Phelps. That was far too hoity-toity for someone who gave as little a shit about everything as Doc. She had a hooked beak of a nose, dirty-blonde hair that hung low near her tired-looking eyes, and held a large coffee mug adorned with a huge yellow smiley face, the latter the exact opposite of her own expression. She conducted herself around the morgue as if the freshly bullet-riddled bodies bored her more than watching paint dry. It dawned on me that this wasn't anything new to her. I wondered exactly what condition a body would have to be in to get a reaction out of her.

"Please, come in," she said, her words dripping with disinterest.

The dead shooters from the highway were stripped nude and neatly displayed on their own individual metal slabs. We all started to spread out into the room; Hodges made sure I noticed when he brushed my shoulder hard as he passed. I pretended not to care.

As I stepped closer to the row of tables, I looked over each one of the corpses. On the far left was a younger man with a crew cut, well-maintained mustache, and a face that would've fit on a poster for police officers everywhere if it weren't for the large bullet wound in his forehead. He was the van's initial driver, the first one Kelly had bullseyed through the windshield. Next to him were the remnants of the shooter who had fired on us with a submachine gun from the van's side-door. He'd been shot through the heart and then fell under the wheels of our SUV. Beside him was the guy Hodges had rammed head-on; the same one Billy had spotted the tattoos on. Lastly was the Hispanic man, the one I'd killed.

"I don't suppose I need to go over cause of death for any of them?" Doc asked.

Vaun gave her an icy look. "They have anything on them worth noting?"

"Well, after the heads-up from Billy, I couldn't help but notice *something* peculiar." With a laser pointer in her left-hand, Doc indicated the driver's body. "Eagle globe and anchor, left breast." She then pointed to the submachine gunner. "Fairbairn-Sykes dagger, inside of right wrist. Raiders skull on the shoulder." The double-edged dagger was a symbol for Special Forces across several branches in the United States military, the skull a familiar emblem dating all the way back to World War II.

Next was the one Billy had already checked. "Standard USMC English bulldog, a set of Corporal chevrons, and a couple others."

Last, the Hispanic I'd killed. "Skull with an Airborne beret on his chest, few more 'hooyah' moto tats like this one that say, 'Death from Above' or similar crap." Those all indicated Army Airborne, maybe 75th Rangers or 101st Airborne. I wasn't in the Army, so I didn't exactly know the difference.

"Who are these guys?" I didn't mind being the first to ask the question out loud. There was a pause, during which everyone in the room sat for a moment, nobody wanting to be the one to say it. The second someone did it would give that idea life, and I had a feeling this idea was going to greatly complicate things. Finally, it was Tag who broke the silence when he actually laughed. There was no humor in it.

"We've got Marines, Raiders, and Rangers here. Who are they? I think it's pretty obvious: they're us."

Hodges whistled while starting to pack his can of dip with a shake of his wrist. "Uncle Sam's best-of-the-best all sitting shoulder to shoulder. Damn. It's so much easier when the bad guys are just another terrorist cell from the Middle East."

"If that's the best-of-the-best then consider me disappointed," Billy said with a wicked grin. "I thought you Americans put up more of a fight than this?"

"They clipped Kelly," Tag said. Billy met his gaze but didn't so much as flinch. "I'd say that's plenty good enough."

Then, as if the pressure cooker in the room needed even more tension, Hodges muttered under his breath, "It wasn't these guys that got Kelly shot . . ."

Another pause. Tag stared Billy down, Hodges tense and ready to try and throttle me, and the whole time Vaun gauged all of us with quick evaluating glances. Before things could escalate any further, the quiet was broken by a long obnoxious slurp.

We all looked to the other side of the metal tables where Doc was taking a big swig from her coffee mug. This time the big yellow smiley face on it actually matched her own grin. "Look, kids, you've had a long day and all, but mine's just getting started, thanks to you. As much as I'd love to watch your macho bullshit, there *are* a couple dead guys here I need to take care of. Why don't you all just cool off a bit before one of you turns into another body I need to examine." Doc took another gulp of coffee. "And from the looks of this one, you've all already let off some steam today." She pointed a finger at me. I'd managed to forget my purpling face until just then. "So, what, first-day hazing or something?"

My three new teammates broke into stifled chuckles. Vaun even half smirked but then his phone rang. His posture stiffened as he looked at it. It could only be one person on the other end. Mister Rourke.

CHAPTER 16

Jax was sharpening the six-inch-long blued-steel of his KA-BAR when the satellite phone on his desk started to ring. Sighing, he slid the knife back into the leather sheath on his hip, the blade fitting inside snug as a hand in a glove. Jax found that satisfying in a peculiar way, there was a right fit and place for every object just like there was a right man for every job. His phone rang for a third time and shook him from his thoughts enough to answer the call.

"This is Jax," he said, absentmindedly rolling the sharpening stone back and forth between his thumb and forefinger.

"It's Bats. Brother, we got hit on the way back. It's bad."

Jax considered that for a moment. He gripped the stone tight in his hand and stood up from his chair to pace his office. "Roger that," he said, forcing calm in his voice. "Did the job get done?"

There was a pause on the other end of the line, a little too long for Jax's comfort. He stopped pacing and stood very still, waiting for Batson to speak again.

"Abe," he said, "we lost four men."

Jax felt a pang of anger spike at the bottom of his throat. He was expecting—at the worst—a little police action. Maybe a few local cops getting brave, but there was no reason Batson should have lost anyone, let alone four. Four of *Jax's* men.

"Did the job get done?" Jax asked again.

"Yeah. But Boss... we lost Garza, Michaels, Hoffman, and Davis. It's just me and the Moose now."

Jax nodded to himself, he liked the one they called the Moose. The giant had a brutal nature that didn't fit in with the standard military, yet could perfectly serve in Jax's. This was war, after all. Anyone in Terminal who wanted to kid themselves into thinking that there wouldn't be losses on both sides was simply blind. He just hadn't been expecting it to be this soon.

"We've been burning rubber since they hit us, brother," Batson said. "They were in unmarked black vics. No idea who these guys were, but they were pros. Nobody tailing us right now, but I still think the Moose and I should cool off somewhere."

"Affirmative, Bats," Jax said. Slowly. Deliberately. He would not let himself give in to his own reactions. "Go to the safe house we talked about. I'm sending a squad to rendezvous with you there. We'll debrief via the secure link once you arrive. Jax out."

After he ended the call, Jax stood very still in his office for a long while. He stared out of the large-paned glass window of his office to the desert sands beyond.

This changed things. Unmarked vehicles with shooters capable of taking down four of his own brought him to only one conclusion. It had to be some sort of special outfit. Deep government type. The Centers for Disease Control didn't have shooters. Jax knew the soldiers that made up the U.S. Army Medical Research Institute for Infectious Diseases—USAMRIID—were not made of the stuff to take on his guys. No, this unknown party was something much harder. Maybe some kind of CIA or Homeland joint task force? He hadn't anticipated this type of response until later in the game.

Jax left his office and descended the catwalk stairs to the training grounds. The Terminal Grounds consisted of a shooting range, a few grappling pits, several barracks, a motor pool, reinforced armory and, lastly, the lab. No expense had been spared in the construction of the Terminal Grounds and nearly every building was built out of hard concrete, but the lab was the crowning achievement in terms of security.

The laboratory itself was underground; all that was visible from the surface was the entry bunker which was mostly security gates and filtration systems. Jax walked past the first security checkpoint, which was comprised of an armed sentry and a door. Most in Terminal didn't have access past the sentry, and fewer knew what lay beyond. As he went through and down the first set of steps, he breathed in the cool clean air before coming to the next checkpoint. Here was a keycard reader and another very thick, very strong steel door. Jax produced a red keycard from his pocket, whistling to himself as he scanned it. The door pulled open on hydraulic hinges with a hiss.

Beyond lay the Moses-1 stockpile. Only six men had access to this room, not even Batson had a keycard for it. Jax walked in and looked to the decontamination chamber where his lead scientist was just getting out of his clean suit. The man's name was Steven Chan. He was a former Navy intelligence officer who left the Armed Forces to pursue a career in genetics. Unfortunately, that highly competitive field showed Chan that he wasn't as intellectually gifted as he'd thought. Or it might've been that his God complex ruined his chances since by all measures he was an insufferable prick. That, combined with financial difficulties, led Chan to seek out more lucrative ventures.

It was Chan who had brought Moses-1 to Jax. A major biotech firm Chan worked for had been researching adaptive antivirals and vaccines. A think-tank he was a part of had been developing a cure-all serum but, as is often the case with scientific developments, their actual results had been quite unexpected. Unexpected, and terrifying.

Their goal was to utilize recombinant DNA and stem cells to

create a type of "smart-vaccine." Something that could adapt and fight off any biological agent, something that would only grow stronger the more agents it was exposed to. Inadvertently, Chan's think-tank had created Moses-1. A chimera virus with properties stolen from all of the biological agents they had been trying to treat.

After the group saw the effects it had on a volunteer test subject, another scientist had remarked that it looked like they'd unleashed the biblical plagues of Egypt. Blisters, boils, blood, and even the croaking cough the virus caused in the lungs were attributed to the plague of frogs. The bloodshot effect to the eyes was like the darkening of the sun. Thus, Moses-1 had been borne.

The project was immediately scrapped, all research erased and the samples incinerated. All members of the think-tank had already signed nondisclosure agreements. Due to the sensitive nature of their creation, the biotech firm never announced their results. A pharmaceutical company announcing they'd engineered a doomsday plague? It would have been a public-relations disaster. Stocks would have plummeted and careers ruined. Instead, they disposed of everything. Chan himself carried out the incineration of the samples. Well, almost all of the samples.

While the rest of his group saw total failure with Moses-1, Chan saw opportunity. Just like Jax had said: there was a right fit and place for every object, and Moses-1's fit was with Terminal.

"Mr. Jackson, I hate these fucking suits," Chan said.

He hung his clean suit on a small hook and then heaved his overweight body onto a bench. Chan was not a healthy man. To think that he once fit into a military uniform made Jax's stomach churn. But as much as his appearance upset him, the man had his uses.

While it was Chan's wallet that drew him to sell Moses-1 to Terminal, it was his pride that kept him tethered here. Jax knew this and was not afraid to exploit it. Chan *needed* to prove that he was smart, and Jax needed someone smart enough to handle the virus.

Not only that, Jax needed someone smart enough to perform the experiments he wanted. Moses-1 was perhaps the deadliest contagion in history, but its strength was simultaneously its weakness. Carriers of the virus crashed and bled out before they could effectively spread the virus to a large enough population. Jax and Chan had been making efforts to correct that.

"Good afternoon, Doctor," said Jax. "How goes the work today?"

Chan wiped his sweaty face with the back of his hand. "Why don't you take a look for yourself?"

Jax turned away from the scientist and peered through the observation window to one of the experiment rooms. His face was less than two inches from the window when a bloody hand smacked against the glass.

Jax actually flinched. Chan chuckled and all three of his chins jiggled. On the other side of the glass was a young black man wearing a soldier's fatigues. He was hemorrhaging blood from all of the orifices on his face, his eyes had started to go bloodshot, and blister-like pustules were developing all over his skin. But this soldier wasn't huddled on the floor, slowly succumbing to the virus. He was going berserk. He pounded on the window with both hands, leaving bloody handprints all across the glass. His rancid teeth gnashed at Jax from the other side of the window as reddened foam frothed at the corners of his mouth. With a horrible croaking cough, the man hocked a stream of thick blood onto the window.

"Well now, that is certainly a development."

"I give you Moses-2," Chan declared triumphantly. He gave them both a moment to savor his announcement. "It was the trickiest of riddles, this little problem you gave me," Chan said. "How do you improve upon such a perfect pathogen? How do you make it spread? The delivery system is another factor we still need to work out, but the virus *itself*? Its lethality outweighs its communicability. It kills before it can spread, our initial trial with Mr. Lee-Ray proved that."

Chan fidgeted his fingers as he stared through the glass; the man was nearly salivating at the sight. Jax wasn't going to give the scientist the satisfaction of asking the question he was practically begging Jax to ask. Instead Jax simply waited for Chan to continue.

"Rabies," Chan said. "That was the answer. Despite all our equipment here the riddle was solved by a rabid stray mutt. Administering Moses-1 to it caused the virus to adapt, carriers grow violent roughly one hour after injection. Mental faculties diminish rapidly, of course, eventually you get this here." As he spoke, Chan tapped the glass to indicate the subject.

Jax took another look at the infected soldier in the experiment room. He didn't know him. "Who is he?"

Chan scratched one of his chins for a moment, trying to recall. "Um . . . Freeman, from the motor pool."

"And he volunteered?"

"Yes. I said it was a special position for the cause. I think he thought he was getting an immunization or some kind of covert gene therapy."

Jax considered the young doomed volunteer across from him. He didn't know his story, but assumed it was the same as countless others who had joined Terminal. Chewed up and spit out by the grand military machine, discharged and left unwanted. In the back of his head Jax couldn't help but question if he had become just like the faceless leaders he had lost so much respect for in the past.

No. Jax couldn't let that seed of doubt take root in his head. It was all for the cause. That was all that mattered. History would deem him justified.

A quote from Thomas Jefferson came to mind. Jax recited it aloud. "The tree of liberty must be refreshed from time to time with the blood of patriots." Jax pondered that, then drew a quick salute to Freeman of the motor pool and cut it before turning to Chan. "Take samples as soon as he expires and incinerate the remains."

CHAPTER 17

Rourke's shoulders barely fit into the flatscreen display. Cerberus Squad sat in quite comfortable leather chairs along the conference table, at the very end of which was mounted Rourke's screen. Vaun stewed at the opposite end, a hastily-written field report scrawled before him.

"Every one of the shooters was identified as prior military, most of them special forces," Vaun explained.

"And what does that tell you, Captain?"

"There's plenty of outfits that'll hire on vets. PMCs like Silver Scythe Security, Alpha Wolf Services, Blackwater—or Academi, or whatever they're calling themselves these days—and that's not even counting the dozens of radical militias that have popped up," Vaun answered. "One of the shooters was Hispanic, so that crosses off most White Supremacy militias. And those Minutemen patrols wouldn't be this far north of the border."

"A biological agent like this in the hands of any terrorist makes me uncomfortable," grumbled Rourke. "Put this in the hands of one of our own, and I can't help but be curious as to what they intend. Our diggers are already tearing through these guys' lives, trying to piece together any clues they can. Hopefully soon we'll have something actionable."

A buzzing sounded next to me. Distracted, I looked across and saw Billy with a cell phone in hand. It didn't faze the rest of the squad that our teammate wasn't too concerned with the importance of the meeting. I'm pretty sure Rourke would've made him eat the cell if he were actually in the room.

Hodges fidgeted in his seat. "We're getting behind. Have we pinned down the two that got away yet?"

There was a click-clack as Rourke tapped two unseen buttons, minimizing his image to the upper left corner of the screen as satellite imagery filled the rest of it. "Our eye in the sky tracked their getaway roughly fifty miles south of Los Angeles. McAllister Brothers Press, a defunct printing press until the property was rented out just a few months ago. We're tracking down the name on the lease, but I highly doubt it'll be a real lead."

The fact that we at least had the two remaining shooters' location made me feel better. Even if this was my first day with these guys, they were still teammates. They weren't alone in wanting some closure on today's events.

"At least we have the 'where,'" Tag stated. "Still leaves the questions of 'who' and 'why.'"

Billy spoke next. He just held up a hand like an elementary student, not breaking eye contact with his cell phone for an instant. "Cap, you might want to check this out."

He slid his phone across the table to Vaun, who took a glance at it and tried his best not to let his eyes go wide. "Sir, it's on the news."

In a second Rourke had already tapped a few keys and the McAllister Brothers building was replaced by a live news feed. The video had a single military rank chevron above a skull, the skull was superimposed over two crossed M16 rifles. It had already started playing before Rourke put it up on the screen.

". . . are not the fortunate sons," a digitally altered voice was saying. It was deep, menacing. Whoever the speaker was had a flair for the theatrics. "We are the forgotten ones. We are the overlooked and unwanted warriors of this once great nation, we are the very military might you rely on to sleep safely. We are the ones who have protected you. Who have fought for you. Who have bled for you. We are Terminal."

I became aware that I was no longer sitting, nor was anyone else. We had all risen to our feet and were watching intensely as the video continued to play.

"For too long we have lived in the shadows below both society's attention and care. Our veterans stand neglected, dying homeless in the streets or in VA waiting rooms all across this nation. This inattentive stance is not just a failure on your part, but it is an utter betrayal; one that will be paid for in blood."

The skull emblem was replaced by footage of impressive weapons stockpiles. Countless rows of racked assault rifles and light machine guns, shelves upon shelves of ammunition and ordnance, and several short clips of massive explosions being detonated.

"Do not ask what can be done to stop us," the altered voice continued. "We are everywhere. We are growing." Several images of police, ambulances, fire trucks, and even National Guardsmen filled the screen. "We will unleash a vengeance of Biblical proportions." The video cut to a slow shot of six vials filled with a rust-colored serum.

"That's our virus," I said in a hushed whisper.

"We have bled enough. Now, it's your turn."

The video finished with time-lapsed footage of Matthew Lee-Ray as the unknown virus ravaged his body. The screen cut to black, and then back to the news anchor, whose mouth kept gaping and closing like a fish drowning in air.

I hoped someone on Rourke's team could do damage control on this and keep the public from going into full panic mode.

Before any of us could react, Vaun preemptively put his hand up to signal us to stand fast. "Sir, this—"

"A team is already analyzing it," Rourke said, cutting him off and pointing an angry sausage finger towards the screen. "These Terminal guys want to label themselves, that's fine. At least we know what to call them. So, Corporal Taggart, that answers the 'who' question you had. Now let me answer the 'when' question: we're hitting them tonight."

We all sat on edge, staring like hungry sharks ready to feed. Ready to hunt.

"They want to try and spook us? Let's show them what ghost stories are really made of."

CHAPTER 18

There was a sense of calm in the armored assault vehicle that was outright palpable. The squad's quiet resolve was like a salve against any fear I had going in. Thankfully, these streets were empty. Most people were already tucked away safe in their homes ready to sleep through the night. But not us. The night was ours.

The five of us were eager to kick things off and entirely too wired on caffeine. Rather than get the jitters, it was as if our nerves were coiled tight as piano wire and everything was set for us to start the music. We all wore black fatigues and fully armored ballistic vests. Front, back, and side plates all added weight, but more importantly they stopped rifle rounds. I wasn't sure what they were made of, but they were significantly lighter than the usual standard issue. What I was really thankful for, however, was what we had beneath the armor.

It was called Snakeskin. While I had spent countless hours in different kinds of hazmat suits, this was *the* cutting edge. I had only ever heard of it in reference to the protective garments that special forces like the SEALs used. Unlike the other bulkier ones I had experience with, Snakeskin was thin, comfortable, and surprisingly cool. Best of all, it still protected from bioagents of all kinds. They were essentially like form-fitting onesie pajamas for the biological apocalypse. And boy were they comforting. Top to bottom encapsulation complete with a shielding hood that hugged around the head.

As much as a comfort as the Snakeskin was, it was good to have a back-up plan. Each of us on Cerberus Squad had a small spray bottle of decontaminant liquid readily accessible on our belts. The liquid used absorbents similar to those used in ocean oil spills to soak up the pollutants. Those absorbents were suspended in a strong industrial sanitizer, which could neutralize the contamination. It was strong enough to cause chemical burns, but in the grand scheme of things it remained preferable to what Terminal's virus would do to us.

When I identified the equipment we would need to assault the printing press in case the virus was there, Vaun had simply nodded and produced all of it. That not only did they have the equipment on hand at Angel Site, and seemed to already know what they needed, all but confirmed my suspicions. There was another motive beyond my expertise that Vaun had recruited me for. I made a mental note to figure out what he was up to the next chance I got to catch my breath.

"Two minutes out," said Vaun in a low voice. "Weapons check."

I looked down to do a function check on my new weapon. We each had a Steyr AUG A3 XS 9mm equipped with suppressors and red dot sights. The AUG 9mm was a bull-pup style submachine gun. In the movie *Die Hard,* there's a scene where one of the henchmen assembles a cool-looking assault rifle in an elevator; our AUG 9mms were the latest version of that same rifle redesigned to a compact platform.

Normally I'd complain that the 9mm left a little to be desired in terms of stopping power, but back in the armory Tag had tossed me a case of black-tipped bullets. These were designed to fragment upon hitting a target. Essentially, they acted like miniature grenades stuffed full of shrapnel. It was definitely a step-up from the pistol I'd been issued earlier. I still felt like I was operating with training wheels.

I finished my check and looked next to me where Tag sat. The big man had finished checking his submachine gun and now had a snub-nosed .44 Magnum revolver in his hand. He was examining the open chamber and, satisfied, slapped it shut before tucking it into a leather holster in the small of his back. When he noticed me watching, he said, "Always bring a little extra. Just in case." He then indicated Hodges seated on the other side of the vehicle. Sure enough, Hodges had an old battered set of brass knuckles in one hand, hefting the reassuring weight twice.

Hodges tapped me on the knee. I bent forward to hear what he had to say. "Just in case you want to get froggy on me again," he said, knuckleduster in hand. "I'll make sure to give you a little extra what-for." He gave me an interesting smile, and I couldn't figure out if he was joking or not.

I wondered if I'd eventually bring my own personal weapon on missions; John's voice barged its way into my thoughts to warn me I was getting ahead of myself. I'd have to survive one mission before I would get the chance to worry about what I'd bring to the next.

"Drone-feed and CCTV caught three trucks pulling into the bay doors three hours ago. Other than that, no activity," explained Vaun. He turned a small tablet around for us to see the digital imagery. "Either this is Terminal's home base and those were more of their guys coming home, or they're just reinforcements. Rourke's feelers are out, digging away and trying to scrape together more intel, but as of now it's a time-sensitive issue and we can't hold off hitting McAllister's."

"What does that mean for rules of engagement?" asked Billy as he finished checking his AUG 9mm then proceeded to pull out a very long Tanto-style knife. He eyed the edge to check its sharpness while Vaun answered.

"We're going in quiet. We *need* to come away from this with something tangible. This might not be home base, but if it isn't then those reinforcements had to have come from somewhere. We only need one of them to point us in the right direction."

Shadows moved behind the captain's eyes as he spoke, and we got the underlying message. We wouldn't be taking more than one prisoner.

The armored vehicle lurched to a stop, and Vaun looked the three of us over. "Showtime, mask up."

I took one last deep breath of unfiltered air and then donned my mask. The world was plunged into a fluorescent green hue of digitally amplified night. The lens in our gasmasks had an integrated module that reacted to all ambient light within one quarter of a second. If we passed by any streetlights, or someone turned a flashlight our way, the lenses would register it and lower the light-amp accordingly to make sure we wouldn't be blinded. Tag claimed the module's reaction time was point-zero-two seconds.

Everyone else was hunched over and headed to the back hatch of the vehicle where Tag muscled it open. Cerberus Squad was a team of ghosts, silent as the very darkness that clung to them. I shadowed them. Stalking low as they did, grabbing the handle where they did, and dropping to the pavement nimble as a cat as they did.

With Kelly laid up in a hospital bed, Vaun had appointed Hodges as his acting lieutenant. There were only five of us left on the squad. Thankfully, Terminal wasn't the only unit with reinforcements. Achilles Squad, another San Diego team from Home Site, had choppered in to back us up. They were ten strong, three of them posted as snipers on rooftops from different vantage points to act as our own personal guardian angels, four more staged in an alley across the street from the front door, and the last three on standby in an unmarked vehicle on the backside of the building in case anyone tried to make a getaway. The front, back, and all the windows were covered. Our route was from the top.

"Kage, take point," Vaun said.

Billy took quick short steps to get in front. *Kage* meant "shadow" in Japanese, and I could see why it was Billy's callsign. The man simply glided on his feet in absolute silence. His gear didn't rattle nor did his heavily-obstructed-gas-mask-breathing make a sound. The thought of what a man so quiet could do with that Tanto knife of his gave me a chill.

Billy led us to the fire escape on a building adjacent to McAllister's and began to climb. Vaun was next up, followed by Hodges, then me, with Tag bringing up the rear. I kept my feet from shaking through sheer force of will as I climbed the rungs one by one. I just hoped that any second now the adrenaline would kick in and take over.

I reached the top and readied to haul myself over the ledge when a gloved hand shot down to help me over. Surprisingly, it was Hodges. "Stay low, rookie. Don't need anyone spotting us before the fun begins."

Thanks to a compact mic in Hodges's mask and a small earbud in my left ear, he could speak in nothing more than a whisper and I would hear it clear as day. Each of us had a set that allowed the squad to communicate on a secure channel.

From our vantage point six stories up, we could see the top of the McAllister Brothers building, which topped out at three stories high. Hodges dropped a black duffel bag he'd brought along, then he opened it and Billy set about assembling a zipline frame. Vaun tapped his earbud twice to open a channel to Achilles Squad. "Achilles, this is Blackbars. Roof drop in forty seconds."

"Achilles Two, copy," one of our snipers responded.

"Achilles Three, copy."

"Roger," was all the third sniper said.

Hodges slid the last piece of the zipline tower into place with a quiet *clack*. Billy stood next to him, holding what looked like a short grenade launcher. There was a cable attached to the end of it, and I realized it was a grappling gun. Billy pulled the trigger, and with a low *POOM* the hook was shot over to the McAllister Brothers rooftop, trailing the line of cable behind it, and then anchoring itself deep into the roof.

Before we hooked up to the zipline, we all activated small infrared emitters on our belts. They were invisible to the naked eye but they would mark us to our snipers with bright blinking white through their scopes.

"Kage, hook up," said Vaun.

I watched as, one by one, Billy, then Vaun and Hodges linked up to the zipline and gracefully slid across the night sky. They all moved smooth as glass. Then, it was my turn.

Tag had talked me through it earlier on our drive over and he instructed me step by step a second time. "Hook up to the line like this," he said, "Good, now attach the safety line to your waist just like I showed you." I tightened the carabiner attachments of both lines and then looked to Tag for approval. He gave a single nod. "You're ready to fly. Alright, one hand on the line, one hand on your weapon. Just like that." I took that step out onto the ledge of the roof. I know I shouldn't have, but I looked to the bottom. Even in the dark of night I could tell: it was a long way down.

"Need a push?" Tag asked.

I heard one of the other squad members give a short laugh on the open channel. I squared my jaw, and stepped off. Tag grunted in approval, it sounded pleased.

I don't know where Black Spear got their zipline cables from, but I slid down it as if it was made of oil. Cold wind, unfelt due to the complete encapsulation of our protective gear, buffeted against my Snakeskin as I rushed down the line. My heart beat rapid-fire in my chest, and I had to remember to hold onto my weapon. Otherwise, I surely would have lost it in my excitement.

The McAllister Brothers's roof, which was a distant picture seconds ago, quickly filled my vision as I neared. I was coming in fast—too fast—and next thing I knew I was hitting the roof and tumbling into a roll. As I started to somersault over my shoulder, SMG and other gear clattering against the hard roof, Hodges stepped in to brace me and stop my roll.

"Make noise like that again, and I'll ghost you," he said, pressing his mask against mine.

He pulled me back to my feet then gave me a quick pat down to make sure none of my gear was damaged. Satisfied, he shoved me away then stalked low over to where Vaun and Billy waited.

I tried to shake off the shame and went to join the squad. Tag zipped down a moment later—a sight to behold such a massive man flying through the night—then turned around to give our distant snipers a thumbs-up. He gave me an encouraging pat on the shoulder.

"Everyone tumbles the first time."

There was only one service door on the roof, which had a lone small light above it. We approached with the dark as our cover. On point, Billy moved in a combat glide with his weapon trained at the door. He paused and held up a fist to halt us. I froze in my tracks and all I could hear was my own heartbeat. Had we been spotted already? Or had our mission been compromised thanks to my clumsiness?

Before I could mentally tear myself apart any more, Vaun pulled the door open and Billy stepped inside. He fanned his weapon left and right. Hodges and I followed. The room we found ourselves in was an empty storage area filled with dozens of old pallets of paper. The lens in my mask adjusted to the bright industrial bulbs above, the world's *Matrix*-like green hue vanished.

"New Guy, readings," said Vaun.

I looked at the device on my hip. It was a Bio-Aerosol Mass Spectrometry detector, which was a fancy way of saying it was a sort of smoke-detector for biological agents. Even though it was pre-programmed for all of the agents we suspected Terminal's virus had been engineered with, we had no way of knowing if the detector would work. The science of desorption, ionization, and lasers was designed by people much smarter than me, so I couldn't explain exactly why it might *not* work for the chimera virus, but it was the best we had on short notice so it had to do. I checked the device and saw it was registering negative.

"We're in the green," I answered.

Vaun nodded.

We moved farther down the storage room. It ended against another door, which I knew from our mission brief would lead into a long hallway. The hallway split from there, one end heading in the direction of the actual printing press floor and the other to several office areas. Billy's hand moved to the doorknob and started to turn it just as it was pushed open from the other side and a man walked in.

His eyes couldn't even finish going wide with surprise before Billy chopped him quick in the throat and then swept him into the room. Vaun quietly closed the door again after making sure no one was behind him.

The man had a short beard and wore Army ACU bottoms and a dirtied plain white T-shirt. The AK-47 slung over his shoulder told us that he was no paid security guard. Billy had him pressed against one of the pallets of paper, one hand covering his mouth and the suppressor of his AUG 9mm pressed against his temple.

Hodges covered the door while Vaun walked up to the man and pulled the AK-47 sling from his shoulder. "You flinch, you die," the captain said, "Now: one blink for yes, two blinks for no. Is the virus here?"

The man's frantic eyes darted back and forth, looking at us and all of our weapons, looking at the door he'd come from just a second ago, and then finally coming to rest on the black-tinted lens of Vaun's mask. He blinked twice.

I checked the detector in my hand once more just to confirm. Still green.

"Good," said Vaun. "Next question, and you only get one try.

Blink once if you understand." The man blinked hard, as if blinking harder was the equivalent of a scream. "Who is in charge here?"

Billy carefully pulled his hand away from the man's mouth just far enough so he could answer. Shaky lips uttered one name, "Batson."

Vaun's pistol whispered mere puffs as he fired two rounds point blank into the man's face. The black-tipped rounds were already fragmenting in his skull before he had time to release a death rattle. Billy eased the body down to the ground, the man's head leaving a long red trail on the stack of white paper behind as it went down.

"Blackbars to Father," Vaun said after tapping his earbud twice. "So far negative on the virus. Run a check on the name 'Batson.'"

A moment later Mr. Rourke uploaded a package of images to Vaun's wrist-mounted computer. "Blackbars, this is Father. Diggers have already registered a match. We've located digital footprints of the militia group calling itself Terminal. Traces are all over the social media gamut."

Vaun cycled through the imagery as the Director narrated.

"A few different groups had similar names but Batson cross-references a possible to a Robert Batson; USMC, received a less than honorable discharge. Surface details make this group look like just another veteran support group, but we've found traces of messages that clearly indicate active recruiting."

Vaun fixed his computer on an image of the supposed Robert Batson. It was the same man with the moustache and bomber vest from our highway shootout.

"Blackbars, be advised: if this is the *real* Terminal then their numbers are much greater than we anticipated."

We all looked at each other, though we could see nobody's eyes through the masks.

"Father, can we track how many they've recruited from the messages?"

"Difficult to say. They're clever enough to delete their messages and run a bleach program, which they've been doing for months. We've already uncovered some, still digging."

"Father, please advise: can you estimate how many men Terminal has?"

There was a pause before Rourke answered. "Hundreds, Blackbars. They have hundreds."

CHAPTER 19

Robert Batson. 11:49 p.m.
McAllister Brothers Press
Santa Ana, CA

Batson was thankful for the reinforcements Jax had sent over. The thirty or so capable shooters were reassuring, though truth be told he would've preferred a single good vehicle that he could use to leave this place. It was the waiting that was getting under his skin. Batson was not one prone to plotting or deep-thinking; he was a man of action and sitting around stewing went against his very nature.

But he had his instructions. One of the men Jax had sent had delivered the message: sit tight. Wait the night out.

"Hurry up and wait" was not a new concept to Batson, or any of the other men in Terminal, for that matter, but to him it always had and always would leave a sour taste in his mouth. That Jax was the one making them do it struck Batson as funny in an ironic sort of way. After all, back in the Corps it was Jax himself who had been the loudest voice in the room to call "hurry up and wait" an utter waste of time. The ensuing confrontation with Batson's and Jax's Platoon Commander, Lieutenant Kim, had cost Jax a promotion. Yeah, funny that now Jax was the one making them do it.

Batson wondered where their old lieutenant was these days. More importantly, what would he think if he could see them now. The sheer *magnitude* of what Jax had created was something Batson didn't have the words for. Terminal was the unrestricted might of American military potential, but even this force would inevitably be prone to some of the less desirable borrowed aspects of the U.S. military. Batson chuckled to himself about that, then shook the thought away as he continued walking his rounds of the building.

He was currently on the ground floor of the printing press building. Several foldable cots had been set up and a few of Batson's reinforcements were on a sleeping break, rifles propped up against their frames. One of the men looked up at Batson as he walked by and shot him the peace sign. The huge printing machines took up a majority of the area, but it offered the most space so they'd made it the resting area.

Batson finished his rounds and made his way to a catwalk that overlooked the rest area. Moose was leaning against a guard rail, smoking a cigarette. He nodded to Batson as he approached. "Interesting night. Figured we would've cleared out of here by now."

Batson stopped in his tracks and faced him. "Jax says we stay. We stay."

"I thought nobody ordered anyone in Terminal? We all get a say, right?" Moose flicked his cigarette over the guard rail, its ash raining down on the men below. Batson's posture didn't change.

"You're right," Batson said. "You're your own man. You don't like it, then head on out. Jax might not be in charge of me, but I will tell you one thing. He's smarter than both of us. So, feel free to boogie your giant ass out the door."

Moose shifted around so that the two hardened men stood squared up face to face.

"I think you should stay, too. Or do you want to challenge that?"

The offer held in the air for a moment. A muscle at the edge of Batson's jaw twitched. He readied to dropkick the Moose over the railing if he so much as flinched.

The Moose's hands, large as baseball mitts, clenched into rock-like fists.

The offer was there, and Batson actually wanted him to take it. One swing. Hell, give him something to do other than wait until daylight. Give their reinforcements a show and add another notch on his belt. He was Jax's hammer, but the Moose would just be another footnote in the stories the men told of Batson.

The moment passed. The Moose's stance softened, his fists relaxing. Moose pulled another cigarette from his pack and shrugged, "Hell nah, Jax is the man. Ain't nobody questions him. It's just the boredom."

Batson nodded. "Maybe you should get some rest. Plenty of fight left to go. We're gonna need all the energy we can get."

The Moose thought it over as he flicked his lighter. "I don't know, man," he said, using his cigarette to point at the men below. "Seems like some of our 'back-up' looks rougher than we do." Batson couldn't argue with that. He'd thought the same thing earlier when the reinforcements had arrived. Batson simply shrugged and walked past the big lug, leaving him to whatever mischievous thoughts he had.

Past the catwalk, he entered a long hallway. Old vending machines gathered dust. A few bulletin boards that hadn't been updated in years adorned the walls. Another handful of troops were hanging out here, one used the buttstock of his rifle to break the glass on a vending machine and snatch up a decades-old bag of Doritos. Batson gave them a few seconds of a stare that was all needles, then pushed by them towards the room he'd turned into his office. It brought him a certain level of satisfaction that the men parted before him like the Red Sea.

As he strode into his modest accommodations, which had previously been the factory foreman's office, Batson closed the door behind him and then let out a long sigh. He tried to breathe out all the built-up frustrations of the day. He tried. He failed.

He collapsed into an old leather chair and started to replay the day's events in his head. Garza. Michaels. Hoffman. Davis. Four dead in their first mission. Batson had seen Garza get gunned down last, right before the Moose had torn a young woman from a stopped vehicle and literally pulled Batson into it. Part of him still felt like he should've stayed and finished their enemies off, or at least taken more of them down before retreating.

On the desk in front of him was a secure laptop in a ruggedized case. After the excitement on the freeway, Batson and the Moose had burned their phones in case the GPS was being tracked. The laptop was currently his only secure form of contacting Jax and vice versa. He'd told Jax that he'd be standing by the laptop for any further instructions, but all night there had been nothing. He considered booting it up one more time and checking if Jax had sent him a message but decided against it.

Instead, Batson placed the three magazines for his 1911 on the desk in front of him and slowly began reloading them from a box of .45 ACP. He needed an activity to keep his hands busy while his mind continued to process everything. As he thumbed a round into a clip, his eyes fell on the nickel-plated pistol. Jax's colt, now his. Jax must've lost some faith in him. Maybe that was why he'd sent so many men— some of whom looked more haggard than he did—to meet him here. Maybe the "hurry up and wait" of it all was a form of punishment. Or maybe Batson was reading too much into things.

While his right hand continued to thumb rounds into the clip his left scratched his mustache. He was getting way ahead of himself. Thinking things out was Jax's game. Batson knew his place. He also knew his role in this game. His thumb finished loading the last magazine, something his hands accomplished all on autopilot. Resolved, Batson slapped a fresh mag into the 1911 and slid the gun back into his holster.

For a second his tired eyes closed. It was so tempting to let that seductive power of sleep take him over. Before he gave in, a loud pounding sounded at the door. The Moose barged in as Batson snapped to his feet.

"Bats," said the Moose, eyes frantic and wide. "Something's wrong. You better come quick. It's one of the guys downstairs, it's weird. He's really sick, man."

CHAPTER 20

I took one last glance at the man Vaun had executed, then followed the others out of the storage area.

"Robert Batson is the target," Vaun said. "All other hostiles are expendable."

We approached the end of the hallway that split into a T, Billy still taking point, when two men paced into view from the left. Both had AK-47s slung over their backs, and one was stuffing his face from a small bag of Doritos. Billy sprang out at the closest man, wrenched him around the corner, and slammed him against the wall before sinking his large Tanto knife into the side of his neck. I hadn't even seen him draw it from the sheath. The man's eyes bulged in panic, but Billy withdrew the knife and then buried it into the soft palate up under his chin.

The other man coughed out a breath of Dorito crumbs, scrambling for his weapon when Vaun unloaded a hammer pair from his submachine gun. Black Spear's suppressors put all else to shame: each shot sounded equivalent to the snap of a BB gun. The inner mechanics of the weapon cycling were louder than the gunshots themselves.

Both rounds caught him in the sternum, Vaun followed up with a third round that struck between the man's eyes. Each fragmenting shot left a grisly mess of exit wounds on its way out. He tipped over backwards, dead yet still stiff as a board when Hodges stepped in and caught him by his shoulders. He pulled the body back around the corner and quietly set it down next to the other. It all happened in the span of two seconds. Aside from the sound of three brass casings hitting the floor, it had been deathly silent. The only evidence that anything had happened at all were patches of blood left on the tile floor and opposite wall.

Vaun's squad was a well-oiled machine, and they moved flawlessly. While Billy sheathed his blade, Tag moved up to take his position in the lead. "Going left," he whispered and pied the corner with his weapon before moving past the T-junction. Vaun aimed down the hallway on the right, which ended in a janitor's closet.

An office door was on our left, the room beyond it, empty. From its appearance and decoration, it looked to have been a manager's office once upon a time. There was a half-empty box of .45 ACP next to a ruggedized laptop on the desk. Tag approached it. Robert Batson had used a .45 Colt on the freeway. The glance Tag gave to Vaun said that he'd made the same connection I had.

"Boomerang, check the laptop," Vaun said, but Tag was already pulling up a chair and connecting an external hard drive to the laptop. "Crash, stick with him. Kage, Rookie: on me."

Vaun was directing us out of Batson's office when the door pushed open from the other side. The three men entering all looked as surprised as we were. Batson wasn't among them, which was a death sentence for all three. In the half-second I hesitated, I saw the silvery flash of Billy's knife and one of them went down with a cut throat. At the same time Vaun had wrapped his hands around the second man and swept him to the floor; a quick and violent twist after that and the man's neck gave a wet snap.

That left the third guy for me. I fumbled with my weapon, considered taking a shot, but then realized I didn't trust myself to get a clean enough one with my two squad mates so close. I defaulted to my hands instead.

My left hand flew out and jabbed my hooked fingertips into his eyes. At the same time my right hand reached for his shoulder; twisting and pulling to bring his backside close to me. Disrupt, attack, finish. I didn't give myself time to plan what I was going to do. I just did it. Moving more on autopilot than conscious action, I drew the combat knife sheathed on my belt and ran its edge along the man's neck. For some reason I looked down as I did it, and was rewarded with a bright red arterial spray that blinded me.

Feeling like an idiot, I pushed the dying man aside and tried to wipe the blood off my mask's visor. Once my lens was clear I saw Billy in front of me. Even behind the mask I could hear him laughing.

"Today's lesson: the carotid is here," he said and tapped me on the neck. "Next time, you don't need to look for it."

I thanked him for that little bit of advice, which felt weird because usually I thank people for advice on stuff like how to best cook a steak as opposed to how to best slit a man's throat.

A pang of panic ran through me. My eyes shot to the detector on my hip, but I saw only the welcoming sight of bright green LEDs. I blew out an uneasy breath and gratefully patted the detector.

I wanted to look down at the man I'd killed to see if I'd feel any type of remorse or self-disgust. I'd never get the chance to, though, because out of nowhere we heard gunfire. We all dropped to a crouch with our weapons trained on the door, but the gunfire wasn't directed at us. Vaun crouch-walked to the door. Tag went back to downloading the laptop's files.

Another automatic burst clattered off in the distance.

Vaun keyed his earbud to alert Achilles Squad, "Achilles, this is Blackbars. What's spooked them?"

There was a pause. "Achilles-2 to Blackbars, it wasn't us. They aren't shooting our way either. It looks like . . . Blackbars, it looks like they just executed one of their own."

That didn't add up. It doesn't take two bursts of automatic fire to execute a man.

Vaun considered that for a moment and pushed out of the office. That prickly feeling in my gut was warning me to keep the detector I'd brought handy. I even caught Billy checking it as we followed the captain.

More gunfire. And now, shouts. And screams. It occurred to me that there was a difference between the two. One was all fear, the other anger. I shadowed behind Vaun and kept my finger outside of the trigger guard of my weapon. I didn't want to accidentally pull the trigger on account of jumpy nerves. Back in the hallway there was another door that led closer to the source of the gunshots. Vaun held up his fingers, then gave us a three-count before pushing through.

We came out onto a catwalk overlooking the actual printing press floor. Large machinery filled most of the room. Four men occupied the lower level. One was Batson. The big bald man stuck out like a sore thumb. Next to him was a guy I could only describe as gigantic. He even made Batson look small. But despite positive confirmation of our target, my attention was drawn instead to a door that two Terminal shooters were braced against. Cerberus was the only team inside the building, and we hadn't been made yet, so just what in the hell were they dealing with down there?

I heard another gunshot and realized it was coming from behind the door. Something slammed against it from the other side, nearly throwing down both men. A bloodcurdling scream emerged from the room beyond. There was something wrong about it. This scream wasn't one of horror, nor anger or pain. It was more primal than that.

"This is a mistake . . ." Batson muttered.

The door shuddered as it was struck again. I looked down to my hip and saw the green light on the detector had been replaced by a blinking yellow light. Caution. Billy noticed it, too. He muttered an impressive string of swear words.

"Crazy, they're going fucking crazy!" one of the men on the door stammered. "I don't know what happened, they went nuts and started tearing each other apart!"

"Moose, we need to get out of here," Batson said to the giant man. Despite his size, the man called Moose looked visibly shaken. I saw him reassert the two-handed carry he had on a M4 carbine. It looked like a Nerf gun when held with his ape-ish hands, but neither the weapon nor the man's size gave him any sort of comfort.

Moose took a step back from the door, raising his weapon, "What's wrong with them, Bats? Did you see their faces? Did you see their goddamn faces?!"

Before Batson could answer, the door took another hit. There was a creak, a crack, and then a second and third hit. The door came off its hinges and fell atop one of the men that had been bracing it, pinning him to the floor. The detector on my hip flashed red. Danger. The virus was here after all. Unfortunately, it was not in any form we had expected.

There were roughly ten of them, squeezed shoulder to shoulder and filling the doorway, but quickly scrambling over each other to get inside. The ones in front had blood leaking out of the corners of their eyes and pustules splotched across their exposed skin. Their hands were balled into fists, which immediately began raining down furious blows onto the man's face who was pinned under the door. Hard knuckles pelted his face again and again, and his head continued to buck back into the hard cement floor with every hit.

It was then that I saw it. Bloody froth at each of their mouths. Despite all of the other conflicting symptoms—hemorrhaging from the eyes, developing lesions across the skin—I was focused on these new ones. Foaming of the mouth. Uncontrollable spasms of the jaw and throat. And most notably: pure mad rage. I said it into my mic without even thinking.

"Rabies . . . they've got fucking rabies."

I stood transfixed as one of the infected, whose eyes were so bloodshot they'd gone black, began to drive his thumbs into the man's eyes. When he tried to scream, the infected grabbed his jaw with one hand and started to pull it open. Wider, wider, until there was a crack when he forced it open past the stop of the hinge. I heard a sound like bedsheets tearing and the man's jaw was ripped free from his head. His wailing turned to a wet gurgling as he choked on the blood of his ruined maw. Even when his eyes rolled back dead, the rabid man showed no sign of satisfaction. Instead, as his hands clawed and tore at the corpse's chest, he leaned in with wide snapping jaws and tore out the man's throat with his teeth. But he wasn't feeding. No, that would've made some sort of crazed sense. He spat out the raw flesh, the front of his shirt soaked in gore as he leapt to his feet ready to kill whatever he could next.

"Like a damn zombie movie . . ." Billy muttered next to me.

Batson and Moose backed away and opened fire, trying to thin their numbers as they poured through the doorway two at a time. The slide on Batson's pistol locked back on an empty chamber just as an infected soldier approached him. Blood-frothed teeth gnashed six inches from Batson's shocked face—and then the infected man's forehead opened up in a red blossom as Vaun's bullet found its mark.

"We need Batson *alive*," Vaun reminded.

Our weapons were suppressed, and at the moment Batson was left with the belief that Moose had been the one to save his skin. Luckily, the situation at hand didn't afford him the opportunity to turn around to give his thanks and catch us on the rafters behind him. The room was loud with gunfire, the *crack-cracking* of Moose's assault rifle rattled the room while Batson's Colt pistol drowned it out with its deeper *bang*.

Billy and Vaun were putting me to shame. Their shots were precise, their accuracy flawless. It was all going so smoothly until Batson took a quick glance over his shoulder. Before I could take a guess at what caught his attention he turned and started emptying his clip at us.

The shots were fast, but wild. They weren't meant to hit any of Cerberus Squad, just to keep us back. It did the trick. Vaun went down into a roll and came up in a crouch with his weapon ready, Billy dropped prone with the barrel of his weapon canted over the edge of the catwalk, and I took a few steps back to the safety of the back wall.

Batson and Moose took advantage of the reprieve to climb the metal-plated stairs to a separate catwalk that ran perpendicular to our own, the infected quickly trailing behind. As I steadied to take aim again, I happened to lock eyes with one of the rabid men moving toward Batson. His blackened eyes leaked red out of each corner and there was a moment where he looked at me with confusion, but then a heartbeat later they spread wide with recognition. The horde chasing after Batson split in half: one group continued to chase after Batson up the stairs, the other stampeding towards us.

Vaun shot a glance Batson's way as he made his escape, and then engaged the closer enemy. He lined up a headshot on the nearest one and its skull split apart. Chunks showered behind it, I instinctively took a step back to avoid the spray of blood.

"Watch the backsplash," I said.

Billy grunted acknowledgment through his mic between dropping them one by one. He squeezed off hammer-pair shots with deadly accuracy, each shot hitting center mass into vital organs.

"At least they aren't as hard to kill as zombies," he said happily. He sounded calm, as if fighting a throng of rabies-infected men bleeding from their eyes and developing necrosis across their flesh was nothing new.

The horde pressed forward. They shoved and clawed and fought through each other. To get at us. Instead, they got bullets. Lots and lots of bullets.

Even though I knew it was impossible due to my mask's filters, I swear I could smell both the sting of gunpowder and the stench of the oncoming mass of bodies. A small part of my focus was noticing other little things. Things like an old set of dog tags worn around one's neck before my bullet punched through it and into his heart. I saw a set of combat boots—old and worn from years of service—stomp through blood. I saw men who in another day I would've bought a drink and shared stories with. I saw them all, and I continued to fire. Reload, fire. I lost count of how many I'd put down.

"Blackbars, Blackbars, we have no shot!" one of Achilles Squad's snipers shouted into his mic. The oncoming crowd was thinning, but they were almost on us. Our backs were to the edge of the railing and the last dozen or so of our rabid pursuers were less than six feet away.

My hand reached down to my side for a new clip when I realized I had already used my last. The nearest man reached out to me with arms covered in rot. Both hands grabbed at my vest, and I used his momentum to throw him over the railing behind me. I didn't have time to see how bad his landing was, all I could do was hear the bone-crunching thump when he hit the bottom. Two more had already closed the distance by the time I had turned. Before my hand could draw my sidearm there was a silvery flash of movement from my side and one of them fell, hands grabbing at its slashed throat.

Billy stood next to me with his Tanto knife in hand. The other rabid was swinging at Billy with a wild punch when his head kicked back, his forehead marked with a small hole. The black-tipped round fragmented out the back of its brain and hollowed out the skull. Behind both of us stood Vaun, his handgun now empty.

"Over the rail!" he ordered. I leapt over without thinking, aiming my boots for the body of the man I'd thrown over just a second before. When I landed, I felt bone and tissue collapse under my weight. The Terminal thug who'd had his mouth ripped open was on the ground right next to me. I grabbed his AK-47, trying not to look at the severed jawbone next to it.

I pulled the stock of the rifle into my shoulder and aimed down the sights. Billy had already hopped from the rails and used the same gory landing spot I had to cushion his fall. Vaun was still on the catwalk, four crazies surrounding him. He lashed out with a side kick, a punch, and a chopping knife hand strike to push them back and give him enough space to escape. Any one of the blows would have staggered a normal person. These guys barely seemed to notice their bones breaking. I squeezed the trigger. The AK-47 kicked into my shoulder as the burst peppered their flesh. Vaun didn't have time for a thank you before he had to make his own leap of faith.

Billy was next to me now, an identical AK-47 in his hands taken from the other dead man. As Vaun sprinted back towards us I tossed him the AK-47 and drew my sidearm. "Batson's getting away!"

There was no time for discussion, but Vaun gave me a slight nod before I turned and ran. I came to the stairs and took them two at a time, keeping my weapon aimed in front of me, and all the time paying attention and ensuring I still heard two men firing behind me. They stayed pace with me and then one of us would pause, turn, and fire before turning back and catching up.

"Blackbars to Achilles!" Vaun yelled into his mic. "Take the damn shot already!"

Our unseen snipers hesitated for just a second and then the glass to our left was shattering. The bullets came so close I could hear them zipping behind us—though I dared not turn around—as they slammed into our pursuers. The *pop-pop* of the bullets penetrating the windows followed us down the catwalk. I could still feel the horde's foul breath hot on my back and somehow I willed my legs to pump faster. The door was twenty feet away. Ten. Five. An arm's distance.

And then the three of us were crashing through it, piling through the doorway so fast that Billy went sprawling. All but one of our pursuers had been taken out by the snipers. The last one roared and leapt through the air at us.

I put a single bullet through its left eye. Its momentum carried it into the room with us where it skidded to a stop face-up by our feet.

We sat there for a second and tried to catch our breath. Each of us huffing and puffing through the restriction of our masks in a vain effort to calm ourselves. I kept my weapon aimed at the dead body before us. I didn't want to accept that this was real, that it was possible.

Billy knelt over the body. "Nice shot, dude," he said and tapped his gloved finger on its forehead. "That was a close one."

Underneath my mask I started to smile, and then the dead body spasmed and *vomited* a blast of blackish blood into Billy's face.

"Fuckfuckfuck!" he yelled as he backed away and started wiping his mask off with his gloves.

The dead body twitched its second death spasm while I fired three more rounds into its head. The bullets tore its skull apart until it was nothing more than bits of a lower jaw and half a neck.

I looked at the body and then at Vaun. Billy was shaking and sat against a wall, trying frantically to wipe the splattered gore from his face and gloves.

Vaun pulled his bottle of decontaminant spray from his belt and knelt next to Billy, "Don't move." He went as still as a statue. Vaun looked over his shoulder at me and simply cocked his head further down the room. "It's down to you. Don't let him get away, Rookie."

CHAPTER 21

"Doctor, this is most impressive," Jax said to Chan. Both were fixated on the monitor on Jax's desk. Several cameras in the McAllister Brothers building were sending a live video feed of the mayhem Moses-2 was letting loose.

Dr. Chan excitedly shifted his weight back and forth with his hands held behind his waist. The amusing display made the doctor look like a giant penguin. "They're reacting much faster than expected, sir."

No matter how many times Jax told him, Chan still defaulted to calling him sir. It was strange considering Jax had been lowly enlisted and Chan himself had been a commissioned officer.

"Those that were administered injections still required the three-hour incubation time before the more . . . *aggressive* symptoms began to manifest. But the second group began exhibiting a behavior change within minutes."

Jax pondered that for a moment. "Any theories on why that is?"

"Well, the first group we infected through a controlled dose. A very precise measurement of Moses-2," Chan said. "The others were infected through saliva, blood, and vomit. The viral content of that second-hand infection could have been more potent."

"What do you make of this?" He tapped a few keys and rewound some of the footage to a point when the three men in black had been firing on the infected men from the catwalk. One of the infected's jaw trembled and then it vomited a stream of thick reddish black blood over four feet long towards the men. Jax looked to Chan with a raised eyebrow, eager for a scientific explanation for that particular *Exorcist* reenactment.

"Rabies attacks the nerves in the jaw and throat, it causes uncontrollable spasms. The foaming at the mouth that you see in rabid dogs is a result of that," said Chan. "I can hazard a guess that as the body begins to hemorrhage, blood from the esophagus accumulates in the stomach, then the muscular spasms in the throat trigger the gag reflex and you get this novel form of transmission."

He waved his hands around whenever he explained things, which really got on Jax's nerves, but until Jax had a PhD in genetics he would have to put up with it.

"Of course... there is another simpler explanation," Chan continued, then waited for Jax to turn and look at him. Chan gave him a wide excited grin and walked about while his hands flailed wildly. "Consider a sneeze. In most people's minds, a sneeze is just something that happens when you're sick. But have you asked yourself why you sneeze? The answer is simple: viruses and bacteria *want* to spread. Every symptom the virus causes, from bursting pustules to vomiting, is purely to help the virus spread to a new host. Maybe through the air, maybe through touch, but in the end it's always for the same purpose. So, we can explain away the *how* that thing is vomiting by breaking down the various effects of Moses-2. But the *why* is so much simpler. Moses-2 wants to spread."

Jax's hand went to his KA-BAR knife and gripped its reassuring handle. "That's a scary thought, Doctor."

Chan continued to smile. His fascination with the virus was

bringing him to new levels of unhinged. It occurred to Jax that he actually had his very own mad scientist now. On a positive side, Chan's obsession with perfecting Moses only meant that he would happily continue to serve. Hell, he probably wouldn't even have to pay the man anymore.

"Did Batson know . . . ?" asked Chan, giving Jax a queer look.

He didn't so much as return eye contact. "That'll be all, Doctor."

Chan's smile disappeared. He straightened. After a failed attempt at fixing his lab coat, he turned and hurried from Jax's office.

In truth, Batson hadn't known of Jax's plan. It had only come to him after the phone call they had shared. Despite Batson's assurance that they hadn't been followed, Jax had been sure they were. He'd given Batson express instructions to stay by his secure terminal. After all, Batson was his right hand. He couldn't let his best man get stuck behind in the slaughter that was bound to ensue.

But the big man hadn't listened. And he hadn't received Jax's message to hastily and discretely evacuate himself. Jax had continued to watch with trepidation as he lost control of the events. Now, thankfully, it looked like Batson and Moose had gotten away. Unfortunately, so had this mysterious group in black. Both parties had moved beyond sight of any of Jax's cameras. All he could do now was wait. Wait, and hope he hadn't made a mistake in overestimating Batson's skills.

CHAPTER 22

I pursued them down a dark corridor. Boarded-up windows were on my left, and I couldn't avoid thinking of the fact that I no longer had cover from our Achilles snipers. Even with the digital illumination my lens provided, there was still too much shadow for comfort. For the first time since Vaun had snatched me up from my office, I was truly on my own.

Our small team was compromised and already short-handed after losing Kelly; if Billy was contaminated then our numbers were well and truly fucked. Throughout all the excitement downstairs neither Hodges nor Tag had given so much as a radio check. Had they been swarmed by another group of rabid men? Just about the only comfort I found at the moment was that my detector was back to reading yellow. I forced all of those thoughts from my head and chose instead to focus on the sights of the weapon in my hands.

The Tritium dots atop the pistol's slide glowed, just three little green beads lighting the way in front of me. I kept my finger out of the trigger guard and waited on the edge of my nerves for either Batson or the Moose to pop into view. My finger would have to move less than an inch to close the distance and squeeze the trigger. Less than an inch, yet if both of them got the drop on me even that short distance might be too far.

The hallway ended in a short flight of stairs. I hissed sharply when I saw that it went to the roof. Batson and the Moose could have already made their escape while I'd been jumping at shadows.

I gritted my teeth and pushed up the steps, taking quick short strides to keep my aim from bouncing too much. I shouldered through the door to the roof, covered left to make sure no one was there, then back to the right as I closed the door behind me. The rooftop was a wide expanse of flat surface on a separate level from the one we'd made our initial entry. In the middle was a large glass skylight that overlooked the printing press factory floor. I could see the still-warm bodies of the recent carnage below. A few large air conditioning units were clustered towards the edge of the roof, and beyond those I spotted a fire escape that led down to the street. More importantly, I saw Batson as he bounded towards it.

"Freeze!" I fired a warning shot over his shoulder while running towards him. It dinged off a handrail nearby. He spun and shot a quick round that cracked the glass of the skylight next to me. His pistol locked back on an empty chamber, and he shoved it into a holster on his hip before hauling himself over the fire escape.

I knew we needed him alive, but every ounce of me wanted to empty my magazine into his back. After everything he'd put us through today, I wouldn't have lost sleep over it. As if he could read my mind, Vaun's voice came through the radio into my ear. "We need him alive, Rookie. I'm coming up now, watch your six."

"He's getting away!" I shouted back and went into a dead sprint. All our back-up from Achilles Squad was stationed at exits that neither Batson nor I were near. "He's going—"

A huge black mass separated itself from the air conditioning unit on my left and slammed into me like a missile. *Moose*, I thought to myself as I was sent sprawling, *How did I forget him*? Before I could recover, hands like baseball mitts reached under my armpits and hoisted me up to my feet. I weigh over two-hundred pounds *without* any gear on, so to say it was an impressive feat to lift me, armor and all, so effortlessly was an understatement. His rifle buttstock slammed into my chest like a battering ram and—despite the ballistic plate in my vest, I felt the blow. It staggered me. I tried to take a shaky step back, but found myself falling backwards.

I fell onto one of the large panes of the skylight. It cracked under my weight. My left hand still gripped the pistol. Moose came at me, swinging his empty M4 like a club at my head. Too fast for me to line up a shot. All I could do was roll to the next window pane on my left as the M4 shattered the thick glass and sent broken shards raining down to the printing press floor thirty feet below.

The rifle came down again and I fired a wild shot that went over his left ear. His swing went wide and destroyed the other skylight pane next to me. Pitch black emptiness waited on both sides of me and I had nowhere else to roll to avoid another swing. But I didn't need to. I'd already sighted in.

My attacker stopped mid-swing and glared at me. The bright green of the night-vision tint gave his eyes an unsettling glow. There was nothing but murder in them, and for just a second it broke my heart. Terminal had twisted this soldier until he was unable to see anything in me other than an enemy. If the pistol wasn't in my hand, he would've caved my skull in without a second's hesitation. I knew in my soul then that there was a slight but distinct difference in us. We were both willing to kill each other, that was at least true. That fire in his eyes was pure hate, but if I had to punch his ticket right here? It wouldn't be anything personal. I'd say it would just be me doing my job and staying alive.

He took a step back and dropped his club, chest heaving and out of breath. Gingerly, I eased myself to my feet and up off the skylight. And then he rushed me. He made a grab for the gun and I fired off two rounds, but as the distance closed all I managed were two grazing shots across his ribs. One of his hands snatched up my wrist and the other wrapped around my throat. They clamped down and *squeezed*. His grasp was iron. My bright green vision dimmed as he choked me in a single palm. His other hand kept my gun hand locked in place; I couldn't even cant my wrist and squeeze off a shot to his feet.

Choking for air and desperately out of time, I grit my teeth. "Fuck it," I said and hopped up as I wrapped my legs around Moose's waist and locked my ankles together. With my free hand I pulled his head in close to me. And then, with every ounce of strength I had, I threw my weight back. Two-hundred plus pounds can do one hell of a job fucking with your center of gravity. The Moose's grip on my wrist slackened a little as he saw too late what was happening. We both fell towards the skylight and the thick pane shattered beneath us.

I twisted as we fell and managed to get Moose under me as the darkness below swallowed us up. We went down hard and fast. Moose, who just a second ago had tried to get away from me, now instinctively held on tight to my wrist and the front of my vest. He bared his teeth like an animal as we plummeted down, down, down.

And then Moose's back struck one of the enormous factory presses. Though he took the brunt of it, it still rocked both of us to our bones. My mask slammed into the metal surface of the machinery and I tasted blood inside my cheek. Everything went black and we were rolling end over end, striking every hard surface on our way down, before coming to a rest on the factory floor still slick with blood and gore from our previous action.

I flopped away from Moose on shaky hands and knees. Both of my elbows throbbed, blood welled in my mouth, and I'd knocked my knee bad on something during the last tumble. At some point in our drop, my handgun disappeared. My vest was crisscrossed with deep cuts from the sharp glass we'd crashed through. Slowly, I pushed myself up onto my knees as I tried in vain to catch my breath, and gave my thanks to a very strange God that I'd survived that drop. My vision started to clear. And then I realized with worry that the lens of my mask was cracked. The night-vision lens had failed, and I was fully enveloped in shadows.

A groan came from my left. I could barely make out the shape of Moose as he stirred. Somehow, the fall hadn't killed him. With a jump, I forced myself to my feet before a sharp pain forced me back onto one knee. The pain stabbed like a hot finger in my side, when I looked down there was a two-inch shard of glass pierced through my Snakeskin suit and into my gut.

My suit was compromised. My mask was damaged. And I was blind to the giant moving next to me. I heard the tinkling of glass and knew that the Moose was moving closer. The tinkling turned into a crunch as his boots crumbled the glass underfoot, then to the thumping of heavy footfalls as he ran at me.

One meaty hand clamped onto the front of my mask and slammed my head against the hard wall behind. With a savage tug he ripped my mask clean from my face with one pull, tossing it aside carelessly, and then spreading his fingers across my face as if to crush my skull with his bare hands.

My hands made weak attempts at striking his ribs, going to the spots my bullets had grazed before. I tried kneeing his gut. His hand continued to squeeze around my neck and choke the life out of me. Frantic for air, I eyed my surroundings and came up empty. The handgun I'd lost in our fall hadn't magically landed near my feet. My knife had similarly gone missing.

And then I remembered the blade of glass protruding from my gut. I clenched my jaw and wrenched the shard free. I slashed across the inside of the Moose's wrist in the same motion. He released me with a startled yelp, and I put as much distance between me and the brute as possible so I could catch my breath.

If the virus was airborne, then I had already been contaminated when my suit had been pierced. Besides, the murderous giant in the room was clearly the more present danger.

My eyes had adjusted to the dark more, so I took a better look at my assailant. One of his hands clutched at his wrist, but it was his other wrist that drew my attention. There was a wound there I hadn't noticed before; a very distinct one. A bite mark.

"Oh, shit . . ."

I realized exactly why this man was acting so strange. As Moose rose to his feet again, I saw the other signs. A single drop of blood trailed out of his left nostril, his eyes had gone so bloodshot they'd turned black, and sickly splotches appeared on his skin.

Moose came at me like an animal, swinging both hands in furious swipes I had to backpedal to avoid. Every time he clawed at me, flecks of blood flew from the wrist I'd cut. I dodged out of the way as if his blood were acidic.

"I'm gonna fucking kill you!" He swung wide punches left and right.

"You'd have to hit me first, asshole."

The swipes were clumsy and wild, but there was enough force coming behind them that if he slipped just one in it would promptly knock me on my ass.

"Break every bone in your body!" Spittle and blood flying from his mouth. His gloved fist whistled through the air towards my face, then Tag stepped in with an uppercut that snapped his head back and sent him tumbling away.

"Stay the fuck away from my friend."

Tag glanced at me while I licked my wounds. He was unarmed, which could only mean he'd run up against more of these bastards upstairs.

"He's infected," I said. "Watch the blood."

Tag grunted an affirmative.

Moose scrambled to his feet, hands clenching and unclenching as pustules began to appear along his arms. Then he charged. Tag twisted as the Moose shoved into him, rolling on his heels like a dancer, and using Moose's momentum to throw him face first into a wall.

Moose's nose crunched into the concrete, his face coming away drenched in blood, an angry snarl on his lips. Tag closed the distance and pummeled him with a heavy overhand punch to the side of the head and a hard body blow, careful to avoid the blood drenching his nose and upper lip.

Moose didn't even look fazed by the beatdown. Instead, he bent over and charged like a bull. Tag didn't have time to counter the charge, so he set his feet and braced for impact. Moose pushed him back a few feet, but then Tag's legs fought against the strain and stopped them both. Both of Moose's arms wrapped around Tag's waist in a bearhug and started to squeeze. The pustules that had spotted up on his arms burst from the strain. Bloody fluids smeared across Tag's torso.

Tag popped two quick uppercuts with his left and right under the Moose's chin, following up with a heavy roundhouse punch into the side of Moose's head. It ruptured the eardrum and blood exploded out onto Tag's gloved hand. Moose lost his hold. Not seeing any point in avoiding contact with the blood anymore, Tag threw jabs and crosses again and again.

Moose didn't so much as attempt to avoid the hits. He just took them all to the face with the same blind rage. But then that same unnatural speed came out of nowhere, and he spear tackled into Tag.

The two men went flying back, crashing into a stack of wooden crates that broke under their weight. Moose ended up on top and began to hammer Tag with his fists. It was all Tag could do to keep his guard up and soften the blows. Each hit shocked the damaged crates and splintered them further until Tag was sprawled on top of little more than wooden shards and broken planks.

One of Moose's hands wrapped across Tag's mask and ripped it from his face. He pulled Tag's head to the side and exposed the side of his neck. The Moose's mouth opened wide and Tag realized with horror that he intended to bite him.

Pure bloodlust shone in the man's expression. "Swallow . . . your fucking . . . blood!" Moose growled.

One of Tag's hands dropped to the small of his back. Leaning in to rip a huge chunk out of Tag's throat, the Moose stopped short as Tag pressed the object up into his chin.

Somewhere, deep in the Moose's mind, something recognized what it was, and Moose's eyes went wide.

Tag pulled the trigger on the snub-nosed .44. Point blank.

Thunder, impossibly loud, roared off the walls around us. The heavy magnum round punched up through the Moose's chin before the hollow point expanded, pulling with it huge chunks of bone fragments and brain matter as all of it exploded out the back of his head.

The man was nearly decapitated. Moose's head was nothing but a hollowed-out crater, all that remained was the left side of his face, one remaining eye rolling back in death, and a lower jaw where a single drop of blood dribbled out of the bottom of his chin. Every ounce of fight in the towering man was erased in less than a second.

"Swallow *that*, you son of a bitch."

CHAPTER 23

Cole West. 11:58 p.m.
McAllister Brothers Press
Santa Ana, California

Tag lay frozen. The .44 still hovered in the air, a single drop of blood trailed down the barrel. The big man's other hand was near it; he'd thrown it up as a shield against the blood shower. Tag drew in a sharp breath as he looked at the glove on his left hand. It was covered in gore.

Then the moment passed. Tag started breathing quicker. The man was practically hyperventilating as I stumbled near him. "Couldn't risk the shot because of the blood. Had no choice . . . fuck me. The blood," he said, eyes wide with panic. "Did I get any on me . . . ?"

I looked at his glove, carefully moving it aside as I looked over his face and exposed neck. His eyes darted back and forth. One second following my eyes and the next glancing back to Moose's brutalized corpse.

"Didn't get any on your skin," I said. "You're good." We both let out a sigh of relief and then I collapsed next to him, all my accumulated pains finally beating me down.

"It's not airborne," Tag said. He pulled out a bottle of decontaminant from his belt and sprayed his glove. Then he spot-cleaned the areas near his waist where Moose's rotting arms had hugged him. I used bandages and duct tape to repair the breach in my own suit from the glass shard, wincing as I wound it tight over the wound. "I managed to glance at a file from that laptop upstairs. Bodily fluids only."

"Blood and saliva?"

"Yeah," he said. Already I was feeling relief about my broken suit, thankfully the only blood on me was my own.

"What about semen?" I joked.

He shot a look my way, and then I actually got the big man to laugh. He shook his head. "It has to enter the bloodstream, the file didn't say anything about *ingesting* so you'll probably be fine."

"Oh good, I was getting worried for a moment."

We laughed a little of the tension away before getting to our shaky feet. It was a poorly disguised coping mechanism, and we both knew it. After what had just happened, I'd take any bit of levity I could get. Every breath lit a fire in my side, but all the same it felt good to share a laugh with him. You know, as if we hadn't just executed thirty or so grown men with rabies?

I retrieved my pistol from a far-off corner. Tag just stood amidst all of the carnage and blood decorating the room. "Hmm," he said, back to his typical grunting self. "Lot of cleanup. Captain'll be happy."

His ears must've been burning, because Vaun's voice was suddenly in our radios. "Boomerang, this is Blackbars, do you copy?"

Tag rubbed his sore neck where the Moose had strangled him and tapped a fingertip to his ear. "Boomerang. Rookie's still breathing, too."

"Status?"

I gave Tag a very unconvincing thumbs-up and then had to wince and clutch my side. "He's banged up but alive. Blackbars . . . it's about Batson: he got away."

Despite everything, the insanity of the past hour and the bloodshed, Vaun actually chuckled through the radio.

"Negative, Boomerang. I've got the target right here."

✯ ✯ ✯

We found Hodges waiting for us outside the front door as we exited. His arms were folded across his chest, his head cocked to the side with confusion when he saw both of our unmasked faces. He just jammed a thumb in the direction of a blacked-out van. "I don't know what the fuck happened to you two, but Kage's loaded up in the back. We've got a medical bay prepped for the three of you."

"Batson?" I asked.

I could feel Hodges staring behind his mask. "You let him slip away and he almost made it to a getaway vehicle. I handled it, then Blackbars bagged him up. And we have maybe four fucking minutes before Rourke's phone call magic wears off and the cops are swarming down here. Get. In. The. Fucking. Van."

I was too beaten down to argue with the man. As if to make sure I was going, Tag pushed me forward towards the van. I reluctantly climbed inside.

Billy sat in the back and shook his head when he saw neither of us wore masks. "Oh good. For a second I thought I was the only one who was going to fuck up tonight. Maybe we can all share a quarantine room?"

Tag moved to seal the doors behind us when Hodges moved in. As I thought of something witty and unnecessary to say, I stopped when I saw the pistol that lay across his lap. My eyes met the black tempered plate of his mask. "You saw how fast that infection spread. Don't make this a thing, just pass over what you're packing."

I pulled the handgun from my belt and slid it down the bench to him. Tag undid his belt buckle and slid off the .44 magnum's holster. He held the weapon up in one meaty fist then opened the chamber. Five rounds and one empty casing rattled to the ground. "Nobody touches this but me." He placed the empty revolver snug back into its holster.

"Come on, big guy, you know it's not like that," Hodges said. He took the holstered weapon, careful to only touch the leather and not the weapon itself. "Order came from the top."

Tag gave a characteristic grunt and patted my knee. "You did good in there, man. You did real good."

I nodded to myself and rested the back of my head against the cool metal of the van. The weight of the day's events finally took its toll on me. I felt myself getting drowsy.

Nothing else mattered in that moment. Not the chimera virus I'd learned of just this morning. Not the building that had exploded in front of my eyes earlier that afternoon. Not even the bodies of all the dead we'd killed tonight.

Hell of a first day on the job.

In the back of a separate vehicle, bound and gagged and a hood thrown over his head, Robert Batson lay still. He'd almost made it. Almost. He'd been ten paces from his vehicle when one of those black-ops guys had tackled him out of nowhere. He'd been sent sprawling, and before he knew it a second man had taken him down and had him zip-tied in an instant.

This wasn't part of the plan. Despite the turn of events Batson didn't worry; underneath his hood he was actually smiling. Jax would come for him, then these guys would be sorry.

DAY 2

EARN YOUR STRIPES

*"The only person you are destined to become,
is the person you decide to be."*

—Ralph Waldo Emerson

CHAPTER 24

Cole West. 5:48 a.m.
Angel Site
Los Angeles, California

Men in white bubble suits ushered us out of the van as the first rays of sunlight broke through the cityscape on the horizon. We had returned through one of the underground entrances to Angel Site. We were promptly stripped bare, doused in a chemical shower, scrubbed vigorously in ways that were just short of pornographic, given a second rinse under the showerheads, had a once-over for all of our various flesh wounds, and then were brought into a cordoned-off quarantine area to wait. And wait. And wait.

I hated waiting.

Waiting is unavoidable in the military. I guess it was chafing me even more since what I was waiting for finally mattered. The past twenty-four hours had been more worthwhile to me than the past twenty-four *years* combined. As much as I was terrified of whatever would come next, the idea of waking up and realizing all of this had been just a crazy dream scared me even more. I'd eagerly face an army of those infected over coasting through my old meaningless life of yesterday.

The room we were taken to was brightly lit and had three freshly made cots with clean white sheets. I imagine if Apple decided to make hospital rooms, they would look like this. Despite our comfortable arrangements, I couldn't put myself at ease. The same couldn't be said for my two companions. Tag was stretched out on one of the cots, catching a few winks. Billy sat cross-legged with his head bowed. I didn't know if he was asleep or just deep in thought.

There was a loud buzz and our attention snapped to the large observation window next to the door. Doc was there with tired eyes and a clipboard. Her soiled lab coat was over a floral purple and yellow shirt that came across as obnoxious at this early hour and not at all in line with her expression. She thumbed an intercom button below the window. "You know, this place is actually quiet most of the time? Most people think the Los Angeles office would be more exciting, but Fog Site up in San Francisco and Gator Site over in Miami get much more activity. Then you guys had to go and fuck up my nice nine-to-five I had going on."

"Our hearts bleed for you, Doc," Tag said. "Any word on when we'll be allowed out of here?"

Doc shrugged. "Twelve-hour quarantine. You have ten hours to go. Believe me, you three are definitely getting the preferred experience. If we could switch places, I would."

I sat up in my cot. "Paperwork that bad?"

"Shit, I wish it was just the paperwork. Thirty plus bodies, all quickly turning into mush? It looks like a dang soup kitchen down there. Not exactly easy to process a body when it can be picked up with a mop. We turned the whole morgue into an icebox to slow it down—which is doing wonders for my head cold, not that you care—but it's a losing battle."

The imagery was vivid enough to renew the importance for our quarantine. Doc seemed to read my mind and glanced down at her clipboard. "Bloodwork looks clean for everyone, but we'll keep running tests. Mister West, do me a solid and please avoid doing sit-ups or anything else that'll pop those stitches. Last thing I need is you opening that little wound up and bleeding on our sheets."

I gave her an unenthusiastic thumbs-up and brushed my fingers reflexively against the bandage on my side. "Any word on Kelly?"

Doc stared at me as if I was the biggest idiot in the room. "You realize you three potentially exposed yourselves to a virus—which has no known cure or treatment, by the way—that turns people into mindless blood-spewing animals, yeah? And said psychos are currently rotting into sludge downstairs? On top of that you took a swan dive through the roof, but hey thankfully some sharp glass broke your fall. Then Mister Taggart there decided to give himself a nice brain matter shower just for shits and gigs. But yeah, Kelly's the one you're concerned about? Jeeze, it was a bullet." She face-palmed, then glanced down to the clipboard in her hands. "Mister Kelly got out of surgery last night and is sleeping it off. He's ordered to bed rest for forty-eight hours, which means I'm sure he'll sneak out of his room any minute now to come by and pay you all a visit." Doc rubbed her temples between her thumb and forefinger while tapping the clipboard against the glass window. "Well, boys, as much as I'd love to hang around, I still have plenty of work downstairs."

With that, she turned and departed, leaving the three of us alone once again with our thoughts.

"Helluva first day, eh?" Tag said next to me. He actually managed to screw his face into his version of amusement.

"Pretty much feeling like I'm completely in over my head."

"Why, oh why, didn't I take the blue pill," said Billy, waking from his meditation. "If it's any consolation, everyone's first day is pretty rough."

"Except for Kelly," Tag corrected.

"Yeah, except for Kelly. He took the transition from his previous line of work pretty well."

"Exactly what did he do before Black Spear?" I asked.

When Vaun introduced me to everyone, he hadn't explained

where Kelly was from. In a team made up of all colors of Special Forces, it was a strange omission. I was surprised to find that Tag actually shrugged and Billy frowned.

"I think he was an admin specialist in the Air Force?" Tag suggested.

"Nah. I think he got lost and found Vaun's office by accident, and he's just so sweet, the Captain couldn't turn him away," countered Billy.

We shared a laugh as they continued to offer progressively more ridiculous suggestions for Kelly's background. My two comrades seemed to consider for a moment whether to keep messing around or if they could trust me with the truth.

"Daniel Kelly is an assassin," Billy finally said. "He was a headhunter for the CIA for a time before he transferred over to Mr. Rourke's side of the pond. Not sure what he did before that, he never talks about it. It's not like he's trying to be all mysterious or anything, the guy just genuinely doesn't feel a need to bring it up."

A thought came to my head. "If he never talks about it, how'd you find out?"

Billy raised an eyebrow in my direction and gave pause, weighing how best to respond. "Let's just say I heard of him, because I was playing for the other team. Word spreads fast when you're as good as he is."

"The other team? Then what are you doing on ours?"

"Community service. We weren't all given a choice in joining this outfit."

Billy didn't bother explaining further, and I felt like I'd unintentionally hit on a sensitive topic. I'd only wanted to better know these guys. It was a good enough sign that they were talking to me at all.

"Sooooo . . . when do I get to hear about all of Tag's demotions?"

Billy's laugh was so loud and genuine, I could tell that Tag would have no choice but to tell me. "Oh dear me, that's up to the big guy."

I've known several Marines who have been demoted, even served with one who'd received a Court Martial. Only one in ten was for real scumbag shit, most stories tended to be on the dark side of entertaining so I kicked back on my cot as Tag grumbled and began his story.

"I was a Corporal then and looking at picking up Sergeant soon, though that kind of hit a standstill when my Lieutenant raised a huge fuss over finding out I brought my forty-four on deployment." I knew the .44 magnum he'd kept in the small of his back held some sentimental importance to him, but I also knew the Marine Corps took a hard stance on bringing personal firearms to combat zones.

"They busted you down for that?"

"Hell, no," snorted Tag. "They busted me down after I cold-cocked the bastard for trying to steal it. So instead of a promotion, I got a demotion. I'll tell you what, though, nobody tried that shit again. Nobody touches that gun but me."

The image of Tag squaring up to an officer brought a smile to my face; the thought that such an offense wouldn't be Tag's last before joining Black Spear made it even more amusing. Tag used his thumb and forefinger to make his hand into a gun, shooting an invisible bullet into the ceiling. Undoubtedly the fact that his trusty revolver had to be processed through decontamination wasn't sitting well with him.

It felt strange knowing that as a Sergeant I technically outranked Corporal Taggart. The thought of the danger he'd survived over the years while I safely climbed through the ranks just didn't seem fair. But I've also never been one to attribute too much respect to rank by default. Respect has to be earned regardless of what you wear on your collar. At the end of the day I firmly believe that everyone, from the highest General to the lowest Private, is still just a man. And in my eyes who you are can be measured by your deeds.

The room got quiet again. No sound was made besides the low hum of the high-powered filtration system in the vents. Eager for anything to break the silence, I turned to Billy. "So, don't suppose you'll tell me what your deal is?"

Billy looked away. "Don't push it, noob. You might be the captain's favorite experiment at the moment, but you still aren't too special to me."

"Is my memory hazy or did I save your ass back at McAllister when you got a face full of virus blood?"

"Yeah, but then I had to save *your* ass from that giant you cannonballed through the skylight with," Tag cut in.

The room grew silent again before Billy broke it. "Shit . . . guess that actually makes me the least useful one of us. Maybe the captain actually made the right pick with you."

Tag sniggered.

"All the same," I said, "I can't for the life of me figure out why the hell Vaun chose me . . . Not like I bring a unique skill set to the table here."

They were quiet. Clearly they had been wondering the same thing.

"You probably just fit the algorithm is all," Tag said.

"Algorithm?"

"Yeah, there's a profile that they use to find most selectees. Things like being an orphan, or if all your family's dead already. Helps with the obits."

I certainly met that qualification.

"Dad was a cop," I said slowly. "He took a .38 to the face one night; regular traffic stop gone wrong, could've happened any other day. Just a scared kid making the worst mistake of his life. The kid's serving life now and that's justice, I guess. My mom . . . yeah she got in a bad wreck. Rainy night, tires don't stick too well, you do the math. She went quickly, just like dad. I'm kind of thankful for that."

They both did a good job of listening. It made it easier to let the floodgates open.

"Early on I found myself wishing there was more to both of their deaths. Like if that kid was part of some larger gang, or if my mom was hit by a drunk driver and not just bad weather. I could've had closure then. After a while you stop wishing for deeper plots and just accepting that bad shit can happen to anyone, anytime. Eventually you stop thinking about it at all. You know it's funny, before Vaun asked me about my parents yesterday, I can't remember the last time I'd thought about either of them."

Tag nodded. "My old man walked out when I was two. Mom tried to find him at the bottom of the bottle. Never did, but didn't stop her from looking. I ended up in the system. I don't think about mine, either."

It felt good to open up, and to have it reciprocated. It reminded me that my two teammates were made of flesh and blood just like I was.

"Okay, so besides orphan, what else?"

"No kids, no girlfriend," added Billy.

"Strong 'moral compass,'" said Tag, using his ape-like hands for air quotes.

"And a certain level of problem with authority," finished Billy with a devious smile. "Usually experience is a qualifier too, but you certainly broke the mold there."

I finished tallying all the things they'd said. "I guess four out of five isn't bad. Out of all the problem children they have in the entire military, I still don't see what makes me special."

"Nobody except Vaun knows why Vaun does anything," Billy said. "He and Mister Rourke have an agreement that only he chooses who gets on Cerberus. Maybe he tried to find the worst candidate possible to see if Rourke would call him on it?"

I shot a look at him.

"Just saying, man."

I decided it wasn't any use trying to figure it out. Maybe it really did all come down to hitting the wickets on some program's algorithm.

The last thought I had before falling asleep was, *Yeah, definitely in over my head.*

CHAPTER 25

Robert Batson waited for Vaun in an interrogation room. He'd been stewing there since they'd returned to Angel Site early this morning. Vaun needed the gravity of the situation to soak into every fiber of Batson's being. They'd stripped him down to his skivvies, thrown a black spit-hood over his head, and locked handcuffs tight across both wrists. Tight enough to be painful, not so tight as to cut off the circulation. Vaun didn't want his hands to go numb. That would be . . . counterproductive.

Three of Vaun's men were in quarantine, another recovering from a gunshot wound to the shoulder, and his last man remaining had been ordered to get some rest. He and Vaun were both supposed to be sleeping everything off and recovering, but Vaun afforded himself no such luxury. Upon returning to Angel Site, he'd given a quick sitrep to Mister Rourke, taken a shower hot enough to boil a lobster, and changed into a fresh set of recently pressed black fatigues. Appearance was key here. Batson had to know and believe Vaun was perfectly at ease and not at all ready to throw in the towel. He needed to realize that Vaun could do this all day.

Vaun took one last breath to compose himself, fixed his shirt collar, and then entered the interrogation room. Batson's hooded head turned towards the sound of the door opening and the big thug laughed out loud. "About time. The silent treatment was getting a bit old."

Vaun pulled the hood from Batson's head, almost delicately, and then placed it on the small table next to them. He eased himself into a seat facing Batson. "No speeches," Vaun said. His voice reflected utter calm. "I'm going to ask you questions. You are either going to answer them or you are going to hurt."

Batson rolled his eyes. "You clearly don't get the point of Terminal. We're a brotherhood. That means you don't just roll over and spill your secrets to the first guy who makes a scary face."

Vaun tilted his head slightly and almost smiled, then turned to the table next to him and unrolled a bundle of black cloth. As it opened it showed various tools inside. Pliers, scalpels, and all manner of sharp instruments. Vaun made sure the silvery metal caught the overhead light to draw Batson's attention.

"Oof. Those look fun."

"You know there are only two types of people in the world. People who think torture doesn't work," Vaun said and reached for a syringe filled with a yellow fluid, "and people who have done it."

Batson's confidence visibly flickered.

This time Vaun couldn't help the half-smile that snuck onto his face. "It's up to you how far we take this. Ball's in your court."

Vaun stuck the needle into Batson's neck and pressed down on the plunger. Batson glared at him as the fluid pumped into his bloodstream; he licked his lips as if tasting the air. "What's this? A little truth serum?" he said, clearly amused. "Barbiturates? Sodium pentathol? Or maybe just some Wild Turkey? I'll tell you that stuff *always* gets me talking."

Vaun set the needle aside and then sat with his hands clasped in his lap, fingers interwoven. "Nothing of the sort. The problem with truth serums is that most of them work by altering the brain chemistry. They slow cognitive processes. That makes it hard to concentrate and thus hard to lie. Or so the theory goes. But I want you to be able to concentrate. In fact, I need it. What's going through your blood right now is a special cocktail made just for you. Similar effects to GHB and MDMA. You see, I want every sensation you have to be heightened. I want you to experience them *very* vividly."

He grabbed a small knife from the tray. The finish on its wooden handle was worn down from use, but its wickedly sharp hawkbill-shaped blade could've been brand new. When Vaun tightly gripped that knife, he felt the coldness of the metal draw into him. He took it in readily and felt all the warmth go from his eyes. Normally they were grayish blue, but when he saw them reflected back by the blade's mirrored edge? Nothing but slate.

"Now, where is the virus?"

Rourke thumbed through the brief prepared for him by Captain Vaun. The man was taking a gamble with Sergeant West, and Rourke was beginning to think it was going to cost them all dearly. He knew Vaun had his own reasons for doing things, and the man had more than earned the right to pick his own men over the years, but all the same last night's events threw up some red flags.

"Thirty plus dead, and two of our operators potentially contaminated," he groaned.

"Three operators," corrected Kara.

"Two operators. West is a tourist out of his element."

His assistant gave him that little grin that said she was about to say something that would really irk him. "Sergeant West was just on one of our operations. On which he operated. By definition, he is an operator. Sir."

Rourke rolled his eyes. "What's the status of the McAllister cleanup?" A less than subtle transition.

"Officially the building is under quarantine by the CDC, which should keep their forensics experts from wanting to poke their noses in our business," Kara said. "The area was mostly deserted at the time of the operation, and the two outgoing 911 calls that were made were rerouted to us. Local P.D. was kept from the scene until we removed the bodies, at which point they were allowed to create a perimeter. They'll keep their distance, though. Our cleanup crew will need the next two days to completely sanitize the building, but beyond that the police weren't aware of even a single gunshot last night."

Anonymity was the name of the game. If they could keep local PD in the dark then they were doing their jobs right. In the modern age though it was getting harder and harder to remain a ghost.

Last night had at least given them a trail to follow. Thankfully, Vaun's man Taggart managed to copy an entire hard drive full of Terminal's files. Rourke had his experts sifting through it and trying to piece together anything valuable. At the moment it was a race between the computer techs with their instruments and Vaun with his to see who would be able to turn up the first lead.

Rourke had his money on Vaun. Although the Captain always demonstrated a cool and collected nature, Rourke knew from experience that the boy had a devil in him. Robert Batson would talk. Of that he had no doubt.

He tapped two keys on his computer and the monitor showed the inside of the interrogation room at the Los Angeles facility. Only Rourke had access to this camera. Vaun's interrogation had begun to get colorful. All sorts of red.

"The janitor is going to need a lot of disinfectant for that," Kara murmured.

"By my calculations, Robert Batson will crack within the hour," Rourke said.

"Sloppy. I would only need thirty minutes."

Rourke reached into his jacket pocket and pulled out his silver cigarette case. Without looking he popped it open and shook one small white pill into the palm of his hand then swallowed it quickly.

Vaun's Terminal business needed to be wrapped up quickly. The only reason Rourke was granted the freedom to run Black Spear as he saw fit was because of how efficiently his teams worked. Every delay was a hit against that credibility. This whole chimera virus—or Moses-2, rather, as the retrieved files determined—was beginning to make his jaw ache. If Vaun allowed this pain in his jaw to develop into a pain in his ass, Rourke would have to draw a line.

Back on the screen, Robert Batson was screaming. The man's howls did more for Rourke's jaw pain than the pill had. "Get it done, Captain," he said to himself. "Get it done."

CHAPTER 26

To say he was disappointed was too great of an understatement. Parents were disappointed when children didn't do well in school, employers were disappointed when sales were down, but this? This was so far beyond that. This . . . was an insult. Batson, his right hand and best man, had failed him. Simply trying to wrap his head around the idea that Batson had screwed the pooch this bad, and had gotten himself captured, felt like drilling screws into his temples.

Jax had lost his composure when one of the men had reported that Batson didn't make it to the rendezvous point. His KA-BAR was still buried an inch deep into his desk where he'd left it. The man, whose name Jax for the life of him couldn't remember, had been so caught off guard he'd been frozen on the spot. It was only when Jax grabbed his shotgun off the shelf behind his desk and ordered him out that the man found his nerves again.

He still held the gun tightly in his hands. The shotgun was a double-barrel 12 gauge; once upon a time his grandpa had used it to hunt deer. Now, Jax very much wanted to do some hunting of his own.

"If you want something done," he said before he broke open the shotgun and loaded two shells into it, "gotta do it yourself."

Jax snapped it closed and kicked open the door. The hot sun of the early afternoon greeted him as he took the catwalk down to the Terminal Grounds. A few men walking by saw him with the double-barrel in hand; they promptly remembered some business in the other direction and turned around. Smirking, Jax reached the building he was looking for and turned the knob.

Inside, Jax's elite awaited him. When he slammed the buttstock of his shotgun twice into the closest locker, the men snapped to attention. Jax smiled. These were the absolute very best he had. Last night he'd hand-picked them, telling them they were on standby for a special assignment. The men here looked more like a biker gang than a group of seasoned veterans. Most sported either sleeve tattoos or lengthy beards, and a few had already started gearing up. There were mountains of salt in the room from how experienced the lot was.

"Is it time?" asked a barrel-chested black man with scars criss-crossing the left side of his face.

Jax was pretty sure his name was either York or Dakota. One of the states at least. He'd been finding it harder and harder to remember names lately. Scars, however, he could always remember. York's were from a vehicle rollover, a cracked window had shredded his face. The lanky beanstalk in the back was missing half a pinky and most of his right ear from an IED blast. Then there was the one with the beard that made him look like a ZZ Top member. The beard and sunglasses hid the scars from two bullets he'd taken to the cheek and eye. All the scars told the same story: these men were survivors.

"We thought you'd forgotten about us."

Jax's grin spread and he slid his shotgun into the leather scabbard slung on his back. "Of course, not."

"So what is this special assignment, anyway? We going to help the others out with whatever is going on with the fat doctor in that bunker?" York asked. "Or are we going to help Batson with whatever is going on up north?"

"Batson's been taken," said Jax. It was like he'd set a bomb off in the room. "Everyone else is dead. Everyone." Jax paused to let them sit with that news before slowly stalking down the middle of the squad bay. "They slaughtered them. Last I heard from Batson, our guys were tucking in for the night, and these ghosts came in to slit their throats in their sleep."

"Shit . . ." York muttered. "What's the play?"

"That's up to you all," Jax said. "I'm up for a little payback, I think we should go get some. Unless anyone wants to challenge that?"

Their roars reverberated off the walls, and Jax relished it. None of the men would challenge him, no one ever had or ever would. These men would follow him into the gates of hell itself and right now all he would have to do is point out the direction.

Whoever these spooks were, they had hurt Terminal twice now. Jax was ready to strike back with his full might. Terminal was more than an amateur band of men with small arms. Jax was done playing it quiet. There was no reason to hide how much violence he was willing to unleash. He had no doubt that the black-garbed men they faced were from a black-ops outfit.

The entire purpose of Terminal was to strike back at the government for their failures, and now the government had sent more of their brothers to stop them and cover up those failures. No more. Jax's rage drowned out whatever sympathy he might have for soldiers and warriors on the other side. They'd all made their choice. If those assassins wanted to drown in their own blood with the rest of the politicians once the virus was released, then so be it.

"Hit the motor pool," Jax ordered. "We're bringing the Brutus twins with us."

York's eyes lit up with mad delight. A voice somewhere deep inside of Jax urged caution. He ignored it, something he was getting better and better at lately.

CHAPTER 27

Captain Vaun. 4:35 p.m.
Angel Site
Los Angeles, California

"Officially, you'll only ever be listed as a missing person case," Vaun said matter-of-factly. He retracted the blade on a boxcutter with a few clicks. "This location doesn't exist, which means you and I don't have to worry about your Congressman making a call and interrupting us." He placed the boxcutter on the metal tray next to a blooded scalpel, the empty syringe from before, a set of pliers, and an off-the-shelf hammer.

He'd been at the task for hours now. Torture wasn't something he particularly enjoyed nor was it anything he considered himself an expert in. But he did understand how it worked. It was a process, one that took time. Human willpower was a well and that well gradually refilled itself. Torture was just an exercise in depleting that resource at a rate higher than the person could renew it. In concept it was a simple enough cycle to repeat: applying pain, easing off to allow a sense of hope to surface, and then dashing it away just as quickly. Vaun knew this man would break, and soon.

Batson's face strained in an effort to look defiant despite the trauma Vaun had already put him through. Vaun had cut him. Vaun had beat him. He had even pulled off a couple fingernails. In short,

Batson's defiant look wasn't very convincing.

Vaun simply removed the latex gloves and took a calm breath. "Where is Moses?"

Batson squared his jaw and straightened in his chair. Ready for more.

Vaun stood and nodded. "We'll just give you a moment to think on this. I've got nothing but time."

He placed a clear plastic bag over Batson's face and cinched a zip tie around his neck to restrict his breathing.

The bag immediately fogged with every breath the big man took. One bruised eye shot Vaun a look full of murderous intent. He didn't flinch.

"You are going to tell me everything, or you are going to die here," he said. He made sure Batson saw the promise in his eyes. "How much of your body is going to be left in working condition is entirely up to you." To emphasize his point, he grabbed two of Batson's fingers and with a quick snap broke both of them at the third knuckle.

Batson roared. Vaun went for the door, leaving Batson behind with the bag over his head. It wasn't tight enough to suffocate him, but it sure as hell would feel like it. He knocked twice and looked to the security camera. A moment later the heavy deadbolt on the door slid out of place and one of Doc Phelps's assistants was waiting on the other end. "Hook him up with some adrenaline, I don't need him passing out on me."

The assistant nodded and began connecting an IV drip to Batson's arm.

Once he was outside and the door sealed behind him, Vaun nearly collapsed against the wall and had to catch himself with one hand. He'd been bluffing: time was not on his side right now. With every second that passed, the ticking only grew louder. Every moment brought them all closer to that proverbial buzzer.

Vaun never could quite stomach this part of the job for long.

Mentally, and morally, it was challenging to get your hands this dirty. As a person who tended to see the world through a very black and white lens, this level of interrogation tended to feel very gray. But it had to be done. His hand curled into a fist and he punched the wall. The pain that shot up the small bones behind his knuckles felt reassuring. It had to be done. Vaun might not have the stomach for extended torture, but the thought of what failure would mean was much more unsettling.

CHAPTER 28

Cole West. 5:48 p.m.
Angel Site
Los Angeles, California

Billy picked up an apple from the food tray we'd been provided and tossed it to me. "You know, as far as first missions go, West. Yours has been quite a full one."

I caught it then juggled it back and forth between my hands.

"Fistfights, car chases, explosions, shootouts . . . hey, who am I to complain? It sure beats making the CO's coffee." Billy nodded in agreement. I passed the apple back to him. "Was your first day this rough?"

Billy caught it and threw it to Tag. "What do you think? That one time in Rome: that was my first day."

Tag scowled, deep in thought. "Hmph . . . It was a little rough."

Billy rolled his eyes at Tag's understatement.

There was a tapping at our observation window. I turned, half expecting to see Doc Phelps again, but instead found Captain Vaun before us. His eyes looked tired and something told me that our fearless leader hadn't gotten a wink of sleep since we'd left the McAllister Brothers building. I felt a little guilty for kicking back, shooting the shit while he'd been hard at work. Then again, he wasn't at risk of suddenly developing necrosis.

"You boys enjoying your R&R?" he asked. "Or would any of you care to actually do some work?"

"Always, Captain," Tag said.

I gave a curt nod in agreement. Billy stood and shrugged.

"Good. Doc tells me you're clean and that's good enough for me." Vaun tapped a few buttons and the airlocked quarantine door slid out of place with a hush of compressed air. "Mr. Rourke's diggers just managed to glean some intel from that drive you swiped. Billy, you'll help me finish up with Batson and then we'll put this Terminal matter to rest."

"Finally, some good news," I said at precisely the same moment that an explosion behind Vaun took the four of us off our feet.

CHAPTER 29

A man in the motor pool had dubbed them "The Brutus Twins" when Jax first brought them to the Terminal Grounds. The Brutus Twins were two Humvees equipped with augmented Avenger Missile Systems. Each vehicle sported four Stinger missile pods on each side of the vehicle turret. The Stinger missiles were packed with six pounds of high explosives apiece. The turret also had an automatic 40mm grenade launcher mounted to its center.

In short, the Brutus Twins were hell carried atop eight wheels. They'd transported the vehicles under tarp on a big rig from the Terminal Grounds and, just as Jax had predicted, not a damn person had so much as batted an eye in their direction. Funny how little situational awareness the average passerby possessed.

York, who had unofficially become the squad leader for Jax's elite, manned Brutus One while another bullish-looking man with a flowing beard controlled Brutus Two. The man had been given the incredibly creative nickname Grizzly—after Grizzly Adams; Jax had trouble thinking of anything better to call him. Both men were currently bombarding the office building they'd tracked Batson to and absolutely relishing it.

Tracking his right-hand man had been surprisingly easy. Robert Batson had a very small GPS tracker roughly the size of a dime lodged beneath one of his molars. Jax had waited a few hours after Batson's capture to activate the tracer to ensure that Batson's captors wouldn't have simply scanned him, found the tracer, and ripped out his tooth. Then, it had only been a matter of following the blinking light on his cell phone. Modern technology was a hell of a thing.

Another Stinger fired from Brutus One collided with the side of the office building and the explosive payload detonated. Two floors of the building disappeared in a ball of smoke. This was the third missile they'd fired and the building was quickly beginning to resemble a burning tinder box.

While York hammered them with missiles, Grizzly rained volleys of 40mm explosives at the ground level. The few vehicles that had been in the parking lot out front had been reduced to flaming husks, the ground floor face of the building's windows completely blown apart, and the grenade launcher still had hundreds of rounds to spare.

So far, the rats still hadn't come out of their burning nest. Maybe they were retreating inward. Jax knew that Batson was being held in a secure room on the third floor of the building, which meant that the levels below were fair game to devastate. It was a delicate game of destruction though. After all, they had to ensure they didn't cause so much damage that the entire building might collapse below their comrade's feet.

"This is Jax," he said into the radio, "We're going in." While York and Grizzly covered them with the Brutus Twins, Jax's vehicle lurched forward. It was a Stryker Armored Personnel Carrier, or APC. The APC was an eight-wheeled vehicle resembling a metal plated clamshell armed with a .50 caliber belt-fed machine gun and a Mk 19 grenade launcher. Jax's vehicle could hit a top speed of sixty-three miles per hour. He had already gotten it up to fifty before smashing head-first through the front doors of the building.

The armored vehicle barely shook as it punched through the already demolished front doors and continued to barrel forward. Jax keyed his radio, "Grizzly: it's crying time."

A moment later, Brutus Two volleyed CS tear-gas grenades into the building. The telltale *thump-thump-thump* of the 40mm cannon firing was followed by the hiss of gas escaping each of the rounds. White smoke blanketed the area around the APC and spread to fill the rest of the first floor. Jax turned around in his seat to face the back of the APC. Nine of his best men sat on the edges of their seats. The smile that fought its way to his face was irresistible.

"All right, boys, let's get some payback."

The men moved up through the fire and darkness, pushing deeper into the building. Barrels up, masks on. Jax strode confidently amid them with grandpa's shotgun in hand.

The rest of his elite wore body armor from head to toe, but Jax walked amid the burning building in the same thing he wore this morning. Warmth spread up the green sleeves of his jacket from the fires creeping up the walls on either side of him. The men were surprised that he hadn't changed out of what everyone knew was his equivalent of a uniform, but Jax was a legend and, as usual, nobody questioned why he did things the way he did. Jax knew the difference between confidence and idiocy though, so he donned a ballistic vest. Beyond that concession, he walked unarmored. He meant for his appearance to be a statement.

"You five clear this level, the rest with me."

"You got it, Jax," one man said.

"Roger, Jax," said another.

They pushed on deeper into the building and took the stairs up before they heard distant gunfire. Controlled bursts, small caliber. Not unlike the rifles his men downstairs carried. They had their own priorities, and Jax had faith in each of the men he'd brought. He ordered those with him to move on.

White smoke swirled in the air of the new floor on which they found themselves. Jax's exposed hands and neck burned from the CS, but his mask protected his lungs and throat. The burn wasn't too bad. If anything, it kept him alert.

When he kicked in the nearest door, which led to a section of living quarters, Jax found that the occupants weren't lucky enough to have masked up. One man floundered about on the floor in his underwear, clawing desperately at his eyes and hocking spit to the floor with every wheezing cough. Another near him had a Glock in hand, but his eyes were squeezed shut to keep the gas out.

The man fired two shots that hit the wall three feet from Jax.

Jax pulled the trigger once, and one of the shotgun's barrels roared as 12-gauge buckshot blew forth and opened a crater in the man's chest. The man's burning eyes gaped wide as he gasped and keeled over onto his chest, revealing a devastating exit wound.

Almost casually, Jax pointed his weapon at the other man before firing again. The buckshot took the man full in the face and his head snapped back so hard Jax could hear his neck bones crack. While he broke the double-barrel open to reload, his men moved in to clear the next room. There must have been more men coughing out their lungs in there, because his men opened fire. A few death gasps later and his men returned unscathed.

Jax pulled two red-cased buckshot rounds from the belt of shells across his chest. He thumbed them into the breech, then snapped the barrels closed. Once his men finished mopping up, he directed them back out into the hallway with a quick tilt of his head.

Somewhere in this building his friend was waiting. God help these black-ops spooks if he wasn't alive. On the other hand . . . every decent cause is only made greater with a martyr. Jax mulled that over while their search continued. His gas mask hid the smile creeping across his lips. Their hunt would bear fruit, one way or another.

CHAPTER 30

Cole West. 6:20 p.m.
Angel Site
Los Angeles, California

"Get up, West." It sounded muted, as if they were either speaking through a wall or I was wearing earmuffs. "Get the hell up!" the voice said, loud enough to pull me out of my own fog.

My eyes fluttered as I tried to focus and I found myself staring at the ceiling. The whole room was painted red from flashing emergency lights. Fires in another room glowed at the edge of my vision, and black smoke swirled above me.

"What the hell . . . ?"

A hand pulled me to my feet. I shook my head twice but the room was still wobbly. Vaun was in front of me, looking right in my eyes trying to see if the hamster wheels behind them were turning yet.

"You good?"

"Yeah . . . yeah. Jesus, what the hell?"

"You already said that."

"Oh, right. I meant what the actual *fuck*?"

"No idea. Somebody's clearly upset with us, though."

Another series of smaller explosions boomed outside as if to punctuate Vaun's statement.

"We need to get to the armory," Tag said beside me and I turned to see that he held an unconscious Billy over one shoulder. "You think this is Terminal?"

"They're the ones we've pissed off most recently," Vaun said.

"Splendid."

"This goes a little above and beyond just another simple ragtag militia, don't you think, Captain?"

Vaun's eyes darkened. "They blew up one of our buildings yesterday in broad daylight. They cornered us in that warehouse with their virus. And now they just showed up at our front door and blew us the hell up all over again. At our front. Fucking. Door. What I *think* is that they have no idea who they're fucking with." Vaun drew a compact .45 from a hip holster then racked the slide back. "The armory."

Holding the gun in his right hand, Vaun slipped a knife from his pocket and tossed it to me with a nod.

I glanced at it, taking just a moment to admire the knife. It was a large Pro-Tech Don, a very nice automatic switchblade with a five-inch blade. I pressed the button on the handle and the blade leapt out in my hand.

"Very nice," I said, reassured by the cold metal of the tactical knife.

I was partial to knives. Maybe it was because I was a native Californian and it was damn near impossible to get a concealed carry permit for a firearm—even for military members—but you could carry a knife in a pocket, no problem. The thing I liked about blades was that they were reliable. They never jammed or ran out of bullets. Millenia later and a sharpened piece of metal is still one of the most effective tools on the battlefield.

Vaun moved out into the hallway, fanning his .45 back and forth as we came up behind him. "I guess our quarantine is over, huh?" someone said behind us.

I saw that Billy had regained consciousness. Blood dripped down from a wound on the top of his head and into his eye, his head drooped back down and I knew that he still hadn't fully recovered.

More booms sounded nearby and the walls shook again. Burning rubble was knocked loose from above, forcing Tag and me to side-step out of the way. Smoke tickled my nose.

Vaun rounded a corner that led to a stairwell, cleared it, then waved for us to join him. The armory was in one of the basement levels next to the underground garage, so the only way to go was down. Billy tried to help Tag as much as he could going down the steps, but he barely managed to maneuver down the stairs with the grace of a drunken sailor.

Though I was thankful for the knife he'd gifted me, I was getting rather anxious for Vaun to get us to the armory. If the explosions were any indication, Terminal came to play with toys significantly bigger than knives. Reliable as a blade is, it has a certain deficiency when it comes to a guy with a gun six feet away.

The smoke cleared a bit as we descended and my nasal passages were thankful for it. We continued lower, until the stairs ended in a dark concrete hall.

"Where the hell is everyone?" Tag muttered as the four of us neared the armory door.

"Angel Site is on a skeleton crew," Vaun answered.

Tag replied with a disappointed grunt and continued to heft Billy down the hall. The door leading into the armory was plated steel thick as a bank vault with a keycard scanner on the wall alongside it. It had its own dedicated power supply so even with the lights out the scanner still functioned and the large hydraulics that opened the door would work. Vaun turned and covered the hallway, then passed his keycard to me. "Load up and make it quick."

I gave a curt nod and slid the card into the reader. There was a soft beep before unseen machinery pulled the solid slab of steel inside. There was a marvelous selection of shelved weapons of every size. I saw lines of assault rifles and shotguns, larger bolt-action rifles with mounted scopes adorned a far wall, and several racks of handguns in multiple calibers to my right. I wanted to drool at it all, but the only thing I was able to focus on was the barrel of the Glock pointed directly in my face.

"Bang, you're dead."

CHAPTER 31

Rourke's jaw throbbed. Three minutes ago, the security feed he'd been monitoring showed an explosion at Angel Site. Two minutes ago, the footage went dark. And sixty seconds ago he'd activated the nearest team he had. After that he'd pulled his phone out and dialed the Secretary of Defense. He'd answered on the first ring.

"At this hour North Korea better be invading . . ." he said.

"Jim, it's Rourke."

"Ah. *Mister* Rourke," the SecDef said. "I'm sure this isn't a courtesy call."

Rourke gave a second's pause to consider how to deliver his request to the man in charge of the entire U.S. military, but neither of them were well known for sugarcoating problems or beating around the bush.

"Jim, I'm borrowing two of your drones."

There was a sigh on the other end of the phone. "All right, which country are they going to?"

"Los Angeles."

Any other man would have balked at that, but the SecDef just chewed it over for half a second. "Terrorists in our own backyard, huh?"

"Front lawn actually. Jim, they're at Angel Site."

"Christ, whatever you need. I'm calling Pendleton now."

"Don't bother, I already did and they'll be on Angel Site soon. This actually *was* just a courtesy call."

"Well thanks, Rourke, don't hesitate to call next time you want to fly a Predator over Beverly Hills. Just promise me you'll talk to Homeland so they know what's happening."

"I will. And Jim?"

"Yeah?"

"It's *Mister* Rourke."

Once he'd hung up the phone he looked across his desk to Mason to gauge how she was handling the damage control. All Black Spear sites were chosen to be somewhat secluded in low-traffic areas. Preferably set in industrial districts that were unpopulated at night. Still, when three military vehicles start shelling a building, it's bound to attract attention. Mason was currently on the phone with the mayor of Los Angeles.

"Sir, with all due respect, this is a matter of national security and frankly you don't have the authorization to know any more," she barked.

Most of the local police and fire department were being dispatched to alternate locations. It's a shame what kind of misdirection is possible if your dispatch system has such poor firewalls.

Heated words came from the phone's speaker, but Mason remained unfazed. She cleaned a fingernail while looking at a tablet that displayed a live satellite feed of the mayor's location.

"Mister Mayor, this is above your pay grade. Now, divert any remaining police from the area, or we'll send one of them to *your* location. That would be inconvenient since the woman you're with is definitely not your wife."

Rourke could tell that the mayor was speechless. Mason looked amused and hung up before the mayor could stammer any apologies or explanations. After switching away from the satellite feed on the tablet, Mason turned it around so Rourke could see a map with several red dots on it. Each dot represented one of LAPD's vehicles, and within moments the few that were near Angel Site were already rerouting.

"I just made a burning building disappear, and I didn't even have to leave your office." She sounded equally bored and proud at the same time.

Rourke looked back to his own computer screen. The Predator drones he'd commandeered were near their target.

CHAPTER 32

I stared at the gun while my mind processed what I was seeing.

"I almost fucking killed you," said Hodges.

"Cut the shit, Hodges," Vaun said. He pulled the armory door shut. "Have you seen anyone else?"

"Just him." Hodges pointed to the corner where Kelly leaned against the wall.

His shoulder was bandaged and his arm was held in a sling. His eyes told me morphine still coursed through his veins. Kelly managed to drag his conscious mind through the haze of painkillers to give us a thumbs-up. "The band's back together," said Kelly with a half-hearted smile.

"Two minutes," Vaun said. "Load up. Tag, make sure the new guy doesn't grab anything stupid."

I pretended like I wasn't looking at the rocket launcher next to me when he said that. Who *hasn't* wanted to fire one of those off?

Instead, I grabbed an M4 from a long rack of rifles. It had an ACOG scope atop it and a suppressor along the barrel. I was comfortable with most firearms, but M16s and M4s I was the most familiar and experienced with. Behind me were rows of shelved pistols. One in particular caught my eye. The handgun was a .45 1911 by Para. What .45s lacked in magazine capacity they sure as shit made up for in stopping power. When I picked it up, I found the skull logo stamped on the side of the barrel indicated it was from their Black-Ops line of tactical handguns.

"Fitting," I said.

Tag handed a vest to me, and I threw it on over the paper-thin clothing they'd given all of us for our quarantine. Vaun tossed a double clip of ammo my way. I caught it with one hand while sliding my new Black-ops 1911 into a holster on my left hip. I shot rifles right handed and pistols left. Strange, I know, but it made for speedier transitions when one weapon ran dry.

Remembering the folding knife he'd given me, I held it out for Vaun to reclaim. He simply looked down at the knife for a moment before studying me with a curious facial expression.

"No, you keep it."

Once I'd finished loading up, I looked at the rest of my teammates. Tag, the strongest of our group, had picked up a Mark 48 lightweight belt-fed machine gun. The large box magazine attached told me that the big man meant business and was ready to dish it out at a cyclic rate. I guess his snub-nosed .44 had been placed here after it was decontaminated, because it was tucked into the small of his back once again. Atop a shelf was a large black duffel bag that Tag grabbed and tossed over his shoulder. I recognized it as the grappling gun bag from last night. When Tag saw my curiosity, he simply shrugged. "Never know what'll come in handy."

Hodges still had the Glock he'd brandished in my face moments ago. He'd also acquired an assault rifle with an underslung grenade launcher. Several 40mm explosive rounds were tucked into little pouches on his vest. Though I couldn't find it possible *not* to hate the guy's guts, Hodges had a demolitions background, which made him my first pick in the room I'd want with hands on things that go boom.

"We'll need these too," Hodges said, handing out gas masks identical to the ones we'd used last night.

"Moses?" I asked with widening eyes.

"Fuck no, just tear gas. Upper floors were filling up with it when I was getting Kelly down here. Looks like Terminal is trying to smoke us out. I glimpsed two assault vehicles posted outside before shit got crazy. Also spotted a Stryker that blew in through the front door."

I think I might've been the only one to visibly balk at hearing that news. Black Spear was supposed to be the terrifying bogeyman of black ops, yet this militia was on their home turf and kicking the hell out of them. "Christ, Talon would be really useful right about now."

Second time a Talon had been mentioned, and I still had no idea what it was. My mind conjured images of some super-advanced drone swooping in to save our skin or an armored tank that was capable of pulling our asses out of this fire. "What's a Talon?"

Vaun shook his head, "Doesn't matter. This is all we got."

Our team's explosives expert sheepishly avoided the Captain's gaze.

Billy was still fighting off his head trauma, Tag had settled him on the ground next to where Kelly leaned against the wall. "I'll keep an eye on him," Kelly said as he slapped a large clip into the well of a machine pistol before deftly working the slide back with his one good hand.

I shot a look at the rest of Cerberus Squad. "He still looks pretty doped. Is it a good idea leaving just him to watch Billy?"

They all actually laughed at me. Vaun included. "Hell, even doped up he's still a better shot than you or me."

"Doped up *and* one-handed," Kelly corrected.

Vaun gave him a nod of acknowledgment and then reached to the rack of weapons to retrieve one of the long guns. At first I thought it was just an oversized assault rifle. Upon closer examination, I realized it was actually a shotgun.

Specifically, it was an Origin-12 by Fostech. I'd seen it before, advertised as "the world's fastest shotgun". Vaun slid ten-shell clips into the pockets on his vest. "Move out, I've got point. Hodges behind, Tag cover our rear and keep an eye on West. Make sure he doesn't hurt himself."

I took my position behind Hodges and tried to tuck my wounded pride in one of the pouches on my vest. Nobody likes being babied, let alone anyone who's served. It was disappointing that, despite everything that had happened in the past twenty-four hours, I still hadn't proved myself. I was still the boot of the team. I was still the squad's weakest link, which was a serious blow to my self-worth, considering one member of the squad had a busted wing and another most likely had a mean concussion.

New guy or not, I follow orders. The four of us left the armory, Kelly sealed it behind us, and we made our way back to the stairwell. Back to the smoke. Back to the fire.

As we ascended the steps, the heat started to rise. My face felt like it was baking behind my gas mask and my sweating palms started to slick the grip and handguards of my rifle. Despite the sweltering temperature, I forced myself to stay focused.

"How many shooters, Crash?" Vaun asked.

"Stryker fits ten plus a driver."

Flames licked at us as we passed the first floor. The entryway that would've led out of the stairwell was completely blocked by burning rubble, so we pushed on higher.

"Push to the third-floor interrogation room," Vaun said. "They had to have come for Batson."

Tag grunted as he swept the stairwell behind and below us with his machine gun. He wielded the heavy weapon around our small surroundings as effortlessly as most people point a flashlight. My shoulders had already started to ache and burn from holding up my rifle. Keeping tension on my upper arms and shoulders worked the muscles in ways I just wasn't used to; they'd gotten more work in the past day than in the past ten years.

"Get that goddamn barrel up!" Hodges hissed at me. Immediately my reflexes snapped the weapon up at the ready. I nodded and pulled the rifle stock back into the pocket of my shoulder. Hodges was right. If someone came at us from our flank, the split second it would take to raise my weapon could get the entire squad killed.

All at once, we heard gunfire. It echoed into the stairwell and drowned out the low rumble of the hungry flames outside. A cry of pain followed the cracks of bullets, then there was a dark chuckle. And another. A third voice said something unheard while the previous two laughed at whatever joke had been made.

Vaun pressed his cheek to the stock of his shotgun and pulled the weapon in tight to his shoulder. "I count three. Crash, stack up."

Hodges moved up close behind Vaun and gave him a slight pat on the shoulder once he was in position. "Ready."

With one hand Vaun lobbed a small object around the corner outside the stairwell. A second later a boom rattled the walls as a white flash spread out just out of sight. It was a flashbang; I hadn't even seen him pull the pin on it. Before the flashing light dissipated Vaun and Hodges peeled around the corner and advanced down the hallway, leaving Tag and myself to move up and cover behind them.

There were actually four men at the end of the hallway, not that it mattered. Each held an assault rifle, wore full body armor, and had a gas mask over his face. Vaun snapped in on the closest and squeezed the trigger. The shotgun made an impossibly loud boom as the man took the twelve-gauge square to the chest. In half a second, Vaun sighted in on the next man and dropped him with another shot.

Though it had been only a beat since the flashbang blast, the two remaining Terminal shooters managed to recover enough to at least point their weapons in the direction they thought the assault was coming from. Not fast enough. Vaun took them both out with one round each to the chest. The whole ordeal took less than three seconds.

All four of the men had worn what looked like impressive ballistic vests, so Hodges cleaned it up with a quick finishing shot to the head for each of them. Cold, yes, but efficient and necessary.

As Tag and I moved down the hallway to where our teammates waited, I saw what the Terminal shooters had been laughing at. The dead body before us was facedown with two bullet holes in the back of its skull. Blood already pooled around the dead woman's face. If you looked at the shards of the broken ceramic coffee mug near her fingers, you could just make out the remnants of what had once been a yellow smiley face. I'd only seen that mug twice: once down in the morgue and later outside our quarantine room.

Doctor Tanya Phelps lay dead at our feet, and every fiber in my being wanted to do some hurting.

CHAPTER 33

"Doc . . ." Tag said sadly.

"Stack up," Vaun ordered. "We clear this floor, then work our way to three. They don't get Batson. They don't get away with this."

Tag knelt down next to the fallen doctor and started to roll her onto her back, pausing a moment to close her eyes.

"Boomerang," Vaun said with more edge in his voice.

"She deserves better than to be left face-down in her own blood."

"Mourn for the fallen later," Vaun said. "Fight for the living now."

Tag gave the Captain a solemn nod as he rose to his feet. Even through the lens of his mask, I saw the fire burning in the big man's eyes. I was just glad he and his machine gun were on my side.

Vaun pointed down the corridor, and we pushed on. More flames and tear gas awaited us, biting at our exposed skin. I guess I should be thankful it was just tear gas, not an engineered virus that turned people into rabid maniacs. One of life's little blessings, to be sure.

Both the threat of more shooters and our hazardous environment were enough incentive to move faster. The damage Terminal had done to Angel Site was mostly superficial so far, but I didn't know how long before the building decided to up and collapse on us. I figured as long as Robert Batson was still being held upstairs, they wouldn't risk completely destroying the building. Batson was important to Terminal. For now, that still counted for something.

We found our friends' bodies down the hall. Achilles Squad had been resting in the sleeping quarters when they'd been executed. It looked as if one or two had managed to put up a bit of a struggle, but none of them had gas masks next to their beds and the gas had taken them out of the fight before the shooting had started.

Vaun shook his head in disbelief.

"This ain't supposed to be happening, Captain," Hodges muttered.

More gunfire reached our ears, this time coming from above. Vaun shouldered his weapon once more and took off with the three of us barely keeping up behind him. Around another corner and up a set of stairs, taking the steps three at a time, and shoving through the door on the third floor. Right into a burst of gunfire.

The Captain's face would've been taken off if he hadn't immediately dropped into a crouch and fired back. I was still midway up from the second floor when the sound of Vaun's shotgun fire rebounded off the stairwell's concrete walls. It echoed, painfully loud, and I had to fight the urge to clamp both hands on either side of my head. The Origin-12 was supposed to be the fastest shotgun on the market, and it certainly lived up to its selling point.

By the time I'd gotten to the top of the stairs, Vaun had already emptied one clip, reloaded, and fired the second dry. Hodges tapped him once on the shoulder, the Captain ducked back into the stairwell to reload, and Hodges advanced out and fired back.

The entire time, the Terminal shooters fired in our direction. Positioned at the end of the hall, they used toppled file cabinets as cover. Bullets whistled through the doorway and ricocheted around the stairs.

Hodges fired back a few bursts before cursing and taking cover back inside. "I see three," Hodges said, then blindly fired a few more rounds around the corner.

"We need an opening," said Vaun.

"Already on it."

Hodges leaned back into the doorway and fired. This time not from his assault rifle, but from the grenade launcher attached to the bottom of it. There was a deep *thump* sound as the 40mm fragmentation grenade lobbed out and into the hallway. From where he stood, it traveled halfway down the hallway before exploding, sending shrapnel and fire in all directions.

The explosion gave us a fraction of a second. It was all we needed. We pushed out into the hallway while Tag unloaded suppressing fire from his machine gun in the Terminal shooters' direction. Spent brass shells rattled against the linoleum floor by the dozens. There was a break in the fire, and we realized our enemy was no longer firing back.

Vaun edged further down the smoking hall. At the end were our three shooters. One had dropped dead on his ass from a face full of shrapnel, a second had taken the brunt of Hodges's grenade and was missing one arm and part of his leg, the third was slumped against the far wall bleeding from nearly a dozen bullet wounds. The holes peppered across his entire upper body, the ballistic vest he'd worn protected his chest but not his shoulders, arms or gut. One hand attempted to raise a pistol but the weapon's weight was too much to hold. Another second and the last shooter finally bled out.

With the hallway cleared, we approached the interrogation room. As we neared I saw that the door was already ajar. Vaun wrenched it open. We all knew there would be no one inside.

CHAPTER 34

"Father to Achilles, respond."

No response.

"Father to Cerberus, respond."

In a few minutes, Rourke needed to make a hard decision. His men weren't responding to his hails. While there were a million possible reasons for that, the fact remained that a Black Spear site had been compromised. Sensitive information of the highest level was potentially in the open. Workstations with access to Black Spear's digital network were at risk of falling into the wrong hands. And soon, Rourke would make the tough call in that matter.

Rourke calculated a sixty percent chance that Vaun's team was alive. Cerberus was one of his best teams, but that had been before. Now they were undermanned and continued to rack up their own casualties. Rourke determined that his men were still alive and fighting. On the other hand, he figured that there was an even greater chance that, if Angel Site was this compromised, Terminal would walk away with some of their assets.

The information on Black Spear's networks could not be lost. If it fell into the wrong hands, the consequences would be nothing short of disastrous. Rourke pulled up the latest satellite imaging available to him.

"Christ!"

From the feed he could see two Humvee-mounted weapon systems shelling his building. No other activity visible. No return gunfire from the burning windows, no desperate escapes out any of the exit points. No Black Spear vehicles racing out of the underground garage.

"Everyone's dead, sir," Mason said bluntly.

"You know that's not true."

"And you know that, true or not, you still have to make a decision. Sir."

The truth was, there wasn't a choice to make. The dangers made the decision for him. Rourke checked the ETA of the Predator. He remotely armed its weapons systems from his computer. His hand hovered near the computer keys for a moment before he tried to reach his men once more.

"Blackbars . . . this is Father. Last call. Respond."

CHAPTER 35

Chan watched with equal parts delight and fascination as the latest batch of guinea pigs deteriorated before his eyes. He'd never liked referring to test subjects as "guinea pigs", partially because Chan had always liked animals more than people. The thought that the subjects liquefying in front of him could instead be small rodents actually provoked pangs of unease in his stomach. Which was saying something, since the very sight of four men's flesh rotting away while they still breathed hadn't even stopped him from eating his nova lox and shmear bagel.

He took another bite and chewed as two of the subjects flatlined on the other side of the glass. Moses-2 was ravenous in the way that it ate through its carriers Chan continually found himself eager to watch it work. It reminded him of watching a fresh log placed atop a burning fireplace. There was something almost beautiful in its indiscriminate nature, its purity of purpose, something Chan admired in an increasingly confusing world.

A heart monitor let out a long, high-pitched tone as another subject flatlined. Chan took another bite of his bagel and checked his watch. Twelve hours. Genetic engineering was a fickle science. You tamper around in one area of genetic coding and something entirely different was affected. When they'd made the jump from Moses-1 to Moses-2, their goal had only been to increase aggression and a means of spreading the virus, and yet now their creation burned through its carriers at twice the rate.

This was a problem, as Jax had given him the very curious assignment of creating a way to delay the onset of the virus's symptoms. All these subjects were given antiviral injections to slow the symptom's developments. It had no effect on Moses-2. A simpler solution could be a gel capsule similar to over-the-counter cold medication. A pill could be swallowed, and the time required for the pill's coating to break down might suffice for Jax's purpose. He hadn't yet been made privy to the reason why Jax needed a delayed virus release, but Chan only took this new assignment as a challenge to his abilities. It was one he knew he could best.

Chan pulled a small digital recorder from his pocket and thumbed the button. "Going to need more volunteers."

Mr. Jackson had given him free reign to pull as many men as he would need for his studies. Initially, he had been hesitant to let Chan run the tests on his own men, but that had been weeks ago. Since then, the man had acknowledged the necessity of their tests. Jax had originally suggested they simply start picking up vagrants. Chan had quickly dismissed that idea. Random kidnappings would eventually draw attention, attention drew investigations, and this was too delicate a time to have anyone looking in their direction.

It only took a little coaxing for Jax to reluctantly agree. That was roughly twelve subjects ago.

Chan brushed his fingers off on his lab coat as he made mental notes. He would prefer a wider range of subject's demographics for trial. More specifically, he'd like to see any differences in infection rates for infants or adolescents. Of course, he'd have to run that idea by Jax once he returned from his little rescue mission, but Chan expected the request to be approved.

Chan quickly became lost in his plans for further experimentation. He whistled cheerfully as the last of the subjects flatlined on the other side of the glass.

CHAPTER 36

Batson was gone. All that remained in the interrogation room was a loose set of handcuffs and a tray littered with bloody instruments. The sight of all the blades and tools twisted my stomach into knots.

"Exactly what kind of interrogation was going on here . . ." I asked quietly. I picked up a particularly gruesome knife, its hooked blade was stained red.

"The kind that gets results," was all Vaun said.

"So this Guantanamo Bay type of shit is what we do?"

Nobody responded. The lack of an immediate response spoke volumes, though. Vaun avoided looking at me, instead focusing on the various torture instruments strewn on the cart.

"Technically, Angel Site doesn't exist, so you can't violate the Geneva Convention in an area that doesn't exist," Hodges chimed in.

"This is fucked. I'm just going on record as saying that I don't have the stomach for this type of bullshit. This isn't what I signed up for."

"Time and a place for everything," the Captain said, as if that justified what had happened in this room.

I knew the world I'd stepped into wasn't going to be so black and white, but being faced with something this gray wasn't easy. Facing a man with a gun takes a level of courage most don't have, but this? What type of man can brutalize anyone in this manner? The more important question in my mind was how long before I'd be asked to participate in something this . . . wrong.

I tried to remind myself what was on the line here. Torture is easily justified when it's us versus them. An outsider threatening your country is so much simpler. Take them to Guantanamo, put razor blades to their fingernails until they talk. Who cares, right? But Robert Batson wasn't a radical Islamist or anything of the sort. He was a U.S. citizen, a veteran at that. He'd taken the Oath of Enlistment just as I had. I guess it was naive for me to think that the bad guy would always be the mustache-twirling type.

Not for the first time, I wondered how much of the old me would be left when this was all said and done. The moral lines I'd already crossed over felt more like a checklist than actual boundaries. If you would've asked me last week what sort of lines I wasn't willing to cross, I would've said something like not parking in handicapped spots. Or not using the express checkout aisle when I have more than twelve items. My whole scale of right and wrong needed to be thrown out the window. It was starting to set in that the old me was already being lowered into a grave, and I was just too stupid to realize I'd missed the funeral.

The military is a brotherhood. While the separate branches like to poke fun at one another, we are still one big dysfunctional family. In this room, the floor was stained with the blood of our own, a wayward ally now turned enemy. Terminal had stolen that sense of brotherhood and perverted it.

Vaun's posture hardened and the moment of mutual unease was gone. "They don't get away with Batson. Seven shooters down, let's bag the rest."

As I followed Hodges and Tag, Vaun's hand latched onto my

upper arm and pulled me next to him. Tag noticed, but the Captain dismissed him with a nod.

"This is the reality, West," he said. "This is what the war is. You can't stomach this then tomorrow we can send you packing back to your fucking desk job. If we even make it out of here. But *until* tomorrow, I'm still supposed to try and keep your sorry ass alive."

Conflicting emotions flared inside. I wanted to break Vaun's self-righteous face for somehow managing to take a moral high ground when it came to torturing American citizens. At the same time, I wanted to prove that I had what it took to roll with the big dogs. Lastly, it hurt like hell that the Captain could so readily kick me back to the minors. I had thought the team was beginning to warm to me, but just like that Vaun let me know they had all been operating together for far longer and I was still just the inexperienced rookie. Pride can be a confusing thing.

Both shame and anger kept me from looking him in the eyes. "Fall in, Marine," said Vaun. He pushed past me. The torture table hooked my gaze once more on my way out. It hurt just looking at it. If that's what it took to be Black Spear, then I almost hoped they were right about me not belonging. Or was I just frightened to find out that I did?

CHAPTER 37

"Almost there," Jax said as he and Batson neared the bottom of the stairs.

Batson weighed nearly two-fifty, so it was a good thing he was still able to walk on his own with just a little of his weight on Jax's shoulder. Mobile as he was, the man was truly a mess. Batson's face alone was testament to whoever the Men in Black were.

A few tears streamed down Batson's face and Jax had to wonder whether it was from the gas still present in the building or if he was just that thankful they'd come for him. Maybe it was a little column A and a little column B.

Two elites accompanied them, taking point. The other seven of his men were elsewhere in the building, but hadn't responded to his comm checks. Jax assumed the worst.

They reached the bottom of the stairs. Jax stowed his shotgun across his back to continue helping Batson. Fuck, he was heavy. Even with the big man trudging along on his own feet, it was still becoming unbearable. "Next time you're getting tortured, make sure they cut off some of your love handles first, yeah?"

The back hatch of the Stryker opened. They loaded up. Batson went down like a sack of bricks. With a simple cock of his head, Jax directed one of the other men to start administering first aid. Jax signaled for another man to get behind the driver's seat. With the other three stowed away, Jax tried one last time to reach the rest of his men inside.

"Sorry, boys," he said when nobody responded. He waited another half second before getting into the Stryker and pulling away. As the armored vehicle backed out of the burning building, Jax felt a swell of pride. Despite their losses, this was still a victory in his mind.

The Stryker turned around and started to pass Brutus Two. They were close enough that Jax could see the face of the large grunt, Grizzly, behind the driver's seat. Jax was close enough to see a triumphant smile.

But a second later he was close enough to see Grizzly's eyes go wide as a 40mm grenade punched through the windshield and exploded inside.

CHAPTER 38

"Hit them again, Crash!" Vaun ordered.

Hodges reloaded his grenade launcher as fast as he could, fingers moving fluidly from drilling this motion a thousand times. Another frag round loaded into the underbelly of his rifle and a *thump* rang out. The explosive arched through the air and detonated along the side of the Stryker vehicle out front of their building. Unlike the Humvee though, the Stryker shrugged off the explosive round.

Cerberus Squad was still on the third floor, but from this vantage point we had clear sight of the enemy vehicles below. One of the Humvees was already reduced to a burning metal husk. Tag was propped up on a window, spraying the second Humvee with his machine gun, hoping that by sending enough rounds down range he'd manage to hit something critical. So far the vehicle was proving to be more resistant to bullets than Hollywood would have me believe.

Over the gunfire we heard a chirp. Vaun backed away from the windows to hold his radio up to his ear. Somehow, it had begun to work again.

"This is Blackbars!" he shouted into the receiver. "Please tell me you have backup en route?!"

Mr. Rourke's voice came in even louder than Vaun's had been. "Blackbars: get out of the building! Get out *now!*"

Vaun's face crinkled into confusion, and then looking out the window he saw a bright light, far too low and fast to be a shooting star. A fucking missile. And a big one at that.

Tag wrenched something out of his pack and threw it against the wall. The zipline mount from last night. It anchored itself into the wall. A second later Tag had the grappling gun in hand, firing the line out of the window to the street below.

"Go! Go! Go!" Vaun shouted.

The four of us leapt out the window, hooking to the zipline midjump. At the same time the weapons system on the Humvee below found our position and started shelling the side of the building. Already we were away from the fire, the ground was coming up fast, and I had to remind myself that last night I'd tumbled into a mess at the end of the zipline.

The black asphalt of the parking lot neared. I unhooked, sticking the landing this time and using the momentum to carry me into a run. Behind me the missile slammed into the burning building that had once been Angel Site. The explosion was a magic trick: where once there was concrete, steel, and glass only light and fire remained.

I dove behind one of the Stryker's wheels as the giant blazing thing punched out in every direction. The force of the blast buffeted everything around us. I actually felt the Stryker next to me shift along the asphalt an inch. Every sound was silenced, except for a ringing in my ears that went on and on.

In that split-second I knew that it had been Rourke who'd sent the missile. Of course he had. To him we were surely dead, or captured, in which case to him we were better off dead anyway. I had to remind myself of the type of company I was in. I knew from the beginning of this that Black Spear was willing to kill whoever they had to in order to keep the nation safe. I guess I just hadn't considered that that might mean Black Spear's own men.

The other Humvee's turret turned, adjusted itself, and then two Stingers fired off into the night sky. Rourke's Predator that had sent the missile was just now coming into view. I watched it bank and roll, dodging one of the Stingers—but not the second.

The drone exploded into pieces and fell to the street less than a block away from us. So much for air support.

From where I lay crouched, I could see the rest of my team. The blast that had erased Angel Site had hit them hard. Tag helped Vaun to his feet, firing his machine gun one handed as they both made shaky steps behind the downed Humvee for cover.

But it was Hodges that I was looking at. He'd been closest to the blast and it had knocked the hell out of him. Hodges was just pulling himself to his knees, one hand outstretched towards his rifle, which lay just out of reach. The Humvee's turret was rotating its cannon towards him.

Hodges drew himself onto uneasy feet and retrieved his rifle. His face didn't change as the cannon fired right at him.

I tackled Hodges, rolling as I did, pulling him away from the 40mm round that exploded right where he'd been standing. The blast carried us clear away from the Humvee, reducing my insides to jelly. I think one of my eardrums was blown at that point. With a quick wrench under his armpits, I hoisted my teammate back to his feet. The two of us lurched towards the Stryker. We stuck close to its wheels on the backside, out of range from both the Stryker and the Humvee's weapons.

Tag and Vaun were behind a concrete road barrier at the edge of the parking lot. Tag's weapon was laid atop it, and Vaun took a knee with his radio to his ear. I hoped that meant reinforcements were on their way, but I wasn't holding my breath.

Four men with small arms against two vehicles armed with

grenade launchers, heavy cannons, and .50 caliber machine guns. How long could we really last?

CHAPTER 39

Jax was losing his patience. Grizzly was gone. Seven of his men who had entered the building were gone. And like cockroaches, the Men in Black refused to go down. Technically, two of them were men in white medical scrubs at the moment. If his losses hadn't been so high, Jax might've laughed at that.

Terminal had filled the building with tear gas, they'd gone floor by floor killing everyone they encountered, shelled the entire side of the building with explosives. Still the black-ops guys walked away. Still, they represented a serious pain in his ass.

Not even when the drone leveled the entire block did any of them die.

"York," Jax said into the open channel. "Put some bodies in the *ground*."

York gave a grunt before the turret atop his vehicle began to fire off rounds at the barrier two of their enemies hid behind. Just as Jax started to feel good about the situation again, his peripheral vision caught an orange object streak across the parking lot towards York's Humvee.

The vehicle exploded, showering sparks and shrapnel in all

directions. Jax followed the trail of smoke from the Humvee to two men who had emerged from the underground garage ramp. One had his arm in a sling, and the other was loading another missile into a rocket launcher.

"God *damnit!*" Jax bellowed and punched his fist into the dash of the Stryker. He turned to the driver and nearly broke his neck turning his head to face him. "Get us the fuck out of here. *Now!*"

The monstrous engine in the Stryker roared to life, the massive wheels starting to pick up speed. Furious, Jax popped the top hatch leading to the .50 cal. As the Stryker pulled away from the burning remnants of the parking lot, Jax hunkered down behind the machine gun, holding the trigger down. The heavy rounds chewed through everything in sight. Concrete parking barriers crumbled, small craters in the ground popped up everywhere as asphalt was drilled out in chunks. Nearby cars in the parking lot were turned to swiss cheese.

The barrel of the .50 cal glowed red hot in the night. Jax hadn't realized he was screaming until his throat was raw. He didn't stop firing until the entire chain of bullets was spent. By that time, his ears were ringing and he was pretty damned sure he'd given himself some permanent hearing damage. It was the least of his concerns.

Satisfied, Jax let go of the heavy weapon and dropped back into the belly of the Stryker. He buried his face in his hands. Two vehicles gone, a dozen men dead. Terminal had taken some losses tonight, but these Men in Black fellas definitely took more. Jax found some solace in knowing that the scales were currently leaning in Terminal's favor.

CHAPTER 40

Cole West. 7:14 p.m.
Angel Site
Los Angeles, California

Surreal. That's the one word I would use to describe the feeling I had. I stayed huddled behind the burning wreck of the first Humvee even after the roar of Terminal's Stryker engine had faded away. For the past two days I'd felt as if somebody else was behind the wheel and I'd just witnessed it all. Like someone else had been in my body, had killed that man on the freeway, and shot all those infected in the warehouse.

And then, like a switch, that autopilot clicked off. All the built-up insanity I'd experienced crashed over me like a wave as I tried to convince myself for the thousandth time that this was real. My heart hammered in my chest, and all the strength in my knees vanished. Despite my best efforts, I lost my lunch right there on the asphalt.

"Hey, come on, get up," a rough voice said next to me. "You've stayed on top of things so far, don't go bitching out on us now." I slowly turned my head and looked up at Hodges, who put a hand on my shoulder and tried to get me back on my feet.

I stood unsteadily, all around me my team just as shocked. Vaun wandered around on his radio, no doubt trying to hail Mr. Rourke. Tag looked to be stuck surveying the area, clearly in disbelief that this attack on home turf had happened; and both Kelly and Billy slowly rejoined our group from the ramp to the underground garage.

"How do you do it . . . ?" I looked to the smoldering ashes that had been a building twenty minutes ago. "This is insane. How do you fight this fight?"

Hodges looked at the fiery remains with me. "Day by day," he said simply and slung his rifle over his shoulder.

"Well, this is a shit show of a day."

"No argument here. Two days ago, you were filling out paperwork. One day ago you fought four top-of-the-line operators hand-to-hand within minutes of joining Black Spear. A few hours later you killed a man on a freeway in broad daylight. Last night you held your own against rabies-infected psychopaths. This morning you went through quarantine for a virus that shouldn't exist. And tonight? Tonight, you survived an assault from the types of vehicles that have never been used on American soil before. If that was just two days, then try and think about what tomorrow could bring." He gave me a sympathetic look. "It's a game of days, West, and the day is just getting started."

Hodges appeared to notice something of interest near the Captain and walked away. I couldn't tell if what he'd just told me was supposed to encourage or demoralize. Maybe there was some fight left in my soul deep down at the bottom, or maybe I was just sick of being hunched over a puddle of my own vomit on the street. Whatever it was, it got my feet moving.

All animosity and bad attitude aside, Hodges had a point. The day was just beginning. I think I could last just one more.

CHAPTER 41

Robert Batson. 7:30 p.m.
Twenty miles outside Angel Site
Los Angeles, California

One of the men had hooked him up with a very nice dose of morphine. Now the wounds crisscrossing his body, which had burned like fire, began to dull into a pleasant warmth. Batson eagerly rode those euphoric waves. In that strange twilight realm, he felt no pain. More importantly, there was no shame.

Batson floated along his high without a care in the world. Retaliation from their new enemies was sure to come, but that was a problem to worry about tomorrow. Maybe there would be a brief calm so that both sides could take the time to lick their wounds and bury their dead. Batson certainly hoped so. Between their disastrous getaway on the freeway and the Moses virus getting loose, they'd lost too many good men. And exactly what the hell was that about, anyway? Jax had always been careful about handling the virus. It didn't make sense how the men could've gotten contaminated.

His thoughts tried to coalesce, but the morphine blew them away just as quickly. Batson let it happen. It had been a long-ass couple of days. Clearly, he wasn't in the best mindset to try and figure anything out.

As the deep narcotic-induced sleep started to pull him under,

Batson managed to cut a glance to Jax with his one good eye. The way his friend was smiling made Batson feel something unfamiliar. Before the morphine finished drawing Batson into the black he was able to put his finger on exactly what it was. Batson was concerned.

CHAPTER 42

Our short helicopter ride back to San Diego had been a quiet one. The squad sat silently without so much as looking at each other. I wasn't sure if it was exhaustion due to the adrenaline wearing off, or if it was because this was unfamiliar territory for all parties involved. Black Spear was made up of ghosts, and ghosts weren't supposed to bleed like we had tonight.

When we landed we hadn't even taken two steps away from the helipad before we were told to meet Mr. Rourke.

The air conditioning did little to stem the tempers in the briefing room. We were all feeling strong emotions about Rourke's play and weren't doing the best job of hiding it.

So far, our debriefing of the attack on Angel Site had gone as splendidly as expected. Rourke gave us a quick rundown of the spin they'd already put on everything they were telling the public. The official story was that an old military armament disposal facility had caught fire. Outdated fire suppression equipment combined with improper ammunition storage had led to several hundred rounds discharging and, ultimately, the building's destruction.

A spokesman for the Department of Defense had issued a statement that they would be doing an internal investigation, and an elderly man named Morris who worked at the disposal facility as a custodian provided an interview. In it Morris spoke of how he'd mopped the hallways for fifteen years and figured the building burning down was just a matter of time. I wondered how many "Morrises" Rourke had up his sleeve for times like this. Judging from the few clips Rourke played on a screen along the far wall, the media had eaten it up. By this time tomorrow, no one would even be thinking of the events as news.

No connections had been drawn as yet that connected last night's events to Terminal's propaganda video. Many news pundits even challenged the validity of Terminal's threats since Mr. Rourke and Mason had done such a good job of erasing Terminal's recent work. I had a feeling in my gut that this would only embolden Terminal to be even louder until they got noticed.

After explaining how last night was being swept under the rug, Rourke admonished us for letting Batson get away while simultaneously justifying his own actions.

"Angel Site was compromised," Rourke said simply. "The facility had access to the entire Black Spear network, the remaining Moses samples we had were being held in the lab, and not to mention the highly-classified material in just about every damned room in the building. I had no communication from my personnel, and I made the only choice on hand. That drone was sent with the belief that you all had already expired."

We all stewed silently.

"The thing about having to eat a shit sandwich is that you don't have to like it," added Mason. "It doesn't go easy, but you swallow it down as quick as you can."

Rourke's eyes narrowed.

I sensed the man's anger at the fact that we expected an explanation from him.

An unblinking Vaun stared at the Director.

Rourke didn't so much as flinch. "Captain, if you want an apology then you're going to be waiting quite a while."

Vaun looked to Rourke and shook his head. "No, sir. I just need to know where this leaves us." He then shot quick looks at each of us.

We instantly knew to lock down our feelings. Shit sandwich swallowed. We still had a job to do, and Rourke was the man currently running the show.

"First order of business, this man here." Rourke rose to his feet, pointing a clicker at the monitor screen. An image from a security feed showed a bearded man with long hair holding a double-barreled shotgun. "This is Abraham Jackson, or 'Jax' as he prefers. We now know that he is the de facto leader of Terminal. According to our intel and what we've gleaned from that hard drive so far, his troops think this guy is their own damn military messiah. He was forced out of the Marine Corps as a Lance Corporal. Back-to-back tours to Iraq and Afghanistan. Records show he was commended for bravery. Take note that I said 'commended', and not 'awarded'. He was denied reenlistment, though, due to an incident involving insubordination and assault on an officer. After a subsequent failure of a psych evaluation, he was shown the door." Rourke looked at the image of Terminal's leader; it was bordered by a copy of his last driver's license photo and an older photo of him in uniform. Then, he tapped a button and the pictures were replaced with new ones.

"Our initial estimates on Terminal's numbers and capabilities were clearly inaccurate. After last night we ran another screening of all bank accounts associated with Robert Batson. They hid most of their major acquisitions through shell companies, but we were able to piece together a rough list of their larger purchases in recent years."

Images started popping up on the screen. Entire fleets of military vehicles with everything from helicopters to tanks, enough weaponry to equip a small nation, and food and water rations sufficient to feed a few cities. A few keystrokes later and a list of names and pictures of all persons currently linked to Terminal began running down the screen. The list was enormous.

"Christ," sputtered Hodges. A tremor ran through his hand, and he almost dropped his dip spit bottle right there on the table. "This isn't some bullshit militia we're dealing with here. They have an actual army. Trained killers. Ex-Special Forces. The real goddamn deal."

"Even if only half of these names are *actually* connected with Terminal, we'd still need more of our shooters. Achilles Squad is wiped out; we need Demon and Hydra Squads at a minimum," said Tag.

"Demon Squad is out on assignment in Mexico. Hydra is overseas. We can't afford to wait for them to get back," replied Vaun.

At that, Rourke tapped his clicker and the images on the monitors changed to the bodies of the carriers from the McAllister Brothers. "Gentlemen, Moses is still loose. This second strain is even more frightening than the first we experienced."

I thought about that. Not that I was an expert in this world of militias and secret organizations, but something about Terminal and its doomsday weapon wasn't sitting well with me. "Doesn't make sense . . ." I muttered quietly.

Vaun caught it. "What do you mean by that?"

I shook my head and started going over the information in my head. "None of it really adds up," I said. "They dosed Matthew Lee-Ray first. Why?"

"The dude was kind of an asshole," answered Billy with a snap of his fingers. "Correction: he was a grade-A asshole. He was a well-known critic of the military, and Terminal is the embodiment of every salty and bitter vet-bro there is. He was the perfect lamb to slaughter to kick this whole thing off."

"The video they released pretty much capped it up, too. Terminal is out to shut up all the voices that have looked down on them or failed to take care of them," added Hodges.

"Sure," I said. "But why did they use the virus on him? They've got plenty of weapons and plenty of guys skilled enough to use them. You're telling me Terminal doesn't have one guy good enough with a sniper rifle to take him out? Simply shooting him on the street or cutting his throat would've been easier. Why use the virus on *him*?"

"Test trials of some sort?" suggested Tag. "Use him as a guinea pig and make sure Moses was working how they wanted?"

"I don't think so." All eyes were on me, and Vaun offered a nod of encouragement. "Something like this—something so powerful and engineered—you don't risk letting loose until you've already tested it and learned its limits. Anything else would be suicide. Think about what Terminal wants us to believe. Everything, from the video released to Lee-Ray, has been to do one thing: scare us."

Tag's eyes narrowed as he picked up what I was getting at. "They want us to think they have the deadliest weapon on earth and killed a celebrity to prove it. They blew up the medical facility and attacked Angel Site just to show us how bold they're willing to be."

"The Moses virus definitely scares the shit out of me. Hell, it frightened all of you enough to make it priority one," I said. "But it doesn't make sense. The lethality of it outweighs its ability to spread fast enough. Beyond a confined space, like the McAllister Building, anyone infected with the second strain will end up dying and liquefying before they can effectively spread it. Carriers are literally beginning to die the second they become infected."

"But it looked like those dudes were also going rabid within moments of infection," added Billy.

Rourke picked it up from there. "Those Bleeders—that's what the gents down in R&D are unofficially calling them for now—carried the second Moses strain. This one is greatly accelerated and, as you all saw, it manifests characteristics of Rabies. It might kill off its carriers quicker, but you put just one Bleeder in the middle of a major city and it will spread it to enough people before it expires that

Moses-2 will still cause mass casualties. We're talking thousands."

"Okay, sure," I said, cutting off Mister Rourke, who scowled at my interruption, "but this isn't the end-all be-all of doomsday weapons. There are too many variables. They're trying to make a statement. There's already other weapons they could've used to prove their point and get us on the ropes, but this virus is new. This virus is unfamiliar. It's all scare tactics directed at the government."

At that, everyone appeared to be looking at their own thoughts from a new perspective.

"They're terrorists, and Moses is just propaganda," Tag said. "There's half a dozen WMDs I can name that could cause more damage without the need for carriers to spread it effectively. Next-generation nerve agents like Sandman, Novichok, or even good old-fashioned VX gas. All of those are just as deadly."

"But no shock factor," countered Vaun. "Nerve gas gets loose, you've got people twitching and dying. Moses gets loose and you've got a front row ticket to 28 Days Later. The general public has become somewhat desensitized against conventional chemical weapons. That's why Terminal used Moses. It fits in with their one goal that they've been trying to shove down our throats this entire time: scaring the public into waking up."

Rourke rubbed his jaw as the puzzle pieces started fitting together. I think he was just now realizing that he'd been playing right into Terminal's hands the entire time. The knee-jerk reaction Rourke had to Lee-Ray's viral assassination, mobilizing Black Spear's teams, and sending constant updates directly to the President. This entire time Terminal was counter-punching us and beating us at their own game.

"If the goal is fear," I asked, now that everyone appeared to be on the same page, "then what's their game-winning play?"

Rourke's shoulders stiffened. His eyes narrowed. He abruptly stood, then turned away from the table. "Before we started this meeting, I was reminded by the President of just how invested we needed to be in this matter." He glanced down at his phone as if remembering a recent call. "Terminal has him rattled. It being an election year, he also needs a big win. He plans on issuing a public statement, but he's also called for an emergency meeting of key personnel to discuss this."

"Who exactly counts as key personnel?" asked Vaun.

"Oh, nobody important . . . just the Secretaries of Defense, Veterans Affairs, and Homeland Security."

CHAPTER 43

Things don't ever go according to plan. This was a fact of life that Jax was very familiar with. All the same, he felt confident that all the contingencies he'd laid out were paying off perfectly.

An Armored Personnel Carrier didn't make a very good getaway car, so they'd ditched it not too long after they'd made their escape. The Stryker had been left behind in the parking lot of a McDonald's. But Jax thought that was good. After all, it left a damn good image for the reporters to snag if they were lucky enough to take one before the Men in Black covered that up, too. At this point it didn't matter anymore if they were able to lift Jax's prints from inside. He was done hiding. He wanted them to know *exactly* who he was. And it wasn't like the APC they discarded was their only one, far from it actually. Terminal's bank accounts were large enough that they still had a motor pool filled with other vehicles.

Terminal wasn't solely funded by Batson's inheritance or the willing donations from its naive sponsors. Jax had taken it upon himself, and a few more social-media-savvy Terminal members, to acquire additional funds in the days of the militia's founding. Under the guise of everything from charities, veteran-based fundraisers, and even a few false non-profits, Jax had managed to rake in hundreds of thousands in donations. There were even a few extremely generous overseas investors whose dislike for the American government were in line with Jax's own. He wasn't about to pass up a free lunch regardless of who it came from.

That constant cash flow was what helped pay for not only more equipment, but also gave them the funding needed to help bribe any people in the Terminal network who weren't full members. It was a bribe like that to some vets in the Los Angeles police force that had aided in their escape. "Bribe" was such an ugly word, but Jax didn't have too much pride to call a spade a spade. As good as Jax's contingencies were, having a little extra green to smooth things over with the boys in blue certainly helped to make things easier. The stashed van they'd switched over to hadn't received so much as a glance from any patrol cars they passed on their way back to the Terminal Grounds.

The men had greeted him like the hero he was. Cheers erupted; a few overly excited even fired a few rounds off into the air. With a snap of his fingers and a stern pointed finger, Jax had secured that trash. Shooting off wildly was something for the Muslims to do in Afghanistan. He expected more discipline from his men.

The initial cheers died down once the crowd realized no one else was returning. It was upsetting to Jax how quickly the mood turned. Disappointing, really. Jax had personally dealt a deciding blow to their enemies yet people wanted to mourn their losses, instead. It was as if they'd never understood the concept of acceptable losses before. By his own tally, Terminal was winning. Jax would continue this fight as long as he drew breath.

He beckoned to one of their doctors, then pointed to where Batson was being pulled out of their vehicle. "Get that man to the medical wing. Patch him up, dope him, give him whatever he needs."

Once Batson was gone, Jax snapped his fingers at two others

loitering around. "Grab that crate," he instructed, pointing at a nearby equipment box. "Now come with me."

Jax scanned himself and his two-man entourage through the security gates and descended into the laboratory bunker. He needed to see Dr. Chan.

The men accompanying him grew skittish the deeper into the lab they traveled. Twice Jax caught one of them almost dropping the crate, because he was too busy looking around at their surroundings. "The contents of that box are pretty goddamn volatile," Jax said. "If either of you enjoy having a pulse, I'd recommend you don't drop it."

Their backs straightened with renewed energy and both of their eyes snapped to in front of them. Good soldiers.

The doctor was in the deepest part of the lab. It was here that the supply of Moses-1, and now Moses-2, was contained behind triple safeties. Dr. Chan looked like he was just getting ready to don his protective suit when they entered.

"Oh, you're back," Dr. Chan said, sounding disappointed.

Jax didn't have any illusions over whether this scientist liked him or not. He was paying the man for his brain, not to be his friend.

"I learned something while there," Jax said. He nodded towards the men, and they set the crate on the ground.

"Oh?" Chan's feigned interest was barely masked as he shifted his suit up his waist.

"You see, we bombarded the hell out of their building with conventional arms and explosives. Real shock and awe to let them know who they were fucking with," Jax said. "But all the same, that opening salvo hadn't really taken the fight out of them. A handful managed to pull themselves together and bring the fight back to us."

"From what I've heard these mystery men are very capable," Chan said. Jax shot a hard look at the doctor, who quickly corrected himself. "But your men are, of course, just as capable."

"Yeah. Of course. But it got me to thinking: why build up with the jab when we've got the knockout haymaker in our pocket?" The look on the doctor's face told him that the boxing term had gone completely over his head. God, it amused Jax just how little fight this weasel had in his body. "Let me put it another way: I want you to put that," Jax said, pointing past the protective glass to the Moses-2 vials, "into these." He signaled the men behind him to open the crate.

Chan's eyes went wide when he saw the box's contents. "Oh . . ." he breathed, "that will be quite . . . volatile."

"My words exactly," laughed Jax.

He then walked towards the door that led to the virus. He went without a suit, ignoring every safety protocol both he and Chan had agreed upon. Upon entering he was pleasantly surprised to find two small gel capsules next to the larger vials. Apparently, his mad scientist had been successful in creating a more controlled time-release for Moses-2. Reaching out with one gloved hand, Jax carefully plucked up one of the pills and closely inspected it.

"The virus itself isn't normally airborne communicable. However, dispersing the vapors like this with a cloud burst may guarantee infection to anyone in the blast area." explained Chan as he touched the box's contents. "But a delivery system like this is risky. Harder to control."

Jax knew that the scientist might say something like that. His hesitancy—after everything Jax had given him—was like a slap in the face. "Doctor, in case you mistake my order or mistake your position here, let me be clear," Jax said. He grabbed Chan's neck then held the Moses-2 pill close for Dr. Chan to see. "Either you put the virus in that box, or I put this pill in you."

The doctor gulped nervously. Blinking several times, he nodded and finished putting on his protective suit.

Satisfied, Jax placed the viral pill back where it belonged and stormed off. He was done playing it lightly with everyone. His enemies, and now his own men, had seen the end of his patience. This was war. War was no place for restraint.

Fucking right.

Shock and awe, baby. Shock. And. Awe.

CHAPTER 44

Terminal's game of fear was already scoring points with me, and they hadn't even made a move. Christ. We all sat there for a second, as if waiting for Rourke to just say "Go!" and we'd be let off the chain to hunt down Jackson and Terminal. But we still didn't have a lead on where they were holed up, and the whole shit-storm had just hit the proverbial fan.

"Sir, what's the call?" asked Vaun.

Rourke rubbed his jaw while looking at his cell phone once more. "I meet with the President tonight."

"We need to be there," Hodges said. "And somehow we need to get Demon and Hydra Squads back here to back us up."

"Presidential protocols won't allow for three squads of black-ops soldiers to just sit in on an emergency cabinet meeting," Vaun said dryly.

"Indeed," Rourke said. "Gentlemen, this completely changes the situation. The President is already displeased with our progress in combating Terminal. Now, this situation has become entirely too *visible* for us." The Brooklyn giant settled his tremendous weight back into his seat. One palm went to his face. "We have to pull back."

Vaun's fists clenched tightly beneath the conference table. Despite his anger, the Captain managed to keep his voice level. "Sir . . . are you benching us?"

Rourke took a long while before answering, for a time just looking at the images of Terminal on his computer. Abraham Jackson was smiling back at Rourke from the screen, mocking them all. Then Rourke waved a hand as if he could shake the anger from the room like a mist. "The President would certainly like me to," he said. "Gentlemen, I need a minute alone with your captain."

As if on cue, everyone bolted to their feet except Vaun. And myself. I was too caught off guard. I pulled myself out of the chair once I realized I was the only one on the squad still seated and followed the others to the door. Billy stood by the door just to lightly kick me in the ass before walking out behind me.

"You know that's some bullshit," Hodges said once the door was closed.

Tag grunted in agreement.

I was having a rough time with everything. From the very start I'd known how far off the reservation this outfit was, but the attack on Angel Site added some new dynamics to the mix. Knowing from the beginning that Rourke didn't have any qualms about killing me was one thing, but staring at a missile he'd willingly sent was another. Add to that the whole torture room thing—which I still had trouble digesting—and you've got one very morally confused Cole West.

On the other hand, there were bad guys in the world willing to do bad things, and I was in a unique position to do something about it. When I'd first interviewed with him, Vaun had promised to show me how bad things really were in the world. I suppose I couldn't fault Vaun on delivering, though all of this thinking would be for naught if this mission was pulled from us.

Black Spear wasn't supposed to exist at all. If our "plausible deniability" was compromised, then nearly every advantage Black

Spear had in its anonymity would be negated. Just because I could see Rourke's point in pulling this mission away from us didn't mean I had to enjoy it. In the words of Kara Mason: shit sandwich.

Vaun strode out of the conference room alone. As usual the man's face betrayed nothing. Was it good or bad news?

"So we've got good news and bad news," he said.

Damn. Well, at least there *was* good news.

"Give us the bad news first, Captain," Kelly said.

"The bad news is we're officially off the case. If we're right, Terminal is going to hit the cabinet meeting. If anyone even near the President gets infected with Moses-2, then there will be no stopping the widespread panic it'll cause. Terminal will get all the attention they've wanted this entire time. They will win. But if they're going after the cabinet, then they're going to have their hands full with the regular players."

Most of the squad gave a resounding groan at that.

"What's the good news?" asked Billy. "Did you find the receipt that came with the new guy so we can finally return him?"

Despite my best efforts, I smirked.

"The good news is that while there is no clearance for a Black Spear squad to support, Mister Rourke is allowed a two-man security escort."

Everyone exchanged glances as if to see who would draw the long straw to go. I felt like I was back in elementary school, and they were picking teams for dodgeball. I didn't want to be the loser to not get picked, but at the same time if I did get picked then that meant things were expected of me that I might not be prepared for. Facing more of the Bleeders wasn't high on my To Do List.

Then again, maybe I was ready. Vaun had chosen me to fill the gapped ranks in his squad. My background in bio and chem weapons would be an asset to have onboard should Terminal attack the meeting. And now not only did I want to be Vaun's pick, but I actually *hoped* I would be.

Rourke had told me there were literally hundreds of potential candidates for the program, yet I was the one who got picked. I could do it. It had nothing to do with the prospect of potentially being the one to save the President and everything to do with knowing I could handle it. I knew I could.

"Kelly, it's you and me," said Vaun.

My heart sank a little. I was ten years old again and the odd man out of the dodgeball game.

Thankfully, the rest of the squad occupied the same boat. Hodges made a big show of packing a wad of dip into his mouth. Tag scowled even harder than usual. The only one who didn't look that disappointed was Billy; he shrugged and gave a "whatever" look.

"The rest of you stay alert, but I want you on R&R," Vaun said. "That's an order."

Rest and relaxation. Yeah. Those two things had never been further from my thoughts.

CHAPTER 45

We were ready for the fight and I was in it to the end, but Mr. Rourke didn't want us involved at this point. Now that Terminal had gone public with their propaganda video, the President didn't want secret government agents taking them out. Something this public would need a public victory.

Homeland was involved now, and apparently half a dozen three-letter organizations were all sticking their fingers in the pie. Everyone was eager to get a bit of the credit for when the big break came in taking down Terminal. Jax's army was poised to unleash a modernized version of the biblical plagues of Egypt—blood, boils, darkness, and death—and we were being told to sit on our asses. Needless to say, we weren't handling our rest period very well.

For the past two days I'd been going full commando, and not in the fun underwear kind of way. I wasn't sure how to move from that life or death at every moment mindset back to playing old video games or watching Netflix. Even hitting the gym wasn't going to help destress. My body was beaten and exhausted. Breaking it down even further sounded like suicide. Just the idea of exercising during my mandated rest and relaxation seemed like an oxymoron.

Restless and exhausted. Ready and yet not needed. I was going crazy in my room just staring at the ceiling above my bed. Right around the time I was wondering how in the hell I was going to get over this feeling, someone kicked open my door. After the surprise attack on Angel Site, I expected Terminal goons. I scrambled to my feet, but it was only Billy and Hodges.

"Grab your shit, nerd. We're getting chicken wings," Billy said and pointed a thumb out to the hallway.

Chicken wings. Hmm. Come to think of it, I was hungry.

Ten minutes later Hodges was driving Tag, Billy, and myself to a local spot called Dirty Birds. It had over a dozen different wing flavors and today just happened to be all-you-can-eat night. Vaun and Kelly had already left with Mr. Rourke for the cabinet meeting, which meant it would just be the four of us. I wondered if the Captain or his acting Lieutenant were at all worried about what sort of trouble their troops would get into without them. I tried to take comfort in knowing that, if anything exciting happened, it would most likely be on their end. Plenty of Secret Service would be involved before either of them would even get a chance to get their triggers off.

"You're looking slicker than Mister Clean," Billy joked and slapped the back of my shaved head a few times.

I made a face and pushed away his hands.

He looked at me in mock surprise. "I hear it's good luck to rub bald people's heads. Ancient Chinese secret."

"Billy, you're Japanese," Hodges reminded him before spitting into the empty soda bottle he gripped in his right hand.

I caught Hodges glancing back at me through the rear-view mirror. He shook his head disapprovingly. "What is it with you Jarheads and your ridiculous haircuts . . ."

I shrugged. "Helps save money on shampoo. Even the Captain sports a fade."

That actually made the rest of the guys in the car laugh. "The

Captain always gets his hair cut like that before he goes on a base," explained Hodges. "It's like the bit of Marine left in him still wants to look the part whenever he's around them."

Our waitress got us a row of seats at the bar. We hadn't been seated thirty seconds before Hodges was ordering a drink and Tag was picking his first order of wings. I decided on their "Dirty Bleu"; basically a mix of buffalo sauce and bleu cheese dressing. Before I could get a good look at the tequila they had on hand, Hodges abruptly knocked the cocktail menu out of my hands.

"You're designated driver," he said, sliding the car keys to me.

I guess I shouldn't have been surprised that, after everything, I wouldn't even be allowed to have a drink to relax my nerves. I decided against reminding Hodges that, if it hadn't been for me, he would've been blown to little red chunks back at Angel Site's parking lot.

I was distracted from my dinner by the sight of Tag devouring his plate; he was less man at meal and more chicken-wing-eating-robot designed in a government lab. He cleaned his entire plate in the time it took me to eat two wings. Billy apparently expected this because he had his phone out and had recorded the whole thing.

"At least you know that if you're no longer useful to the government you could get a job at *Man vs. Food* or compete in eating competitions."

Tag grunted and then waved the waitress over to order his second plate of wings.

"You do look like you could be the next Kobayashi," I agreed.

Billy pointed a finger at me and feigned outrage. "That man's a goddamn national hero." That somehow got a chuckle out of Tag, who nearly coughed up the last half dozen chicken wings.

I went back to my Dirty Bleu while simultaneously using my peripherals to check the rest of the restaurant. Despite the relaxed evening, I was still very much on edge. Terminal's ranks were vast. Its reach was considerable. Hodges's earlier statement of them being an actual army wasn't an understatement. Worse still, they were an army without a uniform.

All around me were everyday civilians, but any one of them could have an SMG tucked into their jacket just for us. Or they could be wearing a suicide vest. Even a small pipe bomb just sitting in their pocket. Christ, paranoia was exhausting.

I guess it didn't help put me at ease that, despite being among trained killers, I was the only one staying sober. It's not like my companions were drinking themselves into a stupor or anything, but even one drink might slow them down. Hodges nursed a beer, Tag sipped from a vodka sprite, and Billy had already downed two shots. Okay, maybe Billy was trying to drink himself into a stupor.

It would've been a comfort if he didn't, though. Billy had what Liam Neeson would refer to as "a very particular set of skills" and that skillset would definitely come in handy if Terminal sent some brawlers to start a good old-fashioned bar fight. A scuffle like that would be far more manageable than if a strike team of shooters ambushed us.

Hodges noticed me squirming out of my skin. "Rest and *relaxation*," he said and nudged me with his elbow. "Try and chill out. If Terminal makes a play at the cabinet meeting, they'd have to claw through a few dozen Secret Service agents before even getting to Vaun and Kelly. This is the President we're talking about. It's not like he's a sitting duck. We've got our orders, and right now I'm telling you those orders are to eat wings."

I nodded and tried to shake it off. Hodges was right. This whole trip was for everyone to decompress. Goddamn, did we all need it.

I couldn't help but laugh to myself about my suspicion. Hell, it looked like I was the only one here tonight who wasn't drinking. If Terminal had sent some people to make our night more violent, then they'd be just as sauced as the rest of Cerberus.

The waitress came down to top off my soda. Seeing my long face, she said, "You know, if that isn't cutting it, a splash of Jack might make it more exciting."

I shook my head. "No thanks. After the week I've had, I could use less exciting and more boring."

"Suit yourself," she said.

She had a good smile. Disarming even. I found myself looking at her longer than a normal patron should. Right around the time I thought I was coming off as creepy, she looked back at me. Our eyes met. Only for a moment. And then her smile again. It happened right then. Right as I was leaning forward. I was going to ask her for her name.

That's when I heard the gunfire behind me. And that's when her smile disappeared along with the rest of her face.

CHAPTER 46

I didn't freeze. Apparently, I was getting used to being shot at. Reflex and the shooter's poor marksmanship were the only reason I still had a pulse.

More semi-automatic gunfire sounded behind me, but I was already hurling my body over the bar top to the cover on the other side. My teammates did the same. Billy had even grabbed his drink before rolling over. He caught me looking at him with surprise, and he just gave me the Shaka sign before downing it in two gulps.

"Never a dull moment," Billy said before tossing the empty glass against the floor.

It being pseudo "off-hours" the only weapon I had on me was Vaun's Pro-Tech Don. Too much distance and too many bullets to get through before a knife would be useful. Still, better than nothing. I thumbed the button and the blade leapt open in my hand.

Sparing a glance in Hodges's direction and expecting orders, I instead saw my teammates with side arms drawn. No one told me I was supposed to bring my gun. The Californian in me still wasn't used to carrying concealed, black-ops exception to state law be damned.

"Seriously, rookie?" Hodges groaned when he saw the knife.

"I missed the fucking memo, all right?"

"Now hold on," Billy cut in and held his hands up. "Let's not get on his case for forgetting his weapon. It was an honest mistake. Could happen to any of us."

I noticed his hands were empty, too.

Hodges rolled his eyes as more bullets flew overhead to shatter the bottles of liquor above us.

Hodges popped up from the cover and squeezed off two shots before ducking back down. "Six shooters at our ten and two o'clock. Semi-autos, looked like one pump-action."

Tag grunted and crab walked farther down the bar. His snub-nosed .44 was gripped in his right hand. With his left he grabbed a loose bottle of booze that had fallen down then slid it over to Billy. He held up three fingers and counted down. Billy tossed the bottle over the counter, gunshots rang out from the enemy shooters, and then both Hodges and Tag popped up to fire off two rounds each.

I still couldn't believe how unbelievably loud his .44 magnum was. It completely drowned out the sound of Hodges's weapon discharging. Both men ducked back down.

"Three left," Hodges said.

I just sat there with my knife in hand feeling even more useless than usual. Which was saying something.

There was a break in the gunfire. In a perfect world that would mean everyone was out of bullets and we'd have to sort things out like civilized gentlemen. Unfortunately, I'm a realist first and an idealist second.

As if on cue, one of the shooters shouted at us from the other side, "You might be nice and cozy back there, but we've got plenty more civilians out here that aren't. Now toss your weapons over!"

I shot a look over to Hodges. He beat his forehead with the slide of his gun a few times while muttering some expletives. Meanwhile, Tag was still clutching his revolver tight. "Nobody touches this but me."

"Tell him your name, sweetheart," I heard the shooter yell to what I assumed had to be a hostage he grabbed.

I heard the soft whimpering of a female voice, "D-Dana . . . Dana Davidson."

"Dana Davidson . . . how cute. I'm going to call you Deedee," the shooter said, "Now just between us guys I gotta tell ya: Deedee is pretty fine."

Add "hostage negotiations" right alongside "clandestine military operations" on the list of things I was grossly inexperienced in. My only knowledge in that department came from a Samuel L. Jackson movie. Last I checked, by the end of that flick it didn't exactly work out for all parties involved.

The sound of someone pumping a fresh shell into a shotgun jarred me out of my thoughts. "You hear that? I've got a twelve-gauge pressed up to Deedee's pretty cheekbone."

"Please . . ." Dana pleaded.

"You know what that fucking means?" The shooter screamed, "Closed-casket funeral, assholes!"

I looked to Hodges, hoping that he was going to call a play that would save the day. But the senior man on the squad was only staring at the handgun he held as if it somehow held the solution. "What the fuck?" he muttered hopelessly to no one in particular.

I felt just as lost. The only thing that kept me feeling the least useful was the fact that I still had a knife while Billy was rummaging through the shards of glass from his shattered cup for one that looked promising.

"You've got three seconds," the shooter promised. "Three!"

When I turned to Tag, he shook his head then held out four fingers. Four shots left, and with the kick the magnum packed it wasn't exactly the go-to for an accurate quickdraw against three hostiles.

"Two!"

Even though there had to be police en route, I knew they weren't close enough. They couldn't get here in time to save Dana's pretty cheekbones from a point blank load of buckshot. For what felt like an eternity I sat on that bar floor, wondering if we would really just wait for them to execute their hostages. In truth it had been exactly one second. The other truth was there weren't any other options on the table.

"ONE!"

"Wait!" I yelled and snatched the handgun from Hodges's hand, "We're coming out!" I dangled Hodges's handgun harmlessly between my thumb and forefinger. My heart was beating so damn fast. I could feel my pulse in my face. I expected to get shot before I'd finished standing.

But the Terminal shooters held their fire. I saw the one who'd been speaking, the one with the shotgun, directly in front of me. Just as he'd promised, the barrel of his twelve-gauge Mossberg was jammed firmly against Deedee's face. Instead of blowing her head off or pointing the weapon in my direction, he glanced at the shooter to his left.

"That him?"

Though the second shooter held a 9mm in his right hand, he awkwardly held a piece of paper in the other that his eyes were focused on. "Uh . . . think so. Looks like one of 'em."

"Okay, now your friends can come out too," the ringleader instructed.

I glanced down to Hodges and Tag, knowing that if they didn't stand up that I'd be shot dead. God, please just stand the fuck up.

Slowly, they both rose to their feet.

"That's them," the shooter with the paper confirmed.

The shotgun boss tightened his grip on his hostage. "I didn't forget about that hand cannon you're packing. Drop it."

Tag's face tightened into a scowl. Instead of tossing the revolver aside, he decided to open the chamber and spill the four remaining rounds onto the bar counter.

"No one touches this but me." He tucked it back into the holster in the small of his back.

The one with the shotgun shrugged and loosened his grip on the woman he held. "Here's what happens next," he said and lowered the shotgun away from the hostage. "You're all coming with us and— AAAHHH!" The man let out a startled scream as a long shard of glass sank into his eye. Billy stood next to me, a triumphant look on his face. "Booyah."

While one of the man's hands went to his face, the other reflexively squeezed the shotgun and accidentally pulled the trigger. The second shooter with the sheet of paper took the blast to his gut. Chunks of his stomach were blown out the other side and he fell to his knees. In the split-second it took the third shooter to glance over at his friend's grisly wounds, Tag had loaded a single round back into his revolver. That last shooter never got a chance to fix his eyes back in our direction, because his head was already blown to chunks.

I hadn't realized I was holding my breath until Hodges patted me on the back and eased his weapon from my hand. "Good call, rookie. Good call."

And here I thought I was going to get my ass kicked for making a play without his say so.

In the end only two of the restaurant's patrons had been killed in the brief crossfire, though four more were on the floor injured. Tag was already calling it in to Mr. Rourke and triaging what he could, Billy was offering calming words to those that were panicking, but Hodges clearly had something else on his priority list. He and I had that in common.

The one who'd taken the shotgun to the gut had already bled out. He sat doubled over on his knees with his face on the tile, eyes lifelessly staring to the side. I feel like it's unnecessary to comment on the third shooter, who'd been effectively decapitated. But the first one, Mister Shotgun Ringleader, remained alive.

Moaning in pain, pawing at the glass still in his eye, and rolling on the floor. But still alive.

Something very dark inside me was waking up. All the people we'd lost so far—though it hurt like hell—were casualties of war. But these had been civilians. Like the people on the highway on day one, they'd been gunned down for no reason at all. They were innocent, unaware, and it pissed me off that they'd died like this. This was San Diego, one of the busiest vacation spots in the country, not some war-torn village in the Middle East. My hands clenched into fists as wicked thoughts brewed in my mind.

Somewhere in the back of my head the ghost of John urged self-restraint, reminding me of *Rei*. *Rei* is a tenet of Bushido; it refers to always giving respect to your opponent. According to this virtue, true warriors have no reason to be cruel and are expected to be courteous even to their enemies. In this particular moment, I didn't feel like listening to John. I didn't feel like being a "true and noble warrior". I felt like hurting this man and getting answers. *Rei* might've worked well in older times when a samurai would bow to another after a duel, but the current stakes were a little higher. Little by little John's voice faded away into nothing.

"Don't go into shock just yet. You and I need to have a quick chat first," I said. I sounded like this was something I'd done a thousand times before. I made my best effort to replicate that stony emotionless stare Captain Vaun seemed to do so well. "I need you to know that I'm not fucking around." With that, I wrenched the shard from his eye. He howled and tried to throw a punch, but Hodges was there and stamped it down with his boot. He nodded at me to continue.

Outside police sirens approached, undoubtedly creating a perimeter that Black Spear would have authority over. I'm sure Tag's phone call to Rourke had already seen to that. Given that our assigned R&R was equally to give Rourke a rest from the headaches our public antics created, I'm willing to bet he was less than pleased to take the call. Sorry to disappoint, boss, but this fight found us this time.

My hand had readied the Pro-Tech knife before I'd even realized it. I looked down at it, then to the shooter, and forced myself to smile. It felt wrong. It felt like a mask. The whole time my heart was pounding at the thought that this man would see through the act. Somehow he might realize how new I was to this.

To convince us both, I stuck the tip of my knife into his remaining eye.

I didn't thrust too deep, just the point of it near his tear duct. Just enough to hurt and bleed. One red droplet started to form and his eye squeezed shut.

"How far in the knife goes is up to you." I put the lightest amount of pressure behind the knife's handle. "Who sent you?"

The man struggled for a moment, but only a moment.

"Jax . . . Jax sent us!"

That wasn't too surprising. Terminal's leader had an ax to grind, but that was far from new information.

"How did you know who we are?" I gave the blade a little twist. We were supposed to be ghosts, getting hit in public like this was all kinds of wrong. He tried to thrash and squirm underneath me, but Hodges kept him good and pinned.

"Don't know who you are," he groaned. "Don't care. Jax sent your pictures to everyone. Said to take you out however we could. Everyone's looking for you." Despite the knife pressed against his eye, he actually smiled. "Everyone we have in SoCal is looking for you fuckers. We're just the ones that got lucky and found you first."

He laughed. Maybe it was because he knew that somebody else from Terminal's ranks would be able to try again where he and his friends had failed. Maybe it was a bluff, and he just wanted me to see how tough he was. I saw his ante and raised him an inch of steel through the eye socket.

Before he could scream I clamped my hand over his mouth. "You only get to speak when I say so." Fuck. It was like I was on autopilot and someone else was saying this hardcore Gitmo shit. I pulled the knife out and wiped the blood on his shoulder. The damaged eye darted left and right, while I kept the blade still in sight.

"Where is Terminal holed up? Where's the goddamn Moses?" I demanded. His lips mumbled against my hand, but I didn't move it yet. "I swear to God if I move my hand and you don't tell me *exactly* what I want to hear then I'm going to get creative here. You know what that means? Closed-casket funeral, *asshole*."

He pissed himself. I felt the warmth against my knee and when I smiled that time it was genuine.

"He's in the desert. Jesus, that's all I know!" he sputtered as soon as I moved my hand. "I've never even been there! I just heard it's near Twentynine Palms! That's all I know, you've gotta believe me! Ross was the only one who's been there!" He looked to his right where his headless comrade's body was twitching. I glanced to Tag, who just kind of shrugged in an "oops" kind of way. Not sure what else to ask, I looked to Hodges. He frowned, then drew a line across his own neck with his finger.

Clamping my hand over his mouth once more, I leaned in close enough to whisper in his ear. "You see all these innocent people in here you hurt? You got off lucky." I jammed the blade between his ribs and into his heart, then ripped the knife out. I felt the warm arterial spurt against my chest and waited for his eyes to go dead before I stood up.

My hand started shaking when I looked at the brutal scene beneath me. Hodges stood there, examining me, a strange look on his face. "I thought you said you didn't have the stomach for this 'torture type of bullshit'?"

I wiped the bloody knife off on my pants, retracted the blade, and slipped it into my pocket. "Time and a place for everything."

CHAPTER 47

Everywhere

There was a firebombing at a VA clinic outside Junction City, Kansas. When the local fire department finally quelled the flames, they found a single doctor deceased inside. A later autopsy would show that he hadn't died from the fire or smoke inhalation, but from acute toxicity brought on by forcibly ingesting lethal amounts of antidepressants. Evidently someone had wanted to quite literally give him a taste of his own medicine.

In Spokane, Washington, a truck had driven head-on into an Army Recruiting Office. All of the motivating posters on the walls had been marked with red spray paint that said "LIES" and "BULLSHIT". The one Staff Sergeant working inside at the time was beaten to death for whatever perceived part the assailants felt he had played in the Army's deception. According to the spokesman for the United States Army, the Staff Sergeant had just started working there three weeks prior.

Two-thousand miles from there in Grand Rapids, Michigan— coincidentally where Matthew Lee-Ray had originally been infected—a disgruntled, out-of-work vet had taken a shotgun to an employment agency. Police on scene had been forced to shoot him, but only after he'd already taken the life of three employees at the agency. A woman later identified as the man's sister said in an interview that his actions came as a complete shock and that she had no idea he was so angry.

The worst incident occurred in the morning's early hours outside Phoenix. A gentleman described as having a "friendly face" made four separate trips to large home improvement stores like Home Depot and Lowe's. Each time, he picked up a few migrant day laborers under the pretense that he needed a semi-trailer cleaned out. Once they were in the semi, he promptly chained it shut and lit it aflame. The police found him sitting calmly in front of the burning wreckage where he made no attempt to escape. In the interrogation room he proudly boasted that the nation stood by and watched as twenty-two veterans committed suicide a day, so he'd decided to kill twenty-two immigrants to see if anyone noticed.

The chaos Terminal inspired was spreading like a disease. Not even Black Spear could apply enough media smokescreens to cover everything up. The late evening news had already bought into Terminal's presence, and families everywhere in their homes tucked their children in just a little tighter for fear of what madness tomorrow would bring.

CHAPTER 48

Cole West. 10:58 p.m.
Dirty Birds Bar and Grill
Pacific Beach, California

I sat on the back bumper of Hodges's car, drenched in another man's blood. The police perimeter was being maintained and so far the news vans hadn't shown up. For that I was grateful. The last thing I wanted was my face plastered all over the evening news. Something told me that Mr. Rourke had a way of ensuring that would never happen.

Times like this, I wished I smoked cigarettes. I've always thought it was a truly vile habit, but this seemed like the perfect occasion for taking long drags of nicotine and staring dramatically off into the middle distance. But since I was far too health conscious to ever take up cigarettes, I just looked at the blood soaked into my shirt while I rubbed the sore spot on the back of my neck.

Whomever Tag had rogered up to apparently worked faster than I expected. A cleanup crew was already on scene. Another team made up of our own doctors and trauma counselors checked the injured, while a couple other figures resembling very important authority-types talked to the rest of the witnesses. No doubt explaining the gravity of the situation. Using terms like "national security" and "non-disclosure agreement". In this day and age of social media, those men must be very convincing to get these people not to tell the entire world their side of the story.

"You okay?" someone asked.

I'd been so deep in my own thoughts, I hadn't noticed anyone walk up. I expected to see Hodges or maybe Tag when I raised my head. Instead, I saw Captain Vaun, his eyes filled with concern. He did a double-take on my bloodstained clothes before refocusing on my face.

"Yeah. I'm good," I lied.

I let out a long sigh then rested my head against the back windshield. Red and blue flashes from the police lights ruined what could have been a calming view of the stars.

"You weren't the only ones hit," Vaun said. "We're getting word of as many as six different Terminal-related attacks. Intel is sketchy whether it's actually Terminal militia or just lone wolf sympathizers, but whatever spark Abraham Jackson was looking to light has already caught flame."

I was feeling rather numb so I just nodded.

"Hodges told me what happened. You did good in there," he said, trying his best to reassure me.

He sat next to me on the bumper. I felt like I was five years old again. It reminded me of when my dad would sit down next to me after losing a Little League game and try to convince me that the world hadn't ended.

"Word of advice. Next time you have to do something like this, I wouldn't recommend starting with the eye. It's good to leave them with at least one so they can still see what you're doing to them."

I scoffed, "That's an interesting choice of words. 'Good'. I just tortured and killed an American on home soil."

Vaun nodded. "You're right. It wasn't a good thing, but it was the right thing. Necessary."

Good and evil. Right and wrong. A man could go crazy

discerning the minute differences in morality in things such as this. I buried my face in my hands. For all my moral posturing back at Angel Site, I was willing to get my hands just as dirty.

"Any of that intel even pan out?" I asked.

Vaun took a moment before answering. "You remember that hard drive Tag mirrored at McAllister Brothers?" When I nodded, he continued. "Rourke's diggers finished decrypting it. We've got hits for everything from their bank accounts to the number of size ten boots they've purchased. It also gave us five potential sites for where their Terminal Grounds might be."

"All right, did any of that match up with what he said? Twentynine Palms and the desert?"

"Yes. One of the locations leads to Colorado; a second to Arizona. The other three are all in the vicinity of the Twentynine Palms and the Mojave Desert."

"Great. All that dirty work and we learned next to nothing."

Vaun frowned. "Not necessarily. I've been doing this long enough to tell you with all honesty that any bit of intel you can get is useful. Process of elimination. We had a list of five sites, now there's only three. One is near Needles and the other on the northern edge of the desert by Barstow. Homeland is hitting those two first thing in the morning. Everyone wants a piece of this action, and word from the very top is they want a sample of the virus. Defensive research, if you believe it."

"Homeland, guess that means we're still off the case. Wait a second, I thought you said there were three locations?" I asked.

Vaun did that little half smile thing like he already knew the punchline to a joke you hadn't picked up on yet. "Well . . . *our* satellite scans of some heat blooms and that hard drive confirm that this third site is Terminal's home base. Everyone else thinks that the third site didn't look that promising. Homeland's people and Rourke agreed that it looks to be a storage facility but little more. Funny how a few misplaced files will alter opinions." He paused. "Although, that location *is* the closest to Twentynine Palms. I'm sure it's nothing, though." He gave me a look to make sure I was still following. "Rourke and I will be boarding our flight for the Presidential cabinet meeting in an hour. A single squad might be able to go and check out that third site while we're gone. Just to make sure it's nothing."

I nodded. Unofficially back in the fight after all. Then again, when Terminal takes the fight to you in a very public way, that decision tends to get taken out of your hands. Vaun again glanced at my bloodstained clothing. "Maybe get yourself cleaned up first."

When I looked down at myself, I was hit with a fresh wave of unease. Here I was getting the go-ahead from the captain to go splash a fresh layer of red paint on me. To go pull some more triggers and cut more throats. The man I'd tortured wasn't even cold yet.

I'd been lucky so far. Thinking of leaping back into the fray made my mouth dry. I'd done better than anyone could've expected or hoped for, so just what in the hell was I still trying to prove? How far were Vaun and Black Spear willing to let me go?

"Is this all just some fucking test?" I muttered, as much to Vaun as to myself. "You trying to prove that even somebody as wet behind the ears as I am can do this shit? Last night I faced off with a goddamn tank in Los Angeles, and tonight I got to pop my torture cherry. Whoopee. What in the fuck are you trying to prove here with me? I mean, Jesus . . . Sir, why the hell did you choose me?"

It had been a question on my mind since day one. The question without an answer that made sense. Several times now I'd been offered the opportunity to walk out the door and leave this whole sordid business behind. That sounded good to me now, but before I walked I needed to know why my name was the one Vaun drew out of the hat.

"Why do *you* think I recruited you?"

"My chemical and biological weapons specialty means next to nothing to you, and everyone I've met so far finds me grossly unqualified.

Billy and Tag let slip about the selection algorithm Black Spear uses. My money is on random chance and you just wanting to piss off Rourke."

Vaun smirked. "Your chemical/biological specialty is useful but certainly not the biggest factor. Odds are you haven't even heard of half the things we've run into so far. And I'll admit that I do enjoy upsetting the boss and that Black Spear does use those algorithms to aid in the selection pool, but I've never relied heavily on them for my own team. I definitely didn't rely on them to find you."

He didn't say anything for a moment. Maybe he considered telling a lie, or maybe he was mulling over whether I deserved a straight answer. Then, he simply said, "You came highly recommended, West."

I laughed joylessly at that. "Bullshit. There's no way any of my commanding officers would've ever come close to recommending me for this outfit."

"I didn't say the recommendation came from any of your superiors. The recommendation came from someone else, someone I trusted more than you can imagine." Then he said a name . . .

"John. John Crow."

I felt like I'd just been hooked through the gut. Captain Vaun had known John. But he'd committed suicide three years ago. I *knew* that. I'd known that and hated it for years. I'd hated myself for not being there to save him from himself. I'd been to his damn funeral, I'd cried for him. But now the pieces were coming back together in new ways.

"Is he dead?" I asked.

"He is. Yes."

"When did he die?"

"Four weeks ago," answered Vaun. "It's not uncommon to 'suicide' those we recruit. It saves anyone asking questions. We are ghosts, after all. For what it's worth, I'm sorry you had to find out like this."

I'd lost one of my best friends three years ago. Now, I'd just lost him all over again. Feelings of betrayal and outrage battled sorrow and remorse. In a way, I was glad that he hadn't killed himself; it meant he hadn't given up on himself like so many others. At the same time, he'd kept the truth from me. As had Vaun.

"Crow was my lieutenant for the past three years. He was a good Marine, a great operator. And . . . and he was my friend. If you stick around long enough, you're going to lose friends. Brothers. It's a fact of life in work this dangerous. Each time you do, you carry on as best you can with what you have left. But losing Crow? The whole squad's been missing a piece ever since."

More pieces of the puzzle began to come together. "Talon . . ." I muttered, shaking my head. "The past few days the other guys kept mentioning how having Talon would improve our odds. I thought it was just a piece of gear or some advanced weapon, but it was John's call sign, wasn't it?"

Vaun gave a firm nod. "Crow was one of the best operators I've had the pleasure of running with. You could drop him in any situation and the man would adapt instantly—no matter what fight we were in—and somehow he'd still end up on top. Just cold to the core. It didn't matter if we were facing an ambush from an enemy platoon or attacking a convoy of tanks, Crow would just react how you'd want him to. That lack of hesitation was the difference between success and failure. More often it meant whether or not we came back at all. The squad called him our lucky charm." A smile rose as he recalled Crow, not his usual half-smile but a full ear-to-ear grin. "He evened the odds and saved my life more times than I could count. I'd never seen anyone that fluid. You actually remind me a lot of him in that way."

My shoulders fell.

"You asked me why I picked you," Vaun continued. "Truth is, I didn't. Crow did. You're here because he made me a promise. He promised me that if anything happened to him, you were up for this.

That you could fill those boots. He *promised* me that, West. And I promised him I would find out."

For whatever reason, I couldn't look the captain in the eyes. All this time I thought it had been mere luck of the draw and miraculous odds that had gotten me picked from a pool of other dysfunctional candidates. But the truth came heavy. I felt the weight of Crow's promise now. I felt the need to prove his word to be true.

"So, Rookie . . ." He waited for me to look him in the eyes before asking, ". . . ready for the next round?"

Ever since Vaun had picked me up, I'd been holding back. This wasn't my world, and I didn't belong. Everything I'd experienced so far had only reinforced that idea. This was a world of secret wars and very real bullets; it was a world where my mere presence offended everyone. And so I'd held back. I'd avoided rocking the boat and had been choosing to fly under everyone's radar as best I could. Yet, despite that intention, I'd repeatedly thrown myself through the fire and walked away unburnt.

But this changed everything. Vaun hadn't been waiting for me to fuck up so he could kick me back to Pendleton. He'd been waiting for me to show him just how good I could be.

I grit my teeth and pulled myself to my feet. "If you'll excuse me, sir," I said and walked away to find the rest of my squad. "I've got a dead man's promise to keep."

DAY 3
PATRIOT ACT

"A hero is one who knows how to hang on one minute longer."

—Novalis

CHAPTER 49

Cole West. 2:30 a.m.
Mojave Desert, California

The interior of the helicopter was impossibly silent. Whatever tech this bird ran on was years ahead of what the rest of the Armed Forces used. All of Cerberus Squad within the belly of the bird wore earmuffs, but even without them the thrum of the rotors was barely audible. I knew that outside it wasn't much louder.

The helicopter was lovingly referred to as "Charon", as in the boatman of Greek mythology who ferried souls to the realm of the dead. It was fitting. Time would tell whose deaths this trip would bring.

We sat under the soft green glow of the dimmed lights with our heads bowed. Each of us had been given a brand-new set of Snakeskin suits and a squeaky-clean mask. If Vaun was right, then we were headed right to Terminal's source of the Moses virus. Right into the eye of the storm.

This was planned to be just a sneak and peak rather than a modern-day gunfight at the O.K. Corral, but John had once jokingly told me that a plan was just a list of shit that didn't happen. When I said as much, Tag had told me that it was one of John's favorite sayings with Black Spear as well. Plan for things to go off the rails. That's what machine guns and explosives were for.

When it seemed like Tag had fallen asleep and Billy was thoroughly distracted by a book he held, Hodges leaned forward and motioned for me to do the same. "I, uh, never got a chance to thank you for saving my ass back in LA," he said.

I gave him a short nod. There was no point milking this moment.

"I know I've been kind of an asshole. With all the shit going on, the last thing I wanted was to have to babysit you. Turns out you can handle your own."

"Don't go getting soft on me, Crash."

"Never, New Guy." He extended his fist and I bumped mine against it; I think it was the closest I'd ever get to a gentleman's handshake from him.

From the rear of the helicopter Billy threw a water bottle at us. "No chick-flick moments on the helicopter," he scolded.

Hodges reached into one of the small pockets on his vest, then pulled out a silver metal tube. He flung it over and I caught it one handed. "Hold on to it for later. We'll get a chance to enjoy them once this is all over."

On one end of the metal tube was a small cap, I popped it off with my thumb and a rich earthy smell hit my nostrils. Inside was a cigar; a very nice one made by Gurkha.

"Much obliged," I said.

With our destination quickly approaching, I should have been getting my mind sharp. But try as I might, I just couldn't focus on the mission. My thoughts continually replayed everything that had led to this moment.

It was funny. Up until now I hadn't thought once about something as simple as grabbing a cheeseburger or hitting on some girl at a bar. But now my thoughts raced about exactly that and a thousand other trivial things. It was as if subconsciously I knew that those little moments would never be as important again.

"Hey, Crash," I said. "Is it weird that I can't stop thinking about cheeseburgers right now?"

"Hell, no."

"I dunno . . . it just feels stupid. I mean it all does now, right? It's all little shit. Everything. Checking the Facebook newsfeed, watching the game, small-talk with some girl over drinks. In the grand scheme of things, it seems stupid to have any of that on my mind."

"Fuck that, cheeseburgers are awesome," Hodges replied. "Just because you're a part of the real world now doesn't mean that shit doesn't matter. The only thing that's changed is that when this is all said and done, you get to appreciate those little things so much more."

I considered Hodges's words, and then another question came to my mind. "You worked with Talon, right?" I asked. "What was he like?"

Hodges leaned back, looked up, and recalled a memory. "Crow was the best. He was a chess player. Every now and then before a mission, I'd catch him playing Tag; he always won. His word was his bond, too. Didn't matter if he was promising to buy a round later or if he said he was going to get you out alive. If he said it, it was happening. Good guy. A good friend."

I couldn't help but wonder how long Vaun had kept the real reason for my recruitment from the rest of the squad, or if they'd known the entire time. The very air felt heavy. And then I felt Charon's weight lower, which signaled our entry into the belly of the beast.

Tag's eyes snapped open.

Billy carefully slid a bookmark into his book, then placed it under his seat.

"Game faces," Hodges ordered, "Mask up."

We complied.

I tapped my earbud to activate it.

"Crash to Blackbars, Crash to Blackbars," I heard Hodges say next to me.

"Go for Blackbars," Vaun said over the channel.

"We're going in."

Tag slid the door on the side open and hopped out into the desert night. The rest of us followed, guns out in a 360 degree circle. Moments later, Charon rose silently and disappeared into the night sky.

Once the quiet thrum of the helicopter disappeared, Hodges waved us forward. I hugged the stock of my rifle tight into my shoulder, ready to close out the book on Terminal's story.

CHAPTER 50

The body can endure a lot. Up to this point Robert Batson's body had endured a grazing gunshot wound from an enemy insurgent, the concussive blast from a nearby IED, and countless bruises and broken bones from various fights. And now, Batson could add torture to that list.

Morphine was becoming a quick best friend and for that he was thankful. Half his face was still wrapped up in gauze and bandages to cover the intricate crisscrossing of slashes his interrogator had left him. Two of his fingers on his left hand had been broken, the other three fingernails had been pulled off with needle nose pliers, the fingertips now bandaged with cotton. That had really sucked. It's not like needle nose pliers worked well for that job. His interviewer had wrenched the nails off rather than simply pulling them.

His hand instinctively twitched remembering the torture. Yeah, sucked was really an understatement. The whole thing had broken him in every sense of the word. Cut, beaten, and humiliated. The body could endure a lot, but it still had its limits.

The heart operated in the same way. Batson's had taken a motherfucker of a hit. It wasn't the torture or even that he felt he'd failed by cracking from it that was turning his soul into knots. It was something worse.

His mind hadn't processed the rumors. Then he'd confronted Jax's mad scientist Chan. Then he'd seen the reports of just how goddamn many men they'd used. Brothers in arms, reduced to lab rats.

Morphine worked really well for numbing pain. Rage worked even better.

Batson limped along the Terminal Grounds towards Jax's quarters. Oh yeah, the torturer had also smashed both his big and his little toes with a hammer. Big and little so that he couldn't lean his foot to one side or the other to ease the pressure off his broken toes. It hurt no matter how he limped.

The men around the compound parted like the Red Sea. Before, Batson would've chalked it up to equal parts intimidation and respect. Batson was Jax's right hand after all. He was the muscle. Nobody challenged him. Now, he felt like they did it as if he was some kind of leper in their midst. With his one good eye he shot a hateful look at a nearby mechanic, who damn near dropped his clipboard and toolbox before scurrying away.

Any other day that would've amused him. Today, it just fueled the fire in his soul.

Batson walked up the metal catwalk stairs that led to Jax's office. He wasn't sure what was waiting for him inside, and he wasn't sure what he would have to do. With each step a voice inside screamed at him to just turn around and go back to the infirmary.

Batson had never been the praying type, but in that last moment before he turned Jax's doorknob, he said a quick one, anyway.

CHAPTER 51

Air Force One is arguably the most comfortable airplane on the planet. Every accommodation is provided. Every inch of its 4,000 square feet were specifically tailored for the pleasure of the leader of the free world and any guests from among the world's elite. There was an onboard medical suite complete with an operating table, a fully stocked galley that could serve anything requested, and a conference room that could telemeet with anyone in the world the President needed. Rourke had had the pleasure of flying aboard the President's aircraft a total of seven times over the course of his career. Each trip had been the epitome of comfort. This eighth time, however, was not.

For the past thirty minutes he'd been stuck in a chair made of the richest leather possible, but all the same it was becoming a pain in his ass. The Secretaries of Defense, Veterans Affairs, and Homeland Security similarly looked tired from the incessant ranting and finger-pointing of the President. At this inhuman hour, most already looked dead on their feet before the meeting had started.

Mason and Vaun stood across the room, equally agitated. All quietly envied Kelly, who had been told quite unpleasantly to wait outside. When Mason was sure no one but Rourke was looking, she formed her hand into the shape of a gun and shot herself in the head. Patience had never been her strong suit.

The President had just finished recounting the events of the past week leading up to Terminal laying siege in Los Angeles. Simultaneously, he threatened to employ everything from budgetary cuts to a re-evaluation of the authority Rourke held as Black Spear's Director. It was only when the President tried to intimidate everyone in the room by proposing new Executive Orders limiting their power that Rourke decided he needed to speak up.

"Mister President," Rourke said, managing to keep his rising temper in check with considerable restraint, "this Initiative only maintains the track record of success it has due to the freedom of authority and action we have been granted. That being said, the authority we have been granted is only as good as the funding provided."

"I've seen your program's budget, Rourke," the President said. "And let's just say after this embarrassment, it's under review. You didn't just drop the ball, you let a facility that isn't supposed to even exist explode in the middle of one of America's most populated cities."

"Sir, the site in Los Angeles was undermanned," answered Rourke. "If our program has declined, it is only due to fiscal cuts placed on us from your predecessor."

The President shook his head. "The day and age of black budget projects and Cold War spies fighting shadow wars is gone, Rourke. My presidency will not be martyred to history in support of an outdated and ineffective outfit like yours." He then pointed a finger at the Secretary of Defense. "Today we need public heroes and public victories. We need our men and women of the military—the *real* military—to be the ones fighting the battles. We cannot be seen as the villains who work under the table and off the books."

"Mister President, our enemies are *in* the shadows, so we must fight them *in* the shadows. The very nature of what we do is why the military cannot handle this type of fight."

The President only shook his head harder. "Rourke, the only reason you still *have* a budget is because of my predecessor. I asked you to handle this mess before the public turned it into a media nightmare, and you didn't deliver. We've got every agency chomping at the bit to round up these Terminal boys. It's only a matter of time."

Rourke cut a glance to Mason and Vaun. The Captain had remained characteristically silent while Ms. Mason's agitation only grew. They'd all known that the meeting wasn't for the President to hear their side, only for him to voice his disapproval face to face. It was also the reason Rourke hadn't told the President of Vaun's team moving in on Terminal's home base.

"Maybe once upon a time you and your program kept the bogeyman at bay. Now, Black Spear is just a remnant of a bygone era. When this plane lands, I'm cutting your funding."

Rourke's jaw clenched. Underneath the table, his hands curled into fists tight enough to crush a man's throat.

The President squinted at him. "All of it."

CHAPTER 52

It was a brisk fifty-eight degrees out in the desert, but already I was warming up. The soft sand of the rolling dunes around us made our movement difficult; our boots disappeared ankle deep into the powdery surface, which made everything slow going. Intel showed that the supposed storage facility was only about two klicks from where Charon had inserted us, yet only ten minutes into it I could feel the sweat running down my thighs and my back was getting just as slick.

Billy was on point. The lean fighter would make it up the hills with ease, then drop to a knee to survey the area while the rest of us slowly lumbered up to join him. He hadn't even broken a sweat. When we reached the top, he was waiting patiently with his rifle scope up to his eye.

"Compound is below. Looks quiet," Billy said. He fanned his weapon to the left. His rifle had a thermal scope that would highlight any warm bodies in the area. "I spot a guard tower at each corner, two men each."

"If that satellite thermal is right, then the virus is being held in the bunker in the southeast sector," Hodges said. "Kage's on overwatch. Boomerang, New Guy: on me."

Damn, still stuck with the rookie moniker.

As we approached the chain link fence marking the perimeter of Terminal's compound, Captain Vaun spoke through our earbuds. Despite being hundreds of miles away aboard Air Force One, we could hear him clear as day. "Good luck, boys," he said. "Let's hope you're more successful than we are up here."

Hodges paused to take a knee next to the fence. "Things that bad on your end?"

"Not that you need anything else on your mind, but we might be out of a job by sunrise."

I gave a mirthless laugh. "Then that means we still have tonight. Oorah."

Tag moved up to the fence. We crouched directly under the guard tower, yet out of their field of view. From a pouch on his belt he pulled a small spray can then nodded to Hodges. Our acting squad leader tapped his earbud to signal Billy back on the hillside. "Take them."

We didn't hear anything but both men in the guard tower slumping over. The tranquilizer rounds in Billy's rifle were subsonic. There wasn't so much as a zip or crack of the rounds traveling to their destination. I'm not entirely sure what was in the tranquilizers, but Billy assured me it was Black Spear's own special blend and was guaranteed to put people into a sleep so deep so fast that you'd need to check their heartbeat just to see if they were even alive. Hell, the way he described it made it sound like real bullets wouldn't even act that fast. He then joked that when the mission was done, we should dose ourselves with it then put on Dark Side of the Moon. I'd laughed, but I was only half sure he was kidding.

Billy also had a full load of armor-piercing rounds with some serious points on them. If they were anything like the black-tipped frag rounds in our assault rifles, then I had full confidence in their ability to do some damage. I asked if he planned on shooting down any helicopters. The shrug he gave me implied he could if he wanted to.

Now that the coast was clear, Tag held the can in his hand then sprayed it to trace a circle along the fence. The can was a super cold aerosol that chilled surfaces to sixty degrees below zero. Once the fence was frozen Tag gripped it and gave it a violent tug. The fence let out a snapping sound, barely louder than a few matchsticks, then the section pulled away free.

As we stepped through the hole in the fence, Billy's voice sounded through our earbuds. "Kage to Crash. Going to lose visual on you soon. Moving to better vantage point."

"Copy."

There weren't many men about the grounds. A few walked short patrols, uninterested and unaware. We stuck to the shadows to avoid them. Minimal light within the compound made our remaining unseen even easier. As we passed a motor pool, which was filled with more cargo trucks and assault vehicles than I was comfortable with, Billy's voice sounded through our earbuds once more.

"Two-man patrol advancing from your three o'clock."

Before we maneuvered around to face our right flank, I heard the sound of two bodies collapsing. Yeah, the darts worked that fast.

Hodges faced to our front and advanced forward. Half a dozen U.S. agencies would raid the other Terminal compounds at sunrise. As soon as they did, this base would go into full panic mode, and who knew what would happen. The clock on our mission was already ticking.

CHAPTER 53

"The papers are already being drafted, Rourke," the President said. "I've had my eyes on your sordid program since I took office. All I needed was one good reason to shut you down."

It was actually the Secretary of Defense who spoke up first. "Hold on, Mister President," the SecDef cautioned. "We don't need a knee-jerk reaction to this. Mister Rourke has been doing more than his fair share of the fight for decades. Collateral damage aside, I don't think this is a decision you want to make based solely on one incident."

"Jim," the President said with pursed lips, "do you even know his full name? Who he really is? I sure don't. Rourke and his program are frankly dangerous, and to be perfectly honest I can't in good conscience allow his program to continue to run unchecked."

"Mister President," Rourke said, "if—"

"Enough!" The President slammed a fist onto the conference table. He took a breath to compose himself, poorly, then continued, "There is nothing special about them. There is nothing unique. They are a relic, nothing more."

Mason tried to hide an amused smile. She and Kelly had actually made a bet with Vaun before boarding Air Force One, regarding how bad Rourke's presidential ass-chewing would be. As it stood, he owed them both five bucks.

None of this was surprising. Rumor mills had been churning regarding Black Spear's future for months now, but Vaun wasn't worried. A man like Rourke—a man with his level of calculation and planning—would have known this was coming. He'd have secondary plans and tertiary plans and whatever the plan after that was called. Contingencies were something Mister Rourke had in excess. Vaun knew the man was stubborn enough that, if the President himself shut down Black Spear, Rourke would still keep fighting.

That was an interesting thought. A renegade Black Spear, ties fully cut from the official United States government. Hell, that's what all the superheroes did, wasn't it?

The door to the conference room cracked open, and Vaun's eyes darted towards it. Kelly peeked in, and for a second Vaun thought he might be checking just to see if he'd lost the bet. But his eyes said something else.

Rourke nodded at Vaun, who in turn moved over to see what Kelly wanted. "Yeah," Vaun said. "I owe you five. What is it?"

"One of the Secret Service guys was just taken down to the medical bay," Kelly said with widening eyes. "He didn't look too good."

"Okay, well if any plane has Motrin onboard it's definitely this one," Vaun answered.

"No, Captain," Kelly insisted. "He looked *sick*."

Vaun felt his blood run cold.

CHAPTER 54

He'd been waiting for him. Batson pushed the door in, planning for Jax to be asleep on his cot or maybe with his face buried in plans. Instead Jax sat at the edge of his desk as if he'd expected Batson to walk in at this late hour.

"Good to see you on your feet so soon," Jax said. He was meticulously cleaning the same double-barrel shotgun Batson had seen him use in L.A. He ran an oiled rag over the barrel until the blued steel shined. "Trouble sleeping?"

Batson swallowed. "Troubling thoughts, brother."

Jax snapped the shotgun closed.

Batson flinched, then Jax laid the shotgun down across his lap. "Do tell."

Batson's good hand trembled anxiously. "Tell me I'm wrong."

"About?"

"Chan's experiments, infecting one of the guys you sent to me at the McAllister Brothers like some kind of time bomb, the number of our own men you've taken down into that goddamn lab," Batson said. "Jax, tell me I'm wrong. Please."

Jax looked down at the ground for a moment. Batson hoped this wasn't going to go the way he'd first thought. And then Jax laughed, as if Batson had told some kind of joke.

"That's what's got you acting this way?" he said, clapping his hand against his thigh. "Really?" Jax abruptly stopped laughing, his face hardening into an emotionless mask. "Maybe you need to grow up, Bats."

Batson shook his head in disbelief. It just wasn't possible. Batson couldn't help but wonder what had turned his friend into this person, or if he'd actually been this way the entire time. "You can't mean that. This isn't what we started Terminal for. We don't have to go down this road and you know it."

"I started Terminal for the *cause*," barked Jax. "The cause is still the same. I will make them all pay for their fucking negligence. No matter how much blood must be shed, I will shed it and no misguided ideals, no self-righteous committee, no goddamned covert black-ops team will stop me. You think L.A. was a message? What do you think will happen when I take out the President? SecDef? What if I just unleash Moses on an entire city's population? That's what comes next, Batson. Full-on fucking war."

Batson stared at the man who was supposed to be his brother. The words he was saying weren't real. It wasn't him. Batson refused to believe it.

"You just don't see it," Batson said quietly. "You don't see what you've become. We were supposed to be better than the officers and the politicians. We were supposed to put the men before the mission."

"Their lives were part of the cost to complete the mission. Our mission will save countless soldiers."

Batson pulled a pistol from the back of his pants. Despite the clumsy bandages on his fingers, he managed to work the slide. The pistol was the very 1911 .45 Jax had given him. Batson had brought it from his bedside but hadn't believed he'd need it. He didn't want to need it.

"You are so lost," whispered Batson sadly. "I can't let you do this." Jax's hands went to the shotgun across his lap. "Let me? First of all, you don't even know my endgame, anymore. You were never more than a blunt instrument I could point in the right direction. You were good for heavy lifting but came up a little light in the brains department, didn't you? Put your money here, Bats. Tell the men to do this, Bats. Go blow up this, go blow up that. Secondly: Terminal doesn't *need* you, Robert."

"Bullshit. I may have come up light on brains, but I'm still smart enough to know that you need my family's money. 'Full-on fucking war' isn't going to be free. Tanks and bombs tend to get pricey. You can't pay for your war without me."

"Please," Jax said. "We emptied your accounts together. Your money is Terminal's money now. This is the path Terminal is on. I've already given the orders."

"Nobody in Terminal gives orders. Anyone is free to challenge anything."

"Yeah, but nobody challenges me."

Batson's hand twitched on the pistol in his hand. "Abraham . . . don't make me do this."

The two men stood barely three paces away from one another. Near enough to look into each other's eyes, near enough to no longer recognize the person staring back at them.

"You said you were with me till the end," Jax reminded him. "I guess that's now. *Brother.*"

Both men raised their weapons and fired.

CHAPTER 55

Cole West. 3:45 a.m.
Mojave Desert, California

The stillness of the night was broken by a series of gunshots; they came so abruptly that in my surprise I had trouble placing their location. We ducked into the shadows.

No longer hidden, Tag held up two fingers and motioned towards our left. Two shooters. Not far. "Muzzle flashes," Tag said, pointing at the upper floor of a two-story building across from us.

"Three to your nine o'clock, moving fast," Billy said. "Three more from your three o'clock. I think this just jumped up a notch beyond sneak-and-peak. Looks like the whole compound is waking up."

We were smack in the middle of a four-way intersection within the compound, and I could hear shouts coming from two different directions. Shouts growing closer.

"Call it," Tag murmured.

"I see two more groups; they're boxing you in," warned Billy.

I stacked up against Tag with my weapon pointed in the opposite direction. "It's about to turn into a *real* bad day down here."

Hodges's head darted to the left and right. "Fuck, fuck," he repeated.

"Crash, I don't have that many tranqs," said Billy, calm as ever.

"Fuckfuckfuck," Hodges said again.

I found myself wishing we had Captain Vaun with us calling the shots. He never lost his cool. Not when a building exploded in front of him, not when the enemies around us were transforming into things straight out of a George A. Romero flick. But right here, right now, Hodges was cracking. I tried to think of what John would say at a time like this, but the nearing shouts and stomping boots muted everything else out. I think he would've reminded me that if you know certain death is headed your way then the best option is to not be there when it arrives.

The crowd was getting closer. As the approaching danger hit a critical high, Hodges somehow snapped out of it. He whirled around to the building behind us. If the gunshots came from the building to our left, then the one to our right had to be the safest place.

"Get inside, fast." Hodges put an edge in his voice for us as much as himself.

We rounded a corner, searching for the door that would give us shelter from unwanted attention. I got to it first and wrapped my eager hand around the handle. Locked. We were thoroughly fucked.

Then, I felt the handle turn. I shouldered it open and started to take a step inside. I stopped short. It was a squad bay with two dozen men, all armed, all headed out the door in my direction.

"Hey, boys, look what I found!" the nearest man said.

Our entire plan immediately went to shit.

My rifle was firing as I dropped to one knee. I didn't even bother to aim. I just kept the weapon directed into the doorway and unloaded. The man who had been smiling in my direction just a second earlier fell back, stiff as a board, as three rounds punched across his sternum.

Outside, the guards responding to the initial gunshots had reached us and I could only hear the automatic fire from Tag's machine gun. I could barely make out Hodges's voice bellowing directions for Tag to fire in, to which he responded with an enthusiastic grunt. There was no time to focus on it as the inhabitants of the building decided to shoot back.

I rolled back outside just in time to hear the bullets whistle past me. It briefly occurred to me that I had gotten used to people shooting at me. A guy can change a lot in just a few days.

I reached to the side of my vest where three flashbangs were attached. Tugging one free, I looped my thumb through the pin then slipped it out before rolling the grenade into the building. Even outside I could see the blinding white light and the concussive wave thump against the interior walls. I aimed back inside at the disoriented Terminal soldiers and dropped two more with a double-tap to the chest each.

Vaun's insight into what made John so capable echoed in my head. Stay cool, react and adapt to the fluid situation. Most importantly: get everyone out alive. I focused on that, using those words like a guide to my actions.

More and more shooters joined in outside. The rattle of gunfire and the telltale zip of rounds ricocheting soon became deafening. Before I could clear the room and advance inside, additional men had already reinforced the ones I'd stunned, and they picked up the fight.

The situation grew desperate. I could hear Billy relaying something through the commlink, but couldn't quite make out what it was over the roar of combat. I sighted up a shot to the man inside closest to me and squeezed the trigger, only to hear the disappointing sound of an empty chamber.

As I ejected the clip, I glanced back at Tag, who was also frantically reloading his machine gun belt as quickly as he could. Hodges fired two rounds to try and keep our enemies at bay. Then, his weapon was dry as well. Bad luck ran strong tonight.

Before I could slap a fresh clip in I could see a dozen men moving upon us from every direction; each had weapons raised and ready. The nearest one was a mere five feet away when a voice screamed out into the sky and drowned out all other sound.

"STOOOOOOOP!"

The enemy soldiers froze in their tracks, lowering their weapons. They all looked up to the second story of the building across from us—the source of the gunfire just minutes ago. The door exploded outward, kicked off its hinges as if a bomb had gone off. Then, he stepped out.

Abraham Jackson, Terminal's ringleader himself.

"Oh, goodie, looks like we're in the right place after all," I said, defeated.

Jax dragged a bloodied body by its collar with one hand and held a shotgun over his shoulder with the other. Once outside, Jax kicked the body down the stairs, sending it into a lifeless tumble until it came to a rest at the very bottom.

The soldiers around us all gawked at the corpse.

"Is that Batson . . . ?" one said.

"What the hell is going on?" another asked.

Above us, glowering like some triumphant general, Jax allowed himself a smile. "All of you stand down. Now! I'd like a word with our would-be assassins."

Okay, *now* our plan had gone to shit.

CHAPTER 56

Given that Black Spear was already on thin ice with the President, Vaun decided it would be best to check out the sick Secret Service agent before raising the full alarm. For all they knew, the man had eaten a bad egg salad sandwich and just needed some Pepto. If the agent *was* infected, they could radio back to Mason or Mr. Rourke to lock down the conference room in an instant. That room was one of the most secure locations in the country, hitting the alarm and having a dozen more agents bolster the defenses would make it only more so.

As they descended the stairs to the lower hull of Air Force One, both Vaun and Kelly noted the smell in the air: coppery. They both preemptively drew their weapons.

Nothing in the intel reports showed that Moses-2 was airborne. All the same, Vaun preferred to be fully kitted in Snakeskin as opposed to the black and white suit Mr. Rourke had directed him to wear. He felt wholly underdressed for the occasion.

Security measures had forbidden everyone, including Black Spear personnel, from carrying anything more than a sidearm onboard. The Glock 32 pistol was all the comfort he was afforded at the moment. He'd have preferred a larger caliber such as .45 ACP but the

Secret Service standard issue was a .357 SIG P229. If Vaun ran dry, he didn't want to be searching high and low for more .45.

Kelly walked alongside him with a Glock 32 of his own, his shooting hand outstretched and walking with side-steps while his injured arm was still held in a sling. It occurred to Vaun that even if Kelly had long-lasting problems with his wounded shoulder he was still the most accurate shooter Vaun had ever met. Bar none.

"There were two agents posted here before," Kelly noted.

Vaun nodded. "Must've taken something very interesting to get them to move." As if on cue a scream came from farther down in the medical bay before it was cut short by a wet tearing sound. Then, just empty silence. As they advanced, they heard a wet smacking sound every few steps. Step, step. *Smack.* Step, step. *Smack.*

Around the corner they saw a Secret Service agent sprawled on his backside in the middle of the corridor, his pressed white button-up being ruined by the red spreading from the hole in his throat. His face was being beaten into mush by a second agent who straddled him. In the second agent's right hand were the ragged remains of what had once been a human throat; his left hand was curled into a fist that *smacked* into the first agent's face again and again with lunatic persistence.

"He's a Bleeder," Kelly whispered. The agent was completely unaware of them, focused only on beating the body under him. Before the Bleeder noticed them, Vaun put a round through its ear. The Bleeder whirled off the dead body and landed on its rear, its bloodshot eyes still open and looking in their direction. Vaun fired another round that struck true between its eyes.

Moving closer to the grisly scene, Vaun considered the agent with his throat torn out.

Kelly just shook his head. "Don't think that one's coming back, Captain."

"Guess we can be thankful they're not full-on zombies."

"It's the little blessings."

Despite his best efforts, Vaun found himself looking into both dead agents' eyes. They were Americans, American servicemen. Killing his own countrymen had never been something he enjoyed. He was filled with newfound rage for Abraham Jackson and the hell he'd forced onto the world.

"Captain!" Kelly cried from up ahead.

Vaun was pulled from his thoughts, looking up to find Kelly inside the medical bay.

The examination table was upended. On the floor were two severed fingers and a bloody scalpel. A red puddle was spreading by a toppled nurse's cart. One of the overhead lights was flickering, several bullet casings rattled against each other as the plane tipped and they began to roll. But there was something amiss about the bloodshed here. There were no bodies.

"Where the hell are they?"

CHAPTER 57

"Father, this is Blackbars. Best lockdown POTUS. Try to pull everyone you can back to the conference room. Otherwise, this plane is going to be crawling in infected."

Mr. Rourke gave a gruff affirmative, but Vaun and Kelly were already moving on.

Most flyers don't get more than a glimpse at the entirety of a plane. They board, walk down an aisle, sit in their seat, and maybe if they have one or two cocktails, they'll use the lavatory. But they never see the underbelly of the plane, the cargo hold, or any of the other interior sections that the crew sees. Passengers only end up seeing maybe a tenth of what the average plane holds, but Air Force One was not an average plane.

Vaun knew this and was beginning to hate it as he and Kelly explored deeper. There had been no sign of any of the medical personnel nor the patient zero Secret Service agent. Their search led them to a split hallway.

"Which way do we go?" asked Kelly.

"Follow the screams?"

A second later they heard just that. Except this time it wasn't the bloodcurdling cry of a dying man, but screams of anger. Vaun took quick steps down the hallway at the end of which was a door. With a quick shove, Vaun shouldered through.

On the other side they entered the galley. From across the room came the screaming.

Two Bleeders had a cook pinned atop a countertop. One pummeled his chest to the sound of cracking ribs. The other gave its best effort to ripping off the cook's jaw and was halfway done with the task. Wet sputtering gasps escaped what remained of the cook's mouth as the flesh across his jawline continued to tear free.

The other side of the galley produced more chaos. Another Bleeder vomited dark blood into the open mouth of a second cook, while a fourth rabid man used its teeth to rip huge chunks out of the face of a long deceased Secret Service agent.

Despite his training and every ounce of discipline in his body, Vaun hesitated. It was only for a second but that was all it took for the situation to turn. All four of the Bleeders turned their attention to the new prey and flung themselves forward.

The sound of their Glocks firing in the small quarters had their ears ringing. One of the snarling bleeding things snatched up a meat cleaver from the counter. It had just enough time to swing for Vaun's hand before Kelly dropped it with two shots to the head. Vaun fired three rounds into the chest of the next closest one, but it continued to run straight at him with hands outstretched. Its throat twitched for a moment before a stream of bloody vomit shot from its mouth. Vaun had just enough time to back out of the doorway and slam it shut before the virus-filled stream splattered.

"The kitchen crew is supposed to be a dozen, any idea where the others went to?"

The Bleeders inside were already bashing their hands against the other side of the door.

As if to answer his question, Rourke's voice sounded in their earpieces. "Captain, the plane is compromised."

Vaun looked to Kelly while latching the lock on the door to the galley. "The conference room is still secure at this time. We can hold it, but we're dealing with an unknown number of infected onboard."

Vaun started playing through the scenarios in his head. Undoubtedly the President would want to land as soon as possible to get the cavalry into this mess and sort it out, but Vaun knew that meant potentially releasing Moses-2 into an unsecured population. By ensuring the safety of the free world's leader, they would be threatening the safety of the free world itself.

"Captain, the plane is compromised," Rourke repeated. "I have contingencies in place, but you need to get this under control."

There was an underlying threat in Rourke's words. Compromised. That was exactly what Rourke had said about Angel Site when asked why he had sent a missile to erase it. If Rourke was willing to bomb a building to ensure the safety of their sensitive network and classified intel, how far would he go to keep Moses-2 from being released into the general population?

Vaun's sense of dread continued to escalate. Then, all the lights went out.

CHAPTER 58

The three Men in Black were put to their knees with guns to the backs of their heads. Their weapons had been taken, their protective masks removed. Jax wasn't sure which three-letter federal agency they were with, but he would bet they were with one that granted those fabled licenses to kill. For all the good it did them.

All his troops gathered before him. Several gawked as he dragged Batson's body by the ankle. A schism would surely form unless he got a handle on things, and quickly. This was Jax's opportunity to either lose their faith or to see it renewed ten-fold. An idea came to mind and he couldn't help but smile.

"Here they are, boys," he shouted. His voice carried out across the vast empty desert around them. An entire army surrounded him, and it was utterly silent. "We told them we would make them pay for making our brothers bleed and die for nothing. For leaving us forgotten. And how did they respond?"

Yes, that was the key. Always make it a they and them versus us and ours. Base tribalism. Draw a line in the sand between groups, then watch their loyalty strengthen and their hate grow.

"They responded by sending *killers* in the night. By sending these assassins to snuff out our little flame of resistance."

More and more of his soldiers looked fired up. A few nodded while others shouted back to Jax in agreement. They were like putty in his paws; he'd always known exactly what to say to rile them up. Jax pointed his shotgun at Batson's body. His chest was an open cavity where Jax's buckshot had blown through his heart. "This man—our own brother—conspired against us. He led them right to our home!"

Outrage swept across the crowd like a wave. Before they looked at Batson's body with confusion, now they had only disgust. He let them sit in it for a moment; the more it sank in the more Jax would be able to sell them on the next stage.

"Robert Batson was a traitor to the cause. They *let* us rescue him just so he could take us out from within. He came to me and ordered me to stand Terminal down."

Now, Jax paused for effect. He waited until his army was at the edge of their seats.

"I refused."

A resounding cheer echoed through the Terminal Grounds. Fists pumped into the air. Men bellowed like barbarians of old. Not a single shred of doubt could be found anywhere. If he'd armed them all with nothing but toothpicks and ordered them to attack a tank, the only question would be about its location. He decided that this must be what military commanders of old must have felt like. Knowing that he was riding off the same rush that Genghis Khan and Napoleon provoked filled Jax with pride. If the high got any better, he was definitely going to get hard.

"As we speak, one of our brothers has already taken the fight to *them!* We have struck a deciding blow in this war. They sent a wolf in sheep's clothing into our midst, I thought it only fair to do the same. One of our own is aboard Air Force One as we speak with the President *himself* . . . oh, yes. I'm sure you all have heard the rumors of Terminal's secret weapon, of the experiments, of the virus. By now our wolf has released that weapon to the very top!"

Jax decided to leave out the part that their double-agent had done so unknowingly. The men didn't need to know the full truth, after all. "This virus shall be our knife, buried straight into the heart of our enemy!"

Awe and shock washed across his army. Murmuring voices whispered disbelief. It was all so intoxicating. The three commandos in black looked at one another bewildered. Jax's grin grew wider. "We'd already won before you got here. We weren't bluffing when we said we had people *everywhere*."

CHAPTER 59

"What the *hell* is going on out there?" the President demanded.

A nearby Secret Service Agent pilfered through a cabinet, looking for flashlights. "Emergency lights should've kicked on by now . . ." he said.

Rourke remained stitched to his seat at the conference table. Half a dozen agents trained their weapons on the only door into the room, and the Secretary of Defense gripped a pistol in his hand. Rourke tried not to be surprised that the old war dog still had his teeth. Mason had less than politely commandeered one of the agent's submachine guns.

"And here I thought this meeting would be boring," she whispered into Rourke's ear.

He wasn't the least bit surprised that she was relishing this.

The rest of the Secret Service was making its last stand beyond the door. These were the ones entrusted with keeping the nation's leaders safe, nothing short of the very best when it came to trained protectors.

This situation, however, could only be classified as unprecedented. The Bleeders filled the hallway wall to wall, each one flinging bloody vomit in the air, and all of it happening in near darkness? Odds were that at least two agents would be infected. If the men to their left and right hesitated for even a second to dispose of them, they would all be turned. In conclusion, Rourke figured the men outside the door would be done fighting within the minute.

When the lights went out the electronic locks went with them, they'd been forced to barricade the door with a heavy table. Rourke chalked the blackout up to an EMP device of some sort. Air Force One was supposed to have defenses for that kind of attack, but those were for if the EMP was outside the plane. Rourke knew very little about the aeronautics within Air Force One; judging by the fact that it wasn't plummeting out of the air he assumed that most of the plane's mechanics were still functioning. For now.

Of course, that wouldn't matter once the Bleeders got into the room.

At that thought Rourke reached for the small metal pill container in his inside jacket pocket. He popped it open, tapped two painkillers into the palm of one mitt, and swallowed them dry.

The gunfire outside ceased. Now, there were only the wretched screams of the Bleeders. More than before. Whichever agents hadn't been killed had joined the ranks of the infected. Rourke tried to determine how many of them there were. It had been some time since he'd hunted men, but all the same he could pick out roughly twelve distinct screams.

The President shouted orders and questions that everyone ignored. Two agents had him shoved to the back of the room with the Secretaries of Homeland Security and Veterans Affairs. The SecDef was not so easily swayed to stay in the rear.

As the infected threw themselves against the door, the large table shifted half an inch. One of the agents shouldered his weight against it and managed to seal the door again. Even in the dark Rourke could see the agents sweating; the few beams of light provided by the flashlights did little to steady their heart rates.

Rourke tried to contact Vaun and found that his earpiece was dead. There were no other forms of communication available. Phones were down. Hell, even the agents' signature radios wired to their ears were out.

Maybe they could hold the room. Rourke calculated the odds and found them not to be in their favor. Some found it difficult to remove themselves from situations when making altruistic decisions; Rourke never had that problem.

He pulled a small device from his pants pocket. Everyone else had thought it was simply a cell phone. It was small, flat, and rectangular like one. When he tapped the touchscreen on the front, he was pleased to see that the EMP hadn't disabled it. After typing in a four-digit passcode he hesitated for just a second, and then pressed his thumbprint into the screen.

Five red letters popped up onto the screen and began to blink slowly. "Armed".

Rourke wasn't well known for his sense of humor, but he'd allowed himself his own personal joke when years ago he'd dubbed the device in his hands "Plan C." When the primary plan failed and the back-up plan fell through, there was always Plan C. During the Cold War, covert agents had utilized suicide pills hidden inside their teeth. Rourke had Plan C. Though it looked harmless enough, the device was more than capable of completely vaporizing Air Force One and all traces of the virus with it.

The next-generation explosive worked off chemistry that was beyond Rourke. When Black Spear acquired the technology, the layman's explanation of the device was plastic explosives on steroids. Powerful and effective. He'd seen the initial testing first hand. Five ounces of it had been enough to erase a city block. The device contained seven and a half ounces. By Rourke's estimates that would be more than sufficient.

"I've only ever seen you arm that once before," whispered Mason.

"Please tell me you're not considering using it? That won't stop anything, since Jackson has more of the virus up his sleeve."

"Of course, he does. But above all, my duty and loyalty are to the preservation and protection of this country. If the President is infected and becomes the patient zero of a country-wide epidemic, the nation will never recover. By my calculations there is an absolute certainty of a full-scale outbreak should this plane land with infected."

Not even Black Spear could pull off the media blackout that would be required for that cover up, and Mason knew it. Masking the assassination of an annoying filmmaker was one thing, but POTUS becoming a walking biohazard was another matter entirely. Either a stray TSA agent or maybe even a sleeper agent for Terminal itself would snag a photo of the infected President, and what then? He'd become a very symbol to Terminal's already surging propaganda machine. If they could claim the President, they would win. And tomorrow the war would only get bloodier.

But if the President were to . . . disappear? That would be quite a different outcome. Plan C wouldn't cause Air Force One to explode: it would completely atomize it. There wouldn't be so much as a tooth for dental records or the fabled black box to reveal what had happened. The succession of command would proceed, the President would be immortalized as a martyr rather than a victim, but most importantly the nation would carry on.

Rourke slid the Plan C device back into his pocket. He didn't have a problem with this, not at all. There were much worse ways to go out. By Rourke's estimate, everyone in the room was already dead. The only thing left to be determined was how gruesome, or how painless their deaths would be.

CHAPTER 60

They ripped my mask off so hard I thought that they were going to take an ear with it. After that they plucked out my earbud and stomped on it for good measure.

My rifle and sidearm had already been stripped away, but upon Jax's orders they now took the rest. When they slipped the knife from my pocket, I actually tried to grab it back. It was stupid, but Vaun had given it to me and already it held some sentimental value. That got me a smack to the face from somebody's buttstock. My cheek hurt down to the bone. It dawned on me that my face had just started to heal from the initial throwdown I'd had with my teammates. So much for that.

My comrades received similar treatment. Hodges spat at our captors when they snatched away his beltful of explosives. They returned the favor, a solid punch to the nose that caused blood to squirt out both nostrils. It took four men to pin Tag to the ground. The big lug somehow managed to be quieter than usual.

They had us dead to rights. Even if we could communicate with Billy and his very-much-needed sniper rifle, there's no way he could get a clean shot. Maybe he could get lucky and pick off a few of the

Terminal soldiers on the edges of the crowd, but then they would just execute the three of us.

There had to be some way to push them back, to give Billy an opening. I'd hoped Hodges had snuck one of the flashbangs from his belt but we weren't so lucky. At this point I'd even want him to use some of his Semtex and take us all out. I'd never been tortured before, but I'd bet that being turned to red mist by high explosive was preferable.

They'd taken everything, though. All our equipment and weapons were stacked on a table too far out of reach. Jax was looking it over with great amusement.

"Looks like that's the last of it," the soldier searching me said. My pockets should've been empty but I still felt something inside my vest. They'd already taken all my flashbangs, extra clips, and weapons, though, hadn't they? I tried to figure out what it could be but came up blank.

Ever so slowly I reached towards the last unsearched pocket I had on the inside of my vest. The soldiers appeared satisfied that we were disarmed and must have figured I was simply scratching an itch. If I'd pulled out a hidden gun there were fifty more in our faces anyway. Inside the pocket, my gloved fingers brushed against cool metal.

The cigar.

It was the cigar Hodges had gifted me with. An idea formed in my head and I looked to my team to try to give them some kind of signal that I was about to run a risky gambit.

John had once remarked to me that the most lethal weapon on the battlefield wasn't a blade or a bomb, but fear itself. Find a way to use that against the enemy, and their numbers won't matter.

Battle is won in the mind, he'd said. *Break them there, and the fight's yours.*

"All right, then," the soldier said once he'd realized he'd missed something, "Nice and slow now, let's see it."

My hand pulled the long silver cigar tube out of my vest pocket with my thumb pressed firmly against the cap.

"Don't. Fucking. Move." I spoke confidently, as if I held all the cards and they were too dumb to see it. The soldier was confused, then looked at the metal tube and backed away slightly.

"What is that . . . ?" he asked.

The others around us looked just as worried. I rose to my feet and held the tube above my head.

"This is your Moses-2 toxin," I shouted. "We lifted a sample from your lab before you jumped us. Now, back away! If I pop this cap, then this shit hits the air. *Everyone* dies."

The soldiers backstepped a pace, eyes quickly shifting between us and to Jax.

I passed the tube from one hand to the other; they all flinched. "Have you actually seen what this shit does? Have any of you? Or are you just playing follow the leader?"

Whispers. I overheard some admitting they didn't know Terminal was dealing in bioweapons. A few others spoke of the things they'd heard about Moses and the night at McAllister's. Some spoke of brothers that had gone missing down in the lab bunker.

Jax gave me a withering scowl. "Bullshit."

"You think so?" I rolled my thumb along the tube's cap, "You wanted the scariest virus imaginable, Jackson. Did you really think it could never go airborne?"

The crowd stirred uneasily, growing more fearful with every word.

"Do any of you even know what happened at the McAllister building where we took Batson into custody? How many of your 'brothers' Jax's virus killed? What it *did* to them? What it turned them into?"

Fear tilted into burgeoning panic. A moment ago they were cheering and ready to gut us. Now, they were shaking. And then the first one ran. It was just some guy at the very edge of the crowd, but the threat of some plague-induced death sent him running. A few more followed. The rest of the crowd began to break apart. The cocky guard who'd taken all my gear raised his hands, begging for mercy.

"Goddamn it, he's lying!" said Jax. "Stand fast, you fucking idiots!"

"You pull that trigger and every single one of your brothers die."

"Then I guess they'll die," he said. Jax raised his shotgun.

And then Billy took his shot.

The high-powered rifle round drilled through two soldiers. Two birds. One stone. I got a front-row seat to what those armor-piercing tips could do to a pair of human skulls. Not pretty.

The soldiers around us whirled, trying to locate the point of origin for the shot. They failed as Billy fired again and downed another two. As closely packed as our enemies were, Billy could keep picking off multiple enemies with a single bullet. He fired again and again, I could only tell from the spray of blood and whistle of the bullets tearing through the air.

We were moving before anyone could recover from the surprise attack. Tag reached the table first, wrapped nearly all of our gear up in his arms, then dove behind a stacked crate for cover. Hodges had retrieved an M4 from one of the fallen Terminal soldiers and sprayed it into the crowd before sliding to where Tag crouched. I spotted my knife and handgun on the table, I snatched both up on my way to cover.

"Please tell me Billy got Jackson," I said.

Hodges emptied the M4's magazine while checking the bodies that littered the floor. "We're never that lucky."

Looking through the pile of gear Tag dumped on the ground, I spotted one of our earbud radios. I plucked it off the ground and shoved it in my ear.

"That's mine," Tag said.

"Mine's broke."

"It's got my earwax on it."

I tapped the button on the earbud and Billy's voice started to come through.

"-nine o'clock."

"Kage, this is the New Guy. Say again your last?"

"Nine o'clock! I said three are coming up on your nine o'clock!" Before I could aim my weapon Tag had already unloaded a controlled burst with his.

"Jackson's on the move," Billy said. "He's going for the lab."

"Roger." I passed the earbud to Hodges. "Sorry. Your call, Crash."

Hodges nodded and put it into his ear with a twist.

Tag grimaced at the sight of a third person sharing his earwax.

"He's not getting away," Hodges said. "Terminal has only gotten this far because of him. We take him out, Terminal crumbles. Lop off the head of the snake and all that."

"Think he was telling the truth about the President?"

Hodges shrugged. "No idea. Doesn't matter though. Our mission is here."

Behind us the Terminal shooters who had stayed to fight pressed closer. Small arms fire mostly. I suppose it was a blessing that they were still too panicked and caught off guard to go get their really loud toys.

Speaking of which, Hodges held several really loud toys in his hands. He pulled the pins off two of the flashbangs and lobbed them over the crate. There was a brief pause where the only sounds were the shouts of our enemies and their intermittent gunfire.

And then the flashbangs flashed and banged.

We were moving before the burst of light faded. We dropped the enemies directly in our path, evaded those too incapacitated, and maneuvered out of the compound crossroads. There were too many of them, and we had too few bullets. Too little time as it was with Jax making his escape. As we neared the bunker, two guards jumped into our path. They'd barely gotten the stocks of their weapons into their shoulders before both their heads had bullets punch through them. Somewhere, Billy was still covering us. Even if he played second fiddle to Kelly in terms of marksmanship, he was still my MVP right now.

When we finally reached the bunker's entrance, I was slick with sweat. Adrenaline pumped. My fingers white-knuckled my weapon. My cheekbone began to throb from where I had it pressed against my stock. I tried to slow my breathing while scanning around the bunker's entrance for any more enemies. Hodges, alongside me, lowered his weapon once he was sure it was clear.

"Get that goddamn barrel up," I said with a smile, repeating what he'd told me back at Angel Site.

Hodges grinned despite himself and raised it once more as we readied on the bunker's entrance.

Jax was already deeper inside. We followed down a set of stairs to a large security door. Next to the vault door was a sophisticated-looking keycard reader. Tag pondered it while I covered the stairs at our back.

"Looks simple enough," he whispered. He pulled a small device from his cargo pocket and placed it against the card reader. It flashed a yellow light. As we waited for it to complete its work, Hodges and I covered the rear.

"That was a slick move with that 'toxin' trick you pulled back there," he said.

"Viruses and toxins are completely different by the way, but I figured if I threw enough scary buzzwords out it would eventually spook them."

"Wait a damn minute," he said excitedly. "I think we just figured out your fucking war-name."

I spared a glance away from the stairwell to give Hodges a confused look.

"You're Toxin, man."

Tag stopped his work for just a second to look our way. He gave Hodges a grunt of approval before returning to his task.

"I dub thee Toxin!" Hodges chuckled.

And just like that the fucking new guy died, and Toxin was born. I wasn't sure about the exact tradition of getting your Cerberus Squad callsign, but I figured if two teammates gave the thumbs up, then it might stick. Toxin. Yeah, it's a name I could get used to hearing. It sure as hell beat "rookie" and "new guy". All that remained was living long enough to claim it and use it for more than a few hours.

CHAPTER 61

They were coming. Bloody. Rabid. Violent. Vaun had already shot his first two clips dry; Kelly had conserved his ammo by taking slower, more accurate shots. The man was a true deadeye. Every single one of his bullets found its mark between the eyes of one of the Bleeders. Between the two of them, they dropped nearly a dozen Bleeders, Kelly with his headshots and Vaun with double taps to the center mass.

And still they came.

By the time Vaun and Kelly backtracked from the galley to the medical bay, the infection had filled the rest of the plane. Now, it seemed like they were the only ones left still human and sane, besides Mr. Rourke and the others holed up in the conference room. And the President . . .

Vaun grit his teeth and backpedaled as two more Bleeders stepped into view. He recognized one as the Press Secretary, the other looked to be one of the cooks from the galley. They ran on all fours like animals. Vaun put a bullet through the Press Secretary's brow and Kelly shot the other between the eyes.

Every second that ticked by Vaun knew Rourke's finger drew closer to pressing his little button. If that happened Vaun knew for a fact that things would be over before anyone realized it. Here one second, a cluster of loosely associated atoms the next.

"How are you on ammo?" Vaun asked.

"Two clips left."

"There's still more of them between us and Rourke."

He heard their furious cries nearing them. Kelly whirled around to their rear in a flash and fired once. A Bleeder in the corridor twitched once as it fell to its knees, a smoking hole below its right eye. Kelly scowled. By his standards, a poor shot.

More of them stepped into view. Over a dozen, all standing between them and the door to the conference room. They shouted at nothing, raging at the air for a moment. One madly slapped at its own face, another punched an already broken fist into the wall next to it. Knucklebones collapsed further with every blow.

Vaun was just about to suggest a course of action when the one Bleeder slapping itself took notice of them. It stared for a moment, as if unsure that it was looking at uninfected people. A second later it charged.

"Back, back, back!"

Vaun retreated and fired. Kelly already turned and began shuffling as ably as he could. The pack of rabid men was gaining, Vaun took the second to put two rounds into the leg of the one in front. It toppled onto its face, the two behind it sent sprawling as they tripped over it. The rest of the pack simply trampled them underfoot in their pursuit. One paused, trembled, and then vomited a six-foot stream of sickness that missed Vaun's face by inches.

Vaun fired twice more then turned and bolted. He felt hot breath on the back of his neck, heard the gnashing of hungry teeth. Ahead of him, just a mere ten feet, Kelly stood in a doorway with his weapon raised. His finger twitched and the Bleeder that had been right on Vaun's tail fell back.

Kelly slammed the door shut as Vaun barreled in, nearly

knocking the marksman over. Panting and bent over, Vaun examined his pistol. Just three rounds left. Not nearly enough to clear the way to the President.

"I think we might be screwed here, Kelly," Vaun said.

"Ooooh, I don't know about that, Captain."

Vaun raised an eyebrow. Kelly just nodded to the far wall.

They'd found Air Force One's armory.

CHAPTER 62

The light on Tag's device turned green as it finished breaking through the digital lock. A low hiss of filtered air came forth, and the enormous door opened before them.

Tag pocketed the device, then frowned. "Might want to mask up."

Hodges gave a quick nod. We both donned our masks. Tag stood fast. He pulled out his mask to show us the cracked eye-lens.

"They were a little rough pulling mine off."

"You think we're going to just leave you here?" Hodges asked.

"Not like I can hold my breath that long in there."

Hodges considered the options for a second. He looked at me but I had nothing.

"Fine. We're wasting time as it is. Watch our asses, brother."

Tag gave him a queer look, as if he found it insulting that Hodges even felt the need to tell him that.

Now, down to two, we descended into the lab. We entered a sanitizing hallway that misted us. Beyond, we could see a small observation room. Inside was where Terminal's leftovers were kept. Bodies of what should have been their own comrades. Only one or two were even still distinguishable as once being human. The rest were nothing more than red sludge atop metal gurneys.

"They did this to their own brothers . . ." Hodges whispered.

Terminal, whatever their original intent, had been twisted into a gang of madmen.

Hodges turned from the window and indicated the lone door at the end of the hallway. As we neared it, the door slid open automatically. Beyond, the head of the snake himself.

"Took you long enough," Jax said. He stood at the end of a long catwalk with his back to us, appearing utterly unthreatened by our presence. "I was beginning to wonder if one of my boys upstairs got lucky and took you both out."

"Your boys have their hands full, don't worry about them," said Hodges.

He turned to face us. That frustratingly triumphant look hadn't faded one bit and every ounce of me wanted to carve it off. I tried to keep my emotions in check, but here before me was the man solely responsible for everything I'd gone through.

Hodges took a step closer, the red dot of his laser sight hovering over Jax's forehead.

"One chance, Jackson. Where's the virus?"

Jax walked towards us with arms outstretched and palms empty. "Okay, okay, I'll tell you. The virus is through there. I safely packaged them up for you. Well, most of it is in there."

Jax's Cheshire smile dripped with malice.

"No games, Jackson. Where's the rest?"

"As you already know, some of it is probably making its way through your president's bloodstream right about now. Personally, I'm hoping at least one photo of that mess makes it onto TMZ. Being a walking doomsday carrier might actually improve his approval ratings." His grin vanished. "As for the rest of the virus, well, there is another sample right behind you."

Someone slammed into us from behind. I was knocked forward onto my knees and had just enough time to see a portly Asian man in a lab-coat straddling Hodges. They wrestled back and forth, Hodges's rifle fell off the catwalk. Blood and spittle flecked the front of Hodges's mask as he grasped the Bleeder's wrists to keep him from clawing at his face.

"Don't let him get away!" Hodges ordered. Both the Bleeder and Hodges rolled off the catwalk down into the shadowed ground below.

Knowing there wasn't a choice, I went after Jax. I followed him through a door with my weapon at the ready, immediately taking my finger off the trigger.

Jax stood before me, a vial of the Moses-2 virus held carefully in one hand. I stopped dead in my tracks. In the pause that followed, I could hear the sound of my own hot breath filtering through my mask.

"Unlike your stunt upstairs, this really is the virus. Don't suppose you'd tell me who you're with? CIA assassin? Some mercenaries on Uncle Sam's payroll?"

I considered for a second, then realized there wasn't much reason to withhold secrets.

"Sergeant Cole West, formerly of the United States Marine Corps. Today, I'm with Black Spear."

"No shit!" Jax laughed. "Damn. Always heard the stories, the Bogeyman of black ops, the Military Men in Black, yada yada yada, but didn't think Black Spear actually existed."

"No one does."

"Considering *just* how many contacts I have all over, gotta say I'm actually impressed. I didn't have your outfit on my radar."

I sidestepped around the room, examining the surroundings from my peripherals while keeping my eyes trained on my weapon's sights. Computer equipment flanked most of the walls, the center of the room lined with a silver handrail Jax casually leaned against. On the far wall behind him were six large cylinders. I deduced they were virus storage containers. Maps to the left of the room showed Las Vegas and Los Angeles.

I nodded at one of them. "Plans?"

"You know your team pretty much screwed everything for me. So, I figured what the hell, might as well kill a city or two."

I took another look at the six tubes holding the virus, immediately realizing they weren't just tubes. They were short-range missiles.

"Told you I packaged them up for you. You're beginning to make me feel like you don't trust me."

With that delivery system and viral payload, it wouldn't matter that the virus wasn't supposed to be airborne. Anyone caught near the blast would be saturated by the aerosolized Moses-2, penetrating their skin, eyes, and lungs. He could easily infect hundreds with a single missile. Those hundreds would spread. Before Moses-2 burned through them, an entire city would be bleeding. And there would still be five missiles remaining.

"I'm done waiting for the government to fix its fuck ups. I'm done watching our brothers die in VA waiting rooms. I'm done seeing them kill themselves from having the wrong medications. I'm done being ignored while all the homeless die on the cold streets. I'm just *done*. Black Spear is on the wrong side of this." Jax shook the vial with one hand while the other gestured to the Moses-2 missiles. "This will fix this broken shell of a system."

"You really think you're going to fix anything by breaking *everything*?"

Jax shrugged. "You ever do that trick where something stops working so you give it a big ol' smack and it magically starts back up? Same concept. Maybe it works, maybe it just makes me feel better."

The laugh escaped me before I could stop it. "You're unbelievable. All these guys look up to you like you're Jesus. Turns out you're just as selfish as the people you're trying to send a message to. Congrats, Judas."

"You and I have both been to war. Don't lie, you know the

government needs to be taught a lesson in its nature."

"To be honest with you, I hadn't seen combat until Terminal decided to fuck everything up for me. Hell, I hadn't even deployed before. Black Spear just recruited me a few days ago."

Jax's amusement evaporated. His grin disappeared and his mouth tightened to a frown. "You've got to be joking," he said, voice filled with poison. "The Corps lets a Marine who's never deployed stay in and become a Sergeant, while real vets like me get forced out? Tell me how that makes sense. And then to top it off, Black Spear chose *you?* They send some black-ops rookie to stop me? It's a joke."

His hand clenched around the vial so tight, for a second I thought he might actually break it.

I kept going over what Cerberus Squad had discussed, about how we needed to take this man out. Here it was, down to me. The fucking new guy against the very face of Terminal. I wondered if I could get a clean enough shot off. One between his eyes. Lights out. But then he might drop the vial, or worse the bullet could hit the missiles behind him. Bottom line? Couldn't risk it.

Plan B then.

I let my weapon drop by my feet. Next, I reached to my belt and dropped the three grenades clipped to it.

"What do you say, *Lance Corporal?*" I emphasized his rank to make my point as I removed my gas mask. "Why don't you show me what a 'real' vet can do?"

Jax's eyes darted from mine to the weapon on the ground and back. He licked his lips, narrowed his glare, and grinned. Without taking his eyes off me, he carefully placed the vial back on the shelf behind him. Then he reached over his shoulder and removed the shotgun from the scabbard on his back, letting it fall to the floor.

"Oh, I'm going to have fun with you, Rookie." He drew a 6-inch KA-BAR fighting knife and cracked his neck before taking a fighting stance.

The ProTech Don knife snapped open in my left hand. "My name is Toxin."

CHAPTER 63

Billy Ho. 4:25 a.m.
Terminal Grounds
Mojave Desert, California

There was one unbreakable rule in a sniper's doctrine: never fire too many shots from a single position. It let the enemy zero in on where you were and then nearly every advantage you had as a sniper was erased. In the past twenty minutes Billy had repeatedly broken that rule. He knew the risk to himself, but his teammates on the ground would already be dead if he hadn't broken that rule.

Twice now he'd repositioned before the Terminal men could reach him. There was a reason Captain Vaun had dubbed him "Kage", the shadow. He'd more than lived up to that moniker tonight. When they'd maneuvered on his spot at the top of the hill, he'd vanished like a ghost and found a new position atop one of their own guard towers. When the enemy shooters realized the sniper fire coming from the guard tower wasn't friendly, Billy doubled back and took another position on the same hill.

Billy had done more than his share of work in thinning the crowd. Snipers inherently cause fear, the idea of an unseen enemy with a high-powered rifle will cause panic in all but the most disciplined of ranks. It was no surprise that, when Billy started taking heads, a majority of Terminal's men had flat-out run. Some went for the motor pool and loaded up into tactical vehicles, some actually ran for the hills, as if civilization could be found anywhere nearby in this desert. Only about a third actually stood their ground and fought back.

In a strange way Billy found comfort in that fact . He wanted to believe that most of the men drawn to Jackson's mad scheme were simply lost. Hopefully, only a very few were actually willing to engage in full-on biological warfare. The fact that he'd only had to kill a little over a dozen men tonight confirmed Billy's hopes.

Billy was on his last mag, and there were still plenty of shooters fighting. Communications between him and the rest of Cerberus Squad crashed when his three teammates descended into the bunker. That much concrete and steel plating insulation could jam even Black Spear's tech. No word on his friends. As yet, no word on any back-up.

Despite the situation, Billy's heartbeat remained as steady as ever. These weren't the worst odds he'd faced. Not by a long shot. He found that inner Zen, that point where ice flowed through his veins instead of blood. He let his hands work the rifle as they'd done countless times before. A young man's face found itself in Billy's crosshairs. The cushioned buttstock of the rifle bucked into his shoulder. The face disappeared. Kelly would have approved of his accuracy tonight.

Five shots left.

A Humvee with a mounted turret pulled out of the compound. Its gunner started to turn the heavy weapon in Billy's direction as the driver maneuvered the vehicle into position. Billy settled the sights on the windshield, then slowly exhaled. He took out the driver.

Four shots.

The Humvee's dead driver steered the vehicle straight into one of the barricades outside their front gate. Metal screeched as the Humvee ran to a halt, the gunner in the turret was tossed around like a rag doll. He recovered and turned the machine gun to bear. Heavy rounds peppered the sand near Billy but none hit their mark. Clearly the shooter didn't have him zeroed in yet. But Billy had him. The round hit him square in the throat, taking his entire neck with it. His severed head fell over the side of the turret, and his body dropped from view. Three shots remaining.

Billy played with the idea of crawling down into the compound and retrieving any weaponry he could. The heavy machine gun in the turret boasted lots of firepower, but did come at a disadvantage when it came to mobility. He wondered if the rest of Terminal's army had had enough when four additional tactical vehicles exited the compound. Three Humvees, each with a heavy turret, and one very large goddamn tank.

He thought then about just how goddamn large that tank's main gun was when it turned and aimed straight at him.

"And things were going so well."

Billy scrambled to the safe side of the dune. He made it all of two paces before three men emerged from the shadows and aimed their weapons up at him.

One man shook his head. "End of the line. Drop the weapon. You're not fast enough for all of us." He waved an MP5 in Billy's direction, just to clarify his point.

Billy sighed and lowered the weapon. Shooters in front. Tank behind. Then something happened that neither Billy nor the shooters expected.

Charon, Billy's personal angel in the sky, swooped in from behind the shooters. Two Hellfire missiles rocketed off either side of Charon into the four tactical vehicles. All three Humvees, and one very large goddamn tank, blew up in a brilliant ball of fire.

In that split second when the shooters were still caught off guard, Billy fired and worked the bolt of his rifle three times in less than two seconds. He tossed the empty sniper rifle aside before retrieving the MP5 from the lead soldier. The soldier looked up at him in disbelief as he gasped his last breaths.

Billy wrenched the weapon away from him and winked. "Fast enough."

CHAPTER 64

Cole West. 4:30 a.m.
Jax's Lab
Mojave Desert, California

Full disclosure: I've never been in a knife fight before. Surprising, I know. I'd spent countless hours training and running drills but honing skills in practice and being able to perform in the real world are never the same thing. That was especially true when it came to crossing blades. There was a saying I'd heard once: in a knife fight the lucky person is the one that goes to the hospital, the other guy goes to the morgue. I'd already accepted that walking away unscathed wasn't going to happen.

The one hope I had was to provoke Jax enough for him to get sloppy. But even angry, the man moved like an agile feline. We circled the center of the room. Both of us were poised on the balls of our feet. No sound but the low hum of the electronics on the wall and the vents above blowing their icy filtered air. The chill did nothing to dull the fire running through my veins.

For the past few days John Crow's voice had been speaking in my head. Like my own personal black-ops Confucius, he'd whispered wisdom and reminded me of lessons the two of us had learned together. Now, though, the voice was silent. There were no whispers. My friend had no final pearl of wisdom from the afterlife. In this moment there was just me.

I held my knife low, ready to parry and counter-cut. Jax held his KA-BAR out in front of him, his left hand just behind it. There was a certainty to his grip, something subtle about it told me he and his blade had experience together. There was a familiarity in the way he moved it back and forth. I could tell he knew every ounce of its weight, every point of balance, every groove along the handle.

The fingers on his other hand twirled back and forth, baiting me to draw my eyes away from his blade for just a second. I didn't fall for it. He slashed forward, anyway. I parried his arm away with an open palm before drawing my knife up. The edge ran right across the middle of his Service Coat's green sleeve but not deep enough to draw blood.

Jax whipped his arm back away then patted his forearm to check for blood. Satisfied, he lunged forward with a thrust. It was a feint; I fell for it. Damn, he was slick. He reversed his grip mid-thrust and slashed upwards.

I cried out as a hot line was painted across my face. A fine cut ran up from my left cheek through the brow. Somehow, he'd managed to miss my actual eyeball. Lucky me. My hand clamped onto the wound on reflex and I had to take a step back to recover. Blood pooled into my palm, taking half my vision with it.

Not off to a good start. So much for my genius plan of trying to piss him off.

I pulled my hand away from my face and raised my blade. Blood trickled down and threatened to blind me again but I fought the urge to wipe it away. Jax grinned. Bastard was enjoying himself. He lashed out with a back-and-forth slash that was so quick, the glint of his blade painted a blue-steel X in the air for a second.

A quick back step got me clear but nearly had me tripping over an unseen computer chair. I hooked my rear foot around it, then sent it hurtling towards Jax. As Jax pivoted out of the way, I dashed in with a vertical cut that sheared through the top of his sleeve. I followed up with a quick stab into the meaty portion of his shoulder. A patch of fabric with his rank sewn on fell away, revealing the damage caused by my knife.

At least I could die knowing I'd managed to wound him.

Jax whirled back and eyed his wound. Blood ran down the length of his arm and painted the sleeve a deep red. We stared at each other for a moment, as if seeing one another through a new lens. Both of us bleeding. Both reevaluating the other.

"You're out of your element, Sergeant," Jax spat.

"I've been hearing shit like that all damn week."

A muscle at the edge of his jaw twitched. Maybe I could get him angry after all. The man came at me fast, slashing and cutting over a dozen times in the space of a few seconds. I parried what I could, dodged what I had to.

When the distance between us closed, he tried to stab for my neck. I caught the wrist of his knife-hand, stabbing at his gut with my own blade. His free hand stopped me. We stood there, locked in a grapple, both trying to muscle our weapons free and kill each other.

Jax took that opportunity to smash his forehead into my face. It mashed the cut on my brow and sent a fresh wave of blood dripping down my cheek. I responded by kicking him square in the balls. Steel-toed boots and a man's testicles don't mix well.

Jax's grip slackened for just a second. I used that moment to smash his hand into the handrail behind us. Once, twice, and on the third slam he dropped the KA-BAR. Rather than give me an easy opening to finish the fight, Jax drove a knee into my gut and then kicked at my hand. My knife clattered away somewhere unseen. I couldn't spare the time to look for it. Jax followed his kicks with two jabs that caught me right across the nose.

The pressure from the blows had my brain feeling two sizes too big for my skull. When Jax tried to follow his jabs with a wide right hook, I moved into the blow and used his momentum to throw over my shoulder and into the handrail that lined the room.

The metal rail snapped off under his weight. Jax picked a section of it up like a club and swung wildly into my shoulder. White-hot lightning shot up the entirety of my arm before it went numb. Hefting his makeshift weapon with both hands, he thrust it at me like a spear. The jagged end where it had been broken off missed me by an inch.

Behind me were my rifle and the grenades I'd dropped. Part of me wanted to just pull the pin off one and let it blow in Jax's smug face. Another part wanted to prove that I could still take this guy.

"Wouldn't recommend it," Jax said when he noticed me looking at the grenades. "See those sprinklers? Yeah, ain't for water." I risked a glance to the ceiling and saw the fire sprinklers above us. "My personal mad scientist—that was the one who's probably eating your friend's face right now, by the way—made me install a failsafe just in case Moses got loose. Fuel-air system activated by remote. But if a grenade were to go off in a space this enclosed? You do the math. I wouldn't even need to push a button."

I could do the math. It didn't balance out in my favor. "Nah," I said and used my foot to roll the grenade away from our personal fighting ring. "Grenade would be too painless. It's not going to be that easy for you."

"Easy?"

"Yeah."

"Last I checked, you're the one bleeding all over yourself."

"Funny, kind of matches your shoulder."

Jax's lip pulled into a snarl.

"Did you feel anything when you killed your Batson? Or was he ⁀r thing in the way of your war?"

⁀tson knew blood would have to be shed to reach our

ₜt find my knife so I continued to stall. "There's no

way out. You have to know that, Jackson."

"How do you figure? All I have to do is take you down and then load those missile pods up into any of my vehicles up top."

"Then what are you waiting for?" I took up my fighting stance once more. "Come take me down."

Without warning, he charged. He swung the metal pole. Its jagged edge left a grisly cut down my shoulder. Before he could recover from his swing, I threw a right cross to his jaw so hard, I saw spit fly out of his mouth and felt teeth come loose against my knuckles. I followed the right cross with a shovel hook that slipped under his guard and smashed into his gut. Dazed, Jax started to swing more savagely. Each swing I ducked under and countered with another two punches to his face.

It happened in a second. A thought, which seconds ago would've been impossible, took root in my head. I wasn't just going to win. I was going to *beat* him.

One last time he came at me, swinging the pole down like a sledgehammer to cave in my skull. Exactly the sloppy opportunity I'd been goading him for, and it gave me plenty of time to deliver a push kick to his chest that cracked at least two ribs. Jax flew back into the wall behind him, his metal club clattering to the ground. He fell to the floor before me, defeated.

It was over.

He pulled himself to his feet. Panting, he spat blood to the ground and looked at me with nothing but hate.

"Fuck you, West."

I didn't even bother with a witty response. I was too busy relishing the fact that he was beaten. Those bruised eyes of his, overflowing with scorn, left me for just a second to look at something on the ground.

The shotgun.

Jax's goddamn shotgun was just within arm's reach betwe-

For the first time in a while John chimed in. *The best weapon in any fight is the one the other guy doesn't see.*

Time slowed. The span of a single breath stretched out. I became acutely aware of the drop of blood running down my brow. A similar one trailed from the corner of Jax's mouth. Twin rubies in near suspended animation as they descended. Our eyes locked, just waiting for the other to be the first to break the standoff. Both blood droplets spattered to the ground in the same moment.

And then he moved.

Jax ducked down. And so did I.

He reached the shotgun first, but I grabbed the metal pole he'd dropped. The weapon he hadn't seen. Grabbing it like a spear, I rushed forward and rammed its sharpened end through Jax's chest. His eyes went wide as my improvised lance tore through his body and punched out the back of his jacket.

I didn't stop charging until I'd shoved Jax all the way across the room and pinned him to the wall. I roared as I sank it inches deeper through him and into the wall behind him. He tried to curse, tried to cough, but no sound passed his lips. Only blood.

Shaking hands grabbed at the metal pole impaled through his chest; his disbelieving eyes looked into mine. If he was expecting to find mercy in them, he was sorely mistaken.

"Boy," I said, catching my breath, "I bet that grenade is looking preferable right about now, huh?"

I picked up his shotgun, then took another step into what had been our arena. Kneeling, I grabbed the bloodied patch that had been cut from Jax's sleeve. The one that had his rank sewn upon it.

"You built this whole goddamned thing on a lie." I threw the ˙ ⸱s feet.

ʰey . . . *betrayed* us!"

᠄ Terminal's mastermind, staring deep into his eyes.

ɾ about that. It was about *you*. You think you did any

good here? You think they'll look at us in anything other than a worse light now? Yeah, you left your mark alright. Now everyone left is going to have to worry about the stain you're leaving behind."

Those angry eyes of his were changing. I saw something else now. Doubt. Fear.

"You betrayed yourself. Enjoy having that be your last thought in this life," I said.

Abraham Jackson let out one final scream. I fired both barrels into his face.

As the cloud of gun-smoke cleared, I did my best to breathe the fury out of my lungs. I turned my back on Jax's corpse and tried to walk away. After two exhausted steps, I stopped dead in my tracks. Suddenly I thought of something. A funny thought that shouldn't have been in my head at this moment, but I couldn't stop myself from thinking it.

I turned back to take another look at Jax's body pinned to the wall with that metal lance through his heart, fighting the laughter rising in my chest.

"Heh, a Terminal Lance, indeed."

CHAPTER 65

The hinges on the door buckled. Rourke's hand, still wrapped around the Plan C device, began to sweat. It was a natural physiological reaction beyond his control.

He had given Vaun every opportunity to get things in hand. The second the Bleeders got through the door, Rourke would have no options left. The decision brought him no pleasure. Personally, he would have preferred not to have to die today.

"Get ready, boys," Mason whispered. The woman wore a wicked grin.

Laser sights and flashlights trained on the door as it took another hit. Rourke heard a primal scream on the other side of the door. Then it crashed open.

Despite their training, despite the hours and hours spent on reaction drills, everyone in the room froze. Only for a second. Just long enough for everyone to look at the Bleeder before them. Its bloodshot eyes, its pustule-laden skin sloughing off its bones, and the dark bile leaking out of the corner of its mouth.

It charged into the room in the span of that moment of shocked hesitation. Then Captain Vaun appeared. He cracked the back of the

Bleeder's head with his rifle and sent it sprawling.

Everyone let out a gasp while Vaun pinned the infected man to the ground with a carefully placed boot, then put a clean round through the back of its head. Vaun stepped into the conference room and lowered his weapon.

"The plane is ours," Vaun announced.

The man's dirtied suit spoke volumes of what had happened on the other side of that door. Kelly entered behind him, and Rourke was unsurprised to see that his attire was just as ruined. In the hallway behind them were the bodies of dozens of Bleeders. Dozens.

Once the rest of the room's occupants had finished their cheering, Rourke allowed himself a sigh of relief. Vaun stared daggers into him before turning his gaze to the Plan C. Satisfied, Rourke ran his thumb along the scanner once more.

Disarmed.

Mason leaned into Rourke's ear. "And you were worried?"

Vaun left the conference room without a word. Cleaning up the mess was the least Rourke could do for him and Kelly after the hell they had faced.

The President was suddenly front and center, having composed himself and combed his hair back into place. He finished dabbing sweat away from his forehead with a handkerchief. "I want this plane grounded now. Rourke, get a team to meet us as soon as we land. I want samples pulled. Whatever this thing is? I want to know everything we can about it."

Now that the storm had passed, Rourke's jaw began to ache again. The one advantage of having a steady dose of adrenaline was that it had distracted him from the old wound.

"Of course, Mister President. However, there are procedures we need to follow for everyone's safety. Quarantine procedures, you understand? We need to ensure that this was fully contained and that none of us are infected."

"Yes, yes. Fine," the President said. He dismissed Rourke with a wave of his hand and went back to making himself presentable for no one in particular.

The Secretary of Defense stepped close to Rourke. "Quarantine, huh? And how long will your team have to wait before they can come aboard to take samples?"

This time Rourke let himself smile and didn't care if anyone saw. "As long as it takes, Jim."

The SecDef returned his smile, clapping Rourke on the shoulder before he walked away. Rourke found himself looking at the body of the Bleeder that had made it into the room. Already it and the virus within its veins was breaking down.

CHAPTER 66

I've been broken off before. Between sparring sessions, Marine Corps training, and the few actual fights I've been in, I've had my fair share of pain. This moment, however, was by far my crowning achievement in personal agony.

I wrapped a bandage tight over the cut across my face. The laceration on my shoulder from where Jax had cut me was, thankfully, not too deep. I clamped one hand down on it while reaching to pick up Jax's shotgun once more. All the guys on the squad had some personal thing they brought on missions, maybe this would end up being mine.

"Holy shit. You look like hell."

I looked behind me and found Hodges standing there.

"You should see the other guy."

Hodges looked past me to Jax's body. Brain matter and skull fragments splattered across the wall; everything above his neck had been blown away.

"Well, holy shit times two. That Jax?"

"Yup."

"He's dead as shit."

"Yup."

Hodges wandered over to where the Moses-2 missile pods were housed.

"Well, well, well. Here we are at last."

"Virus is secure, Jax is dead, mission accomplished, I'd say?"

I gave him a half-hearted thumbs up and pulled out the cigar he'd given me.

Hodges gave a long sigh and shook his head. "Yeah . . . not quite."

I paused, confused, and put the cigar back into my pocket.

"You know, considering he was a big fat scientist, that last Bleeder that jumped me could actually put up a fight," Hodges said. "You ever hear the saying 'bark is worse than its bite'? Doesn't always apply."

Hodges pulled down the collar of his Snakeskin suit. There was a shallow bite mark at his collar bone. The wound already had black corrupted lines spreading from it. When I took a closer look at Hodges, I saw that one of his eyes was growing bloodshot. The virus was spreading like wildfire through him.

"Hodges . . ." I started to say, but just couldn't find the right words. In my hands the shotgun became very heavy.

Hodges waved the thought away with a shake of his head. He knelt next to the missiles and tapped the tip of one of the warheads thoughtfully.

"It is what it is, West. I bet you twenty bucks we were told to secure the virus so that Rourke's sample team could snag this. Operating directly under the President's discretion means we only avoid ninety-nine-point nine percent of political angles. It's too good a weapon to pass up. They'll claim research purely for defensive purposes but who knows, man? As if this shit hasn't done enough damage." He laughed. "Guess I'll get one last opportunity to give the middle finger to the man."

Hodges picked up the grenades I'd dropped from my belt earlier and got to work.

"You're a good guy, West," he said. "Cerberus Squad's going to be just fine with you. That is, if you decide to stick around."

"Even though I'm still the fucking new guy?"

Hodges shook his head, "You just saved the fucking day, dude. That's certifiable. John promised the Captain that you could hold your own and belonged with us. You proved him right. After today you're off the hook, job's done and all. From here on out, it's your own choice."

I shrugged. The thought hadn't really occurred to me until just now about what I would do after this. Could I really just go back to my office job? Sit around, filing papers for the Lieutenant Colonel all day? The veil had been lifted and a whole other world had been shown to me. Black Spear and teams like Cerberus Squad had been fighting it this entire time while I'd been safe and sound on the sidelines.

"Promise me something, West," said Hodges.

"What?"

"Our squad hasn't been right since we lost John. When the Captain brought you into the fold it was almost like . . . I don't know, we found that missing piece again? The team needs you, whether any of us wanted to say it or not. I wasn't cut out to lead us. I folded like origami when they hit us in P.B., and then I almost got us killed again when they ambushed us up top. Maybe you can do better. Promise me, you'll stay in this fight."

Hodges held out his hand, a first and last handshake between brothers.

"You know we're getting dangerously close to a chick-flick moment here, right?"

"Just don't tell Billy."

I grabbed his hand. It felt hot to the touch; the fever was already spreading. Hodges had been my harshest critic since day one, now here he was being the first to fully welcome me to the team.

Looking down at the explosives he held in his hands, I tried to force a smile. "At least give me enough time to get out of here, yeah?"

Hodges returned the smile and nodded. "No promises." His lip twitched and he stifled a cough. "Go. Not sure how much longer I've got."

I turned and ran.

CHAPTER 67

For nearly a decade now, explosives had been his entire life. Defusing them, planting them, detonating them. And hell yeah, he still got a thrill every time he got to throw a switch and watch the boom go off. To him, that thumping wave that hit his chest was nothing short of brilliance. From the first time he'd seen that blinding flash of light, he'd known that it was the last thing he'd ever want to see.

How right he'd been.

Examining his work, Hodges had to admit that what sat before him was his masterpiece. He'd set a Semtex charge atop each of the virus-laden missiles; perfect placement right outside the agent housing chambers. A single press of a button would trigger the charges, which would in turn set off the additional explosive payloads in the warhead tips and West's grenades for good measure. From there, the lab's failsafe system should incinerate everything else.

Hodges knew full and well nothing would remain. In this confined space everything in the room would be atomized instantly. There wouldn't be any pain, not that Hodges was particularly worried about that. In fact, there wasn't really any concern at all in him at this moment.

In a strange way he was thankful. Being an explosives man meant you could only ever see your art from a distance. His entire career he'd been chasing that high, always wanting to get closer and closer to that flash.

Now here he was, detonator in hand, with the closest seat anyone could ever get.

Hodges felt his nose dripping and wiped the blood away with the back of his glove. Wouldn't be long now. He already felt himself slipping away. Little by little, breath by breath. Blood was tickling out of one of his ears. His thoughts grew hazy, and he felt himself growing angry for no reason at all.

It would still be easy enough to tap a button.

"Hope you're clear, kid."

Hodges hit the button.

There wasn't a spectacular explosion that I walked away from without looking back. I didn't dive out of the lab vault door seconds before a fireball. Our helicopter wasn't hovering nearby for me to leap to as the Terminal Grounds detonated underneath us. It was all quieter than that.

After Tag sealed the lab vault behind me, we simply waited. It was a silent vigil lasting mere moments, but it felt like years. Then we heard a muffled thump from the other side. Nothing more. I'm not sure how long we stood there after staring at the door, which had been flash welded shut. Not sure what else to do, I reached into my vest pocket and pulled out the cigar. Tag held a lighter out for me without saying a word. There wasn't anything to be said that could make it all okay.

I drew the gray smoke in and held it. It tasted sweet, like a fine cognac. "Damn," I said as I breathed it out. "That's good."

"Hodges had good taste."

We walked out of the bunker. Well, Tag walked while half-carrying me—to find the compound filled with federal agents and special response teams. It looked like they'd done a knockout job of rounding up the remaining militiamen, too.

Sure enough, it turned out most of them surrendered when Jax had been nowhere to be found. We limped away from the bunker entrance. The good guys surrounded us, but only a few shot glances our way. Someone far up the chain of command had already passed the word about us.

I could see Charon at the edge of the compound, Billy already loaded up and the door open for us. There was a realization in his eyes as he tried to find our missing third man. Billy wasn't even looking at us; rather, he was looking past. His eyes were locked onto the door to the bunker. Undoubtedly, he asked himself what more he could have done. Maybe one of his bullets could have taken out Jax, and we wouldn't have even had to go down into the lab. And maybe he was weighing and wondering exactly how this was his fault.

We all were. Me, most of all.

I sat with my legs dangling off the edge of the helicopter, just taking in everything around me. When Charon began to lift into the air, it knocked the cherry off the end of my cigar. The embers and ash hit my boot top and scattered to the earth below. For a while I just looked at the cigar still burning between my fingers.

I tried to get Hodges's words out of my head, but they kept repeating. A promise made by John Crow was the only reason I'd been dragged into this mess to begin with, now a promise to Derek Hodges compelled me to stay.

"Okay," I said, pulling in a great mouthful from the cigar. I held it, for just a second, tasting the sweet mix of ash and cognac upon my tongue, then blew it out. When the wind whipped away the smoke, I found Tag and Billy staring at me. I gave them a tight-lipped nod.

No words would ever be enough to speak truth to what it meant.

They immediately understood: a silent promise.

The vow had been made. Who's to say how far down this road it was going to take me.

EPILOGUE

There was nothing in the papers about what we did. Plenty on Terminal, plenty more on the failed attempt on the President's life with a purposefully vague bioweapon, but nothing at all on Cerberus Squad's heroism. Nobody would ever know of the deaths of Achilles Squad or a certain grumpy medical examiner with a smiley-faced coffee mug.

Thanks to Staff Sergeant Derek Hodges's sacrifice, the world would never see a Moses-3 strain surface. All the talking heads in Washington took turns on the news circuit, pointing fingers for who was to blame for Terminal's rise. After all was said and done, they didn't have the decency to find common ground across the aisle even for that.

Thankfully, they did agree that the Department of Veterans Affairs was at least partially to blame. Congress pledged to pass whatever measures needed to be passed in order to improve services for America's veterans. Time would tell if that momentum would lead to anything. Call me a cynic, but I wasn't holding my breath.

All the members of Terminal who had been killed in the week's events were given full military funerals. At Vaun's urging, Rourke convinced the President that, while most had been misguided and misled, they were servicemen nonetheless.

The same courtesy was not extended to Abraham Jackson. Rourke instructed his computer wizards to wipe all traces of Jackson from every record possible. You can't even find a picture of him on the internet anymore. For a man who wanted to etch a piece of his soul into the nation's collective memory, I'm pretty sure being completely erased was the ultimate punishment. Felt like justice to me.

Not all of Terminal's members had been rounded up. We hadn't been so lucky as to have their entirety present in the desert that night, and those that remained were scattered to the wind. Hopefully the ones who got away were smart enough to hang up their guns rather than form back into individual cells.

More troubling was the revelation that an unknown party had deposited millions to Terminal over the past six months. The idea that a second group was not only willing to help Jax break the country, but also had that much money lying around, didn't sit well with any of us. It didn't help that the source of the deposits was completely unknown, and the remainder of Terminal's accounts had vanished. Even our best computer wizards struggled to find exactly where Jax managed to hide all of Terminal's funds before I blew him to hell.

I'm sure one day Terminal's remnants will try to be a pain in the ass again. For now, though, their power and their leadership had been broken. If they or their mysterious benefactor decided to rear a head up, we'd swiftly lop it off for good.

Another fight for another day.

As for me, I wasn't packing my bags. Not yet at least. I'd convinced Vaun that he didn't need to suicide me. There really weren't many people in my life who would miss me to begin with. Part of me still wishes I could've been there to see Lieutenant Colonel Tarly's face when they went in to clear out my old desk. That bastard would have to make his own coffee from now on. I hope he burns his tongue.

Now that the mission was finished, I finally got the time to process everything. And I mean everything. I'd already lost track of how many lives I'd taken so far, which was a scary thing to come to terms with. I found myself wishing Vaun would catch another case for us soon so that I wouldn't have any more time to think. Everyone on the squad said a brief rest would be good for me, though; I tried not to take their concerns as coddling. When I'd cleared the mandatory post-op psyche evaluations, Vaun had been completely unsurprised. He said I was a natural, whatever that meant.

For a few days I kept finding myself thinking about John's promise. I wondered what he'd say to me if he could see how things turned out, or more importantly what I'd say to him. Would I thank him for this opportunity or curse him for stripping away who I was before? I realized the whole point of his promise was so that I would get a chance to figure things out on my own and in my own way.

In the end, I knew there was only one thing he would've said for sure. *Goodbye.*

John would know that for me to truly succeed, I'd have to let his ghost go. Come to think of it, I hadn't heard his voice since facing Jax in the bunker.

The cut Jax had left me across my face was healing, but would leave a scar. I looked at it now in the mirror, tracing a fingertip along its length. I found myself taking inventory on all the minor changes I saw in my reflection. It was the same skin yet a different man wearing it. The eyes were the dead giveaway.

The eyes of the man in the mirror were harder than mine had been. They showed a willingness and capability of great violence. Earlier, I'd repeatedly questioned whether or not I belonged in Black Spear. Those eyes held the answer.

Three people had died down in that bunker: Jax, Hodges, and the old Cole West. The man who emerged would never again be blind to the darkness in the world. He would be right there at the shadow's edge, fighting it back. This was his path, and something told me it was only just beginning.

It had been one week since Terminal's failed assassination attempt. Mr. Rourke sat across from the President in the Oval Office, just the two of them. The week had been consumed by investigations into where the Moses virus had come from, how far Terminal had infiltrated its agents into the government, and most importantly how Air Force One had been breached. Now that the dust had settled, it was left to Rourke to close the book on everything.

"Adam Levins," Rourke said.

The President hissed between clenched teeth. "Levins? Shit, never would have thought."

"Agent Levins had been with Terminal long before he was part of the Secret Service. Autopsy reports show that he ingested a gel capsule. It was a time-released dose of Moses-2. Abraham Jackson had told him that they were going to release a bioweapon onboard the plane and that the pill would inoculate him."

"Jesus . . . All those dead, all from one pill? One man?"

Rourke bit the inside of his cheek. "I cannot possibly overstate how dangerous the Moses Virus is, Mister President."

"Yes, Rourke. I got a pretty goddamned good close-up impression of it, if you can remember."

Rourke tried to force a smile down. It still showed at the corners of his mouth which the President noticed and bristled at. That look on the President's face when the Bleeder had broken into the conference room had made everything else worth it.

"I lost one man at their compound," Rourke said, "Staff Sergeant Derek Hodges died while attempting to disarm the Moses devices there. They were rigged to explode should anyone tamper with them."

The President leaned forward and dropped his voice as if afraid reporters were hiding in the walls around them. "And the virus itself . . . no samples could be retrieved?"

"Unfortunately, the explosives incinerated the virus. I relayed the importance of acquiring a pure sample, as you requested, but when the explosives took Staff Sergeant Hodges they took any chance we had. Furthermore, Terminal's chief scientist—Doctor Steven Chan—perished when the lab's failsafe activated. Any hope of piecing together the science was lost with him."

A disappointed nod was the only response the President gave. Having completed his brief, Rourke stood to walk away.

"Rourke . . ." the President said.

Rourke paused.

"The scientists tell me that they were unable to extract a viable sample from the bodies pulled off Air Force One. By the time we landed they were pretty much mush. Impossible to extract it. I'm told the virus decays not too long after it burns through its host. I wonder, would we have been able to retrieve a pure sample if we hadn't been in quarantine?"

The President tried to glare a hole through the back of Rourke's head. Rourke was immune.

"I hadn't considered that," said Rourke. "I'll have to reevaluate our quarantine procedures."

He'd nearly made it to the door before the President called out to him once more.

"Rourke, you and I both know the virus could've been a useful weapon in the future."

This time Rourke didn't bother to stop.

"You already have a better one. The one that beat it, Mister President. You have the Black Spear."

Mason was waiting for him just outside.

"Admit it, sir," she teased. "Sergeant West did well."

"Beginner's luck."

"Oh, please, you like him."

Rourke chose not to dignify her comment with a response. Even he couldn't calculate what the odds were of things ending this way.

ACKNOWLEDGMENTS

They say behind every successful man is a strong woman and lucky me, I've had one pushing me forward in this writing career since day one. To my mother, who was there at the very onset of this journey when I was a child and met every story I told with unconditional encouragement. And to my wife, who didn't just believe I could walk this path, but was there by my side to make sure I kept stepping. The voice in a writer's head that bring stories to life can be our best friend, other times it can whisper nothing but doubts. She quieted those whispers. Without her, I would never have gotten here. Without her this dream would be mere fantasy.

Secondly, I need to thank all the amazing people that make up the San Diego Writer's Coffeehouse. This huge cadre of creatives, and the support they gave, played a huge part in me staying the course. From the most successful New York Times best-selling author, to the latest eager rookie just learning the ropes, each and every writer is welcomed into the fold and their voice received with equal merit. Specifically, I have to thank Dennis K. Crosby for being an unofficial big brother as I followed his lead and went from aspiring author to now that fabled title of published author. Thanks again for including (and killing) me in your own debut, and for encouraging me to partner with the team that made *FNG* a reality. Also, thanks for just being a good dude overall.

A big shout-out to the entire Acorn Publishing team for all the help and guidance that turned my manuscript into an actual book, and especially to Evelyn! I'm pretty sure for every one email I received from you I sent four unnecessary ones back. Despite all my anxiety-induced questioning, and despite how incredibly particular I could be with how I envisioned certain things, you always answered with reassurance and an infinite capacity for understanding. You wanted my book to be *my* book and—front to back—I couldn't be happier with how it turned out.

And, last but most assuredly not least, this book wouldn't have been possible without all of the amazing service members which I've encountered. You've all come from a myriad of backgrounds, each with personalities and traits as varied as a person's thumbprint. Those thumbprints left a mark behind that, one way or another, lent a hand in creating many of the characters in this book. For some of you it was a piece of a name, others it was an amusing mannerism or saying and hell, for one or two I committed wholesale identity theft with your personality because secretly I'm not creative enough to write interesting characters on my own. Bottom line: a lot more people than yours truly played a part in getting this book published. For that, I am forever grateful.

ABOUT THE AUTHOR

Born and raised in California, Benjamin Spada has had a lifelong passion for storytelling. Benjamin is a dedicated taco aficionado, self-described "Professor of Batmanology", diehard lumpia enthusiast, and served for ten years in the United States Marine Corps. He has been assigned as a Section Leader in the Wounded Warrior Battalion for our nation's wounded, ill, and injured, and served overseas to help train our foreign military allies how to survive against chemical, biological, and nuclear weapons. Over his career he's trained Marines, Sailors, Federal Agents, and other friendly forces in individual survival measures for everything from nuclear attacks to deadly nerve agents. Despite these grim assignments, he has carried on with equal amounts of sarcasm and stoicism. Benjamin is also an avid sci-fi and horror movie fan, tattoo collector, comic enthusiast, and two-time holder of the Platinum Trophy in Elder Scrolls: Skyrim.

Benjamin lives with his wife, Jacqueline, and their three daughters, Elizabeth, Isabella, and Alexandra in Oceanside, California.